*"John, you must ~~~~~
Teri whispered.*

"You can't take her back. *We* can't take her back. *Please!*" She closed her eyes briefly, gathering strength. "Let's not talk about it anymore."

"Okay." John laid his hand over both of hers. "We won't talk about it."

"I have to go back."

He stared at her, wordlessly rejecting the notion.

"John, you can't keep me here like this. It's not good for either of us. One minute you're threatening to do things that make me want to scream in your ears and pound on your head. And the next minute I look at you and I want—" Her hands slid down his arm as she stepped back. "I have to go."

"The next minute?" He turned his hand and caught hers before it slid away. She closed her eyes, but he would not let her shut him out. "What else do you want from me, Teri? Why won't you look at me and tell me what you want from me?"

"Because you already *know!*"

Dear Reader,

The hits just keep on coming here at Intimate Moments, so why not curl up on a chilly winter's night with any one of the terrific novels we're publishing this month? American Hero Duke Winters, for example, will walk right off the pages of Doreen Roberts's *In a Stranger's Eyes* and into your heart. This is a man with secrets, with a dark past and a dangerous future. In short—this is a man to love.

The rest of the month is just as wonderful. In *Diamond Willow* one of your favorite authors, Kathleen Eagle, brings back one of your favorite characters. John Tiger first appeared in *To Each His Own* as a troubled teenager. Now he's back, a man this time, and still fighting the inner demons that only Teri Nordstrom, his first love, can tame. Terese Ramin's *Winter Beach* is also a sequel, in this case to her first book, *Water From the Moon*. Readers were moved by the power of that earlier novel, and I predict equal success for this one. Two more of your favorites, Sibylle Garrett and Marilyn Tracy, check in with, respectively, *Desperate Choices* and *The Fundamental Things Apply*. Sibylle's book is a compelling look at an all-too-common situation: a woman on the run from her abusive ex-husband seeks only safety. In this case, though, she is also lucky enough to find love. Marilyn's book is something altogether different. A merger of past and present when a scientific experiment goes wrong introduces two people who never should have met, then cruelly limits the time they will have together, unless . . . You'll have to read the book to see how this one turns out. Finally, welcome new author Elley Crain, whose *Deep in the Heart* is a roller-coaster ride of a story featuring a divorced couple who still have an emotional tie they would like to deny, but can't.

In coming months look for more great reading here at Silhouette Intimate Moments, with books by Paula Detmer Riggs, Rachel Lee (the next of her Conard County series), Marilyn Pappano and Ann Williams coming up in the next two months alone. When it comes to romance, it just doesn't get any better than this!

Leslie Wainger
Senior Editor and Editorial Coordinator

DIAMOND
WILLOW

Kathleen Eagle

Published by Silhouette Books New York

America's Publisher of Contemporary Romance

SILHOUETTE BOOKS
300 East 42nd St., New York, N.Y. 10017

DIAMOND WILLOW

ISBN: 0-373-07480-8

First Silhouette Books printing February 1993

All the characters in this book have no existence outside the
imagination of the author and have no relation whatsoever to
anyone bearing the same name or names. They are not even
distantly inspired by any individual known or unknown to the
author, and all incidents are pure invention.

Printed in the U.S.A.

KATHLEEN EAGLE

is a transplant from New England to Minnesota, where she and her husband, Clyde, make their home with two of their three children. She's considered writing to be her "best talent" since she was about nine years old, and English and history were her "best subjects." After fourteen years of teaching high school students about writing, she saw her own first novel in print in 1984. Since then, she's published many more novels with Silhouette Books and Harlequin Historicals that have become favorites for readers worldwide. She has received awards from the Romance Writers of America, *Romantic Times* and *Affaire de Coeur*.

For my nephew, Kevin John White Bull.
Teach the children well, John.

Prologue

They called him the Cat, but he was nobody's house pet. The boyhood nickname was most aptly defined by the man John Tiger had become. His smooth walk, his detached gaze, his taciturn approach to all comers, hardly suggested domesticity. Some took him for predator, others for protector. He saw himself as neither one. Cornered and tired of running, the Cat bared his claws simply to stand his ground.

Beneath the pale blue, high-plains sky he paced the eastern boundary of his territory. On the other side of the barbed-wire fence, beyond the right-of-way grass he'd recently cut but not yet baled, was the blacktop highway. That was where the passersby passed, where the gawkers stood, where the waiters cooled their heels. On his own side of the fence, the Cat was effectively caged.

John Tiger was a prisoner on his own property, even though he'd put up most of the barricade himself. Uncle Abner had hauled in two car bodies, both long since picked clean of all usable parts, and rolled them on their sides in front of the wire gate. The cars were backed up by the big green John Deere hay wagon, which would be needed in the field soon if the hay was ever going to get put up. Rounding out the blockade were three half-ton pickups, minus their distributor caps. No one would be moving them anytime soon. Not the local sheriff. Not Lake Sakakawea's cabin owners. Not the Corps of Engineers nor the minions of the Bureau of Indian Affairs, who'd warned John that, since his FBI file was as long as his lanky arm, he would be wise to keep a low profile in local disputes.

Wisdom be damned. There would be no more tooling across John Tiger's land to get to the lake. He was tired of people leaving his gates open and letting his cows wander all over the road. And that wasn't the half of it. He was tired of people advising him as to "the smartest thing for you to do right now, John." Didn't matter what it was about. It always meant backing down or giving something up. What he had wasn't much, but it was his. He was through compromising.

Two weeks back he'd collected his cows off the road again, all except for the heifer calf he'd had to shoot because she'd been mangled by a passing semi. Then he'd padlocked the gate. The sheriff had come by the next day and asked if he'd forgotten that was the gate to the only access road to the lake within, well, quite a few miles. Three summer residents had been unable to get to their cabins. One frankly regretted he hadn't brought a wire cutter along.

No, John hadn't forgotten about the cabins. He didn't know the owners, and they didn't know him. It was nothing personal. He just didn't want them driving across his land anymore. There was no formal easement for the access road. He'd checked. It was something else every-one had taken for granted, an agreement he'd been told had "always been understood."

Well, John Tiger *didn't* understand. He'd made no agreement. Some white guy named Schiller had leased his father's allotted land long before John was born and come to think he owned the place, up until two years ago, when John had decided to claim his right to use his in-heritance.

Apparently people had been more careful about clos-ing Mr. Schiller's gates and asking him for permission to hunt or camp. John had decided that it was his right to refuse. So had Ted LeBeau, John's neighbor, and Woody Whitestaff.

Woody wasn't ranching anymore, not since the local grocer had settled up his charge account by claiming Woody's three-room house. Woody liked the idea of making the Cat's fight *his* fight, and he had become John's right-hand man for the duration of the standoff. He'd rounded up a dozen volunteers to take turns man-ning the barricade. And the summer people—"sun dogs circling the Cat," Woody liked to call them—were howl-ing for their governor to "do something about those In-dians."

"Hey, Cat," Woody called out as his bootheel skid-ded over a tire track molded into the clay road. "Didya see the paper?"

It was day-old news by the time the *Bismarck Tribune* found its way out to Indian country. Some reporter had been taking pictures the week before, the day after John and Woody had set fire to the pickup two guys from the Corps of Engineers had left behind in a hurry. They'd brought their wire cutters. They'd trespassed. They'd gotten no more than what they'd had coming. The walk back to the road hadn't hurt anything but their dignity. John had tried to avoid the cameras, but he knew what good press outlaws made. Still, as long as he stayed on reservation land, he was protected by tribal jurisdiction.

"We make the front page?" he asked as he reached for the folded paper. "What did they say? Indians on the warpath or something?" He started to turn to the bottom half of the front page, but the picture just below the masthead caught his eye. His hand suddenly felt heavy, but slowly he lifted the paper closer to his face.

"It's mostly about how the Corps of Engineers doesn't want any trouble, and how everybody's always cooperated around here and they don't know why we've got our backs up all of a sudden." Anxious for his friend to see what he was talking about, Woody tried to take the paper back. "You're looking at the wrong—"

John did a quarter turn and stepped out of Woody's reach. Woody's voice faded as the blood pounded in John's ears. He studied the face, the chic pose, the faraway look in the eyes he knew to be blue. He didn't have to read a word. He knew it was Teri. God, she looked as though somebody had taken a buffer to her and polished her up, smooth and creamy. She'd been soft when he'd known her, but not the kind of jewel-toned silky he saw in the picture.

"Foxy," Woody intoned over John's shoulder. John looked up quickly, hoping whatever was heating up his face all of a sudden wasn't visible. Woody quirked an eyebrow at him. "We're on the bottom of the page, straight down from her nose."

Figured. No point in denying his interest. He glanced back down, looking for a printed answer to any of the thousand questions the picture spawned in his head. "I used to know this lady," he said.

"What, in a former life?" Woody chuckled.

"*Her* former life. Mine hasn't changed much."

"Says she's in town for...a what? A *shoot?*" The smaller man looked up from the page, beetle-browed. "Shootin' what?"

"Pictures, Woody. She's a model."

"Why don't you call her up?" Woody nudged John's arm with his shoulder. He could already see himself coaching the call from the sidelines. "Huh? Call her up and see if she remembers you."

John stared at the picture. A breeze had lifted her hair, exposing a heart-shaped earring. "She remembers," he murmured.

"H-e-e-ey, the Cat's been prowlin' uptown."

"It was a long time ago, back when the cat was just a kit." Eight years, at least, and the number didn't begin to account for the miles or the choices or the changes that had tumbled like loose coins into that eight-year chasm. "A long time ago."

"Hey, call her up." Grinning, Woody nodded encouragingly and laid his elbow into John's side. "Tell her you'd sure like to see her, but you can't get away from the rez right now." He took the paper from John's hands and turned it over to reveal the picture at the bottom of the page. "You're kinda tied up at the moment. Maybe she noticed."

John sighed. He looked like some kind of wild man in this picture. They'd caught him with his mouth open and his long hair looking wind-whipped and scraggly. "Nobody'd recognize me in this picture."

"Depends on how well they knew you. How well *she* knew you. And whether she can read." He pointed to John's name in the caption. "Or whether she just looks at the pictures."

"Maybe I don't give a damn either way." But he gave in and read the article's first two paragraphs. "Damn, they've got about six charges against me now. What in the...?" He shook his head and skimmed the column, looking for the rest of the story, the part he knew wouldn't be there. "I fired those shots in the air. I wasn't shooting at any cops. They know damn well that shotgun wasn't aimed at them. They weren't twenty feet away. If I'd 'a been shooting *at* them, they'd still be pickin' out buckshot."

There was no point in telling his side of it to Woody, who'd been there, too. But Woody clapped a hand on his shoulder, just so John would know somebody was listening. "You're okay as long as you stay on Indian land. They can't arrest you on Indian land," he repeated, as though saying it twice would make it true. Then he raised his eyebrows, reconsidering. "I don't *think*."

"I'm going to South Dakota, Woody."

The Cat's right-hand man shook his head. "You can't."

"I need one day," John insisted. "Two at the most."

"You won't get past the mailbox."

John looked at the picture again and thought back through the chasm. They'd been kids when they'd first met, one as shy as the other. He'd wanted to be her champion, stronger and brighter and better than any of a thousand other guys who couldn't help noticing her. He'd wanted to possess her, and beyond that he'd wanted to be worthy of possessing her. Assurances of her love had never been enough. Driven to prove God only knew what, he'd tested her at every turn. In his estimation, they'd both failed.

But she was still Teri Nordstrom. She hadn't changed her name. The small gold earring, available at any jewelry counter, might have been acquired last week. But he didn't think so. Unless her glamorous life had changed her completely, she didn't hate him. She might not love him anymore, but she wasn't capable of hating him. And she might be willing to help him if she knew his cause.

John handed the newspaper back to Woody and smiled. "Takes more than a fence to keep a cat in the yard."

Chapter 1

"Teri, you've lost too much weight."

Slender-for-life Lavender Archer should talk, Teri told herself as she sipped the only thing she'd really wanted for lunch, which was a cup of tea. Since she'd started modeling, Teri had learned to smile and innocently demur on the subject of weight. "I haven't lost an ounce since the last time you saw me. Really, not one ounce."

It wasn't quite true, but because so few people understood the demands of her profession, Teri used a mental weight-conversion table that made the claim not quite false, either. Then she deftly slipped into the proverbial best defense. "Anyway, look how skinny *you* are, Lavender. As ever."

"Look at me," Lavender echoed, and she laughed as she waggled her half-eaten chunk of whole-grain bread in the air, as though it were some kind of self-indictment. "Look at *us*. A cartoonist would have a field day with this conversation, wouldn't she? Two women fussing over one of the three topics nearest and dearest to their hearts. Men, clothes and diet." She made a good-natured production of indulging in another bite of bread. "So what do you think of the clothes, Teri?"

Teri's stomach unwound a quarter turn, and her eyes brightened. "Oh, Lavender, that white coat. I love the way it falls from the shoulder. It's a great design."

And it looked great on Teri. She'd modeled many a famous label, but Lavender's handwoven fabric lent a special quality to her unique clothing. It was wearable art. Teri knew exactly how much time and thought went into the making of each piece. She counted twelve years back to the real beginning of her life, when Lavender— she'd been Lavender Holland then—first showed fifteen-year-old Teri Nordstrom how to weave. From that day on she'd spent countless after-school hours working at the loom in Lavender's studio. She'd learned about color, construction and design as her part-time job helped pave her way out of the small town of Glover, North Dakota, and into the big city.

"It's all in the darts," Lavender said. She was still looking at Teri as though the young woman were a neglected child she'd just taken in off the streets, which, in fact, she once had done. But this time Lavender wasn't responding to a court order temporarily removing Teri from Marge Nordstrom's custody. She was looking at Teri's tiny wrist. "What you really need is a little more of my homemade bean soup."

"Your soup is delicious, but I can't...." Lavender's hand hovered menacingly over the bowl Teri had barely managed to empty. It irritated her that Lavender didn't seem to appreciate the compliment, but still she smiled. "No, really, I can't. I'll look like I'm hiding a cantaloupe under that slinky black number. The camera is absolutely pitiless, you know.''

"I do have some cantaloupe in the fridge. How about just a small slice with a little bit of—"

"No more foooood!''

A small giggle turned Teri's attention to the kitchen doorway and the little girl with dark braids who had just appeared. She had a book in her hand, her finger jammed in the middle to hold her place as though she was just taking a moment to check on the adults in the kitchen. She wore a handwoven pink pullover that her mother had made, and her brown eyes danced with delight as she glanced from one woman to the other.

"Rachael, help!'' Teri pleaded. "She's making me eat more vegetables!''

"Cantaloupe is fruit, Teri. It's good for your digestion.'' Rachael marched across the bright white linoleum floor, deposited her book on the counter and hoisted herself on the stool next to Teri. "Don't worry. We're having pizza tonight, and Daddy promised to hold Mommy down while I put the pepperoni on. I like it covered with pepperoni.''

"Me, too.''

"Marriage is just one gastric compromise after another,'' Lavender said with a sigh. Lavender was a vegetarian yogi, and her husband, Wyatt, was a meat-loving wrestling coach. The fact that she was white and he was Sioux Indian was a small difference by comparison.

"But my favorite foods are seven-grain bread, hot from the oven, and fresh green beans,'' Rachael said, duty-bound to sound like her mother's child. She could not have been more so even if Lavender had given birth to her, so hardly anyone but Teri ever remembered that Lavender actually hadn't.

"A young woman of remarkably good taste," Lavender said as she straightened the collar on her daughter's shirt and smoothed it down in an instinctively familiar way. Lavender was a natural mother. Teri remembered the same hands patting her own hair into place or mopping tears she'd refused to shed in anyone else's presence. She missed that sometimes. There were days when she was tempted to hop a plane from Minneapolis to Bismarck just for the chance to cry on Lavender's shoulder. But, of course, she couldn't do that now. She planned her short visits well in advance, prepared herself, restrained herself, and came away aching and envious. She was as much a part of the family as she could afford to be—as Lavender and Wyatt could afford to permit. It was almost enough.

"And apple pie with butterscotch ice cream," Rachael added wistfully.

"Which I was planning to make for supper until you let on about the pepperoni conspiracy."

Lavender tapped the tip of the little girl's nose with a maternal finger, and Teri glanced away as she cleared her throat. "Well, if I'm going to do justice to the fall line, you two will have to stop tempting me with food."

"Mommy says I might be a model someday, like you, if I want to."

"And I might design beautiful clothes someday, like your mommy. Or get into marketing." The small hand on Teri's forearm invited her to look into those adoring brown eyes. Of all the admiration Teri received, this was the most precious to her, and whenever goals were discussed, she made sure to slip in the *C* word. "Someday I might actually use my college degree."

Teri slipped her arm around Rachael's shoulders. "Modeling's okay, sweetie, but I'll bet you can think of

lots of other things you'd like to do when you grow up."
Rachael nodded vigorously, and Teri prodded. "Like?"

"Like being a veterinarian. They get to take care of all
kinds of animals. Dr. Paul took X rays of Jasper after
Daddy accidentally sat on him when he was hiding in the
blankets."

"Oh-oh," Teri said. She loved the breathless way
Rachael had of telling stories about her brawny, soft-
touch of a dad. It was easy to tell by her warm smile that
Lavender did, too.

"Well, Jasper's getting pretty-old, and Daddy was really scared, the way Jasper kept going, 'ye-oow, ye-oow,
ye-oow.' But after Dr. Paul said he was okay, Daddy said
Jasper could get a job in Hollywood. But if I got to be a
veterinarian, I'd want to get a job at Sea World."
Rachael turned suddenly, slackening Teri's embrace, and
tipped her head to one side as she inspected Teri's lips.
"Do models get to wear lipstick to school?"

"Not until they're seniors." She hadn't put any
makeup on, and it was after noon, she realized. She must
have been enjoying herself if she'd forgotten her rou-
tine.

"That's ten more years!" Rachael shoved her hand
into her jeans pocket and came up with a tube of waxy lip
moisturizer. "Daddy bought me some yesterday, see?"

"Daddy bought you some...." Lavender leaned forward, and Rachael turned the tube for her inspection.
"Oh. That *is* a nice color."

"It looks better when I put it over my lips after I eat a
cherry Popsicle. Can I go watch when they take the pictures of you, Teri?"

"We're going to three different places. I thought I'd
take you along when we go to the old farmstead." She

reached for her tea again. "That's not far, is it, Lavender?"

"Just about ten miles out of town. It's perfect. Big old farmhouse, red barn, cows, horses, cornfield. It fairly shouts, 'Natural fibers and handwoven clothing from the Midwest.' " Lavender reached across the counter to give one of Rachael's braids a tiny tug. "And that's early tomorrow morning, so there'll be no staying up until all hours tonight."

"I'll go to bed right after supper," the child said as she slid down from the stool, "I'd better decide what to wear, in case they want to take a picture of me, too."

"I'll definitely want to take pictures of you." Teri shook her head as she watched Rachael skip out of the room. "I can't believe she's already seven years old. She's so smart. Sometimes it's hard to believe she's not seven*teen* years old."

"Don't say that. She's growing up too fast as it is." A quiet moment passed as they furtively watched each other sip tea and wait for the passing of the bittersweet feeling that always followed such statements. Neither was embarrassed by it. It was simply a part of all that they shared.

"They ran a picture of you in the paper," Lavender said when the time was right. "Rachael's been showing it to all her friends. They all want to come over and meet you."

Teri tucked her long blond hair behind her ears and poked at her bangs. "Give me some advance warning so I can be camera-ready. If she brought them in now, they'd say, 'So? Where's this model you've been talking about?' "

"You know, you were a pretty teenager, but you're a fabulous woman." Words, Teri thought, and Lavender, as usual, read her mind. "In your jeans and sweatshirt, without a bit of makeup, you're a *fabulous* woman. You don't have anything to prove, Teri. I wish you could see what I see."

"I do. I see that I photograph well, and for that I get paid quite well." But Lavender wasn't paying her. She'd offered, but Teri had steadfastly refused, and she hastened to head off yet another offer. "I'm so glad you're letting me be part of this catalog. The demand for the Lavender label is going to take off like gangbusters this year, and I want to be able to say I saw it happen."

"I've trained more weavers. I'm taking a gamble, because I want to create more jobs. I know how to increase the supply, and I think I can expand the market. I hope—"

"I hear a car!" Small feet thudded on the carpeted steps as the two women exchanged puzzled looks. "Daddy's home early! Daddy's home!" The door opened, and Rachael's enthusiasm dissipated. "Oh. I thought you were my dad."

"No, 'fraid not," a man's voice said. Lavender shook her head as she got up from her stool. She didn't recognize the voice telling her daughter, "I'm Woody Whitestaff."

"Mommy! It's Woody Whitestaff."

"Woody Whitestaff," Lavender muttered to Teri as she led the way to the front door. "Who is Woody...?"

It was too late to tell Rachael not to let the stranger into the house. The man snatched his cap off and shuffled his feet a little on the small area rug by the door. A chunk of black hair stood at attention toward the back of his head.

"Sorry to bother you, ma'am, but I was wondering if Teri Nordstrom might be here." He was looking right at her, Lavender thought, glancing over her shoulder. Teri shrugged. "An old friend of hers asked me to deliver a message. It's kinda personal."

Even though she'd never heard of Woody Whitestaff, Teri knew instantly who the old friend was. Instantly, too, her pulse pounded in her ears as though she were still hearing Rachael's feet bounding down the steps. She tried to swallow, but her mouth had gone dry.

"To tell you the truth, Woody, we've been awfully busy getting Teri ready for—"

Teri found her voice. "It's okay, Lavender. I can spare a few minutes." She smiled at the man who was a friend of a friend. "Hello."

Woody offered a gap-toothed grin. "You're prettier than your picture. The one that was in the paper."

"I didn't see that one."

"I have it, Teri," Rachael offered proudly. "I cut it out for my scrapbook."

"Then you didn't see the other picture on the same page." Woody's smile faded. Clearly he'd hoped the newspaper had prepared the way for his message.

"No, I—"

Lavender laid one hand on Teri's arm, the other on her daughter's shoulder. The look in her eyes said, *If you need me...* "Rachael and I have some cleaning up to do, back in her room."

"Mommy, I just—"

"Show me what you've decided to wear tomorrow, okay?"

It seemed to take forever for the two to ascend the stairs, Teri thought. Woody shuffled his feet as she twisted her long, slender hands together. Then quietly she reported, "I didn't see the paper, Mr. Whitestaff."

"John Tiger sent me."

John Tiger. More than just an old friend.

"He wants to see you."

More than a mere message, those were the words she would have given anything to hear eight years ago. *He wants to see you.*

"Then why did he send you? Did he think that after all this time I might still feel the urge to throw a large, heavy object at his thick head?"

Woody gave a quick laugh. Teri wasn't sure whether he was just nervous, or whether he actually thought she was being funny. Not that it mattered.

"I really don't think it would do either one of us any good. I can't imagine what we would have to say to each other after all this time."

"I don't know anything about what he's got to say to you. All I know is, he can't come himself, but he'd sure like to see you." He waited for her to ask, and when she didn't, he explained, anyway. "See, if he sets one foot off the reservation, he'll get arrested."

"What's he done?" That doesn't matter, either, she told herself. But she couldn't seem to check the surge of worrisome images.

"Nothing much. We're just tired of people forgettin' we got our rights, same as anybody. Just as well you didn't read about it in the paper, 'cause they told it one-sided. A guy don't mind letting people cut 'cross his property when they show some respect. But they think they own the place, leaving gates open, making a mess of everything. John finally closed off that road across his pasture."

"His pasture?" She was lost. The last she knew, besides the fact that he'd left her, was that he was in the army. "John's ranching?"

"He took over on his dad's allotted land. He still had his per cap money, can you believe it? He bought cows with it."

She remembered the money that the members of the small band of Native Americans to which he belonged received when they came of age. He wouldn't touch his until they were married, he'd said. It would be a down payment on the house they would one day share.

"I haven't seen John in a long time. We lost track...."

"Not him. He didn't lose track. He saw that picture of you in the paper." Woody grinned. "I didn't believe him at first, that he knew a famous model."

"I'm hardly famous, but I am tied up with this—"

"I can drive you up there and get you back in a few hours." When she didn't get a refusal out right away, he pressed. "He just wants to talk. He wouldn't be bothering you if it wasn't important."

"All right." The words surprised Teri more than they did Woody. "I'll be ready in half an hour."

"I'll just wait in the pickup." He slapped his yellow-and-white cap back on his head. "Don't dress fancy or anything. Can you ride a horse?"

"It's been a while, but I'm sure I can manage."

Lavender appeared at the top of the stairs as soon as Woody closed the front door behind him. Without eavesdropping, which Lavender would never do, she had put enough pieces together to prompt her to persuade Rachael to stay upstairs. Lavender descended as though she were easing herself into a tub of hot water.

"If you saw my picture in the paper—the picture Rachael cut out—you must have seen John's picture, too," Teri said, her gaze meeting her friend's. "I understand it was on the same page."

"Who is that man?"

"A friend of John's."

Lavender nodded, offering no pretense of surprise.

"Why didn't you tell me?" Teri asked. A casual reference to the hazards of local woodwork would have been nice. A friendly warning about what might crawl out of it.

"Because we don't usually talk about John. You never mention him. Wyatt wouldn't even read the article. John's been involved in these protests before, and you know how Wyatt is. He's interested in Indian culture, but he steers clear of Indian politics." Lavender smiled almost defensively as she reached for Teri's hand. "Mr. Conservative. Wyatt always made his wrestlers keep their hair short. In the picture John had a bandanna tied around his forehead, hair down to his shoulders."

"You haven't become *Mrs.* Conservative," Teri averred. She allowed Lavender to lead her to the sofa as she tried to imagine John with hair the length Lavender had indicated. She decided it would probably become him.

"Of course not. What fun would that be? John looked fine to me."

"Did you read it?"

Lavender nodded. She sank to the sofa, letting Teri's hand slide from hers. "It was so ironic, the two of you on the front page of the same paper and Rachael holding it up for us to see. Wyatt looked over at me, and I could see—" Teri was still standing over her. Lavender lifted her chin and looked her in the eye. "Alarm. A fleeting brush with the reality we'll have to deal with eventually."

Teri sat down, dazed by the image of the moment Lavender described. She chose to see it from Lavender's viewpoint. She understood Lavender's feelings so much better than she did her own.

"It's one of those things you want to put off thinking about. But, as you said, Rachael is a precocious little girl. Sometimes it takes a big stride to stay a step ahead of her."

"You're wonderful parents," Teri said. "Both of you. I have absolutely no regrets."

"We both know that isn't true."

Teri's gaze slid to the large yellow children's book that lay on the glass coffee table. "I did the right thing," she said wistfully. It was something she said to herself at least once a day, every day. "I did what was best for her."

Lavender took Teri's hand again. "What does John's friend want?" she asked quietly.

"John wants to see me." She could tell her hands had gone cold, because Lavender's felt warmer than it had a moment ago.

"You've spent eight years avoiding each other. Do you want to see him?"

"No." She shook her head, but it made her dizzy, going against the grain that way. "Yes," she whispered. Her head cleared. "There were times when I wanted to see him so badly I thought I would crack. Just crack open like an egg, and all my wanting would spill out all over the floor."

"Do you still feel that way?"

"I didn't think so. I thought maybe it had actually happened. All that wanting had spilled out and dried up." Her laugh was as dry and tight as her throat. "I'm being silly. It was over a long time ago. I've dated other men. Surely there have been other women...."

The last was spoken with forced conviction. No matter how hard she tried, she couldn't picture John with another woman. If she could, maybe the regrets would fade. But it was easier to change the subject than to complete a thought that might dim the memories. "Tell me what the article said. How much trouble is he in?"

"John's bucking the system. He says he doesn't have to allow access to the lake across his land. Apparently the access road was built on kind of a gentlemen's agreement, and John wasn't one of the gentlemen who was in on it." Lavender shrugged. "And it sounded as though the disagreement got a little heated when John closed off the gate. In fact, if he leaves the reservation—"

"He'll be arrested, I know. Woody told me. That's why I have to go up there."

"That's a good hour and a half drive. You'll be going up there soon, anyway."

"To do the shoot." Lavender's comforting hand slipped away as Teri stood up. She was keeping a man waiting. Maybe two men, if John believed she would come. She looked down at her white running shoes. "Apparently I can't just walk in there. Woody asked me if I could ride a horse."

"It's a standoff. The police are waiting to arrest him, but they don't have the authority to do it on Indian land." Lavender peered through the curtain. A white pickup was parked below the stone walkway that led to the remodeled schoolhouse, once Lavender's home and now her expanded weaving studio. She turned back to Teri. "Why don't you wait and talk to Wyatt? He's thought of going up there and trying to talk John into—"

"I'm not going to try to talk him into anything. He asked to see me, and I guess I want to prove to myself that I can handle that now. Like two old friends, putting the hard feelings aside."

It sounded reasonable. It was a far cry from any of the reunions she'd envisioned over the years. The one where she bombarded him with breakable objects. The one where he told her about the army recruiter who drugged him and tossed him into the back of a truck bound for boot camp. Or the one where he came to her, heart in hand, and she stomped the bloody thing flat.

She smiled. "You used to be a counselor, Lavender. Don't they call it bringing closure?"

"They don't say you should dodge a police barricade to do it."

Certainly not without makeup and a fresh blouse. Teri headed for the stairs. "Just the other day I was thinking, 'Wouldn't it be fun to ride a horse again?'"

Woody said little on the drive north, and Teri decided to save her slew of questions for John. She had grown up in North Dakota, but the scenery all seemed new to her. A wet spring had made for lush June fields of green spring wheat, young corn and leafy alfalfa, stretching acre upon acre. There were even greater expanses of pale green and yellow prairie grass in pastures dotted with grazing beef cattle. Stands of fuzzy-headed foxtail barley fluttered near roadside culverts. So few trees, Teri thought, but she didn't miss them. In fact, she'd had a time getting used to them since she'd moved east. She remembered John saying that was one of the things he didn't like about visiting her at the university in Fargo. Too damn many trees, he'd said.

Too many trees and too many people. He'd gotten a job as a truck driver. He wanted to go to college but after his accident—Teri always insisted that his disastrous fall from the train bridge had been an accident—he couldn't get the wrestling scholarship he'd hoped for.

He'd given up on the idea of going back to high school, but he'd taken the GED exams and earned his high school equivalency certificate. He'd said he would work for a year, then enroll at the university, but he never had.

Too many trees and too many people. He would hate Minneapolis, Teri thought.

She knew the way to Lake Sakakawea, but once they left the highway she was unfamiliar with the surroundings. She'd never been to the reservation. After they'd made several turns that took them from blacktop to gravel and gravel to dirt, Teri had no idea where she was. Woody took her to what he introduced as Ted LeBeau's place, which wasn't much more than a house trailer, a barn and a set of corrals. Ted wasn't home, but Woody seemed to know where everything was. He saddled two horses and told Teri to mount up.

They cut across a pasture and followed a cow path until they reached the huge blue lake. It wasn't really a lake at all but the Missouri River, swollen midcourse like a plugged artery. Backed up by the Garrison Dam, the water had flooded fertile Indian-owned bottomlands and become a man-made lake. In recent years it had turned into the state's favorite recreational site.

A cool breeze blew across the water and lifted Teri's hair off her damp forehead. If she sweated off all her sun block, she was going to have a heck of a time camouflaging her cherry red nose tomorrow. Her thigh muscles were beginning to turn rubbery, and she had already chipped a nail. Accepting the fact that none of it could be helped lightened her spirits, and she shook her hair back and turned her face up to the sun.

"There he is," Woody said, breaking into Teri's buoyant reverie. He nodded toward the next hill. "The Cat himself."

John topped the next rise on a big, blaze-faced sorrel and reined in when he saw them coming. Teri steadied herself with the saddle horn and blinked against dancing sun spots, thinking she saw a mirage. His stout stallion pranced beneath him, eager to join up with the approaching horses, but the rider held the high ground. It was to his advantage. Etched against the cerulean high-plains sky, with his long black hair flung back from his chiseled face and his bare, bronze arms handling the high-headed horse, he appeared indomitable.

Teri's heart tripped over her next breath.

"We're on taken land," Woody said, speaking of the border around the lake, claimed by the Corps of Engineers. He pointed to the four-strand wire fence. "Through that gate we'll be on his territory."

John waited for them on the hill. Without a word or a backward glance, Woody delivered his charge, then rode back down the slope, leaving them simply to look at each other, sort out the changes and ache with the memories.

"Hello, John."

The greeting left her throat tingling.

"Thanks for coming."

The words were an accomplishment for a thick tongue.

"You knew I would." She tossed her hair and squared her shoulders, hoping an assertive carriage would offset the bend in her resolve. "You told Woody to say the magic words. That you were in trouble."

"If that's what he said, he used his own words. Not mine." He glanced after his departed friend. "He won't go far, in case you're worried. He'll see you safely back where you came from."

"I'm not worried," she assured him. "You have a problem. I think that's closer to what he said."

"Take a ride with me and I'll show you my problem."

"I've come this far," she muttered as she neck-reined her black mount to follow John's lead. She wasn't sure her increasingly saddle-sensitive parts were up to the ground-eating lope, but she resolved to take her blisters in stride rather than ask him to slow down. When he pulled up in a thicket of buffalo berry bushes, she managed to make her wobbly dismount inconspicuous by putting her horse between them. They left the animals tied to the bushes, and John started up the sidehill on foot. Several paces behind him, Teri stumbled.

"You okay?"

She'd gone down on one knee, and he turned, bracing a hand on his thigh. They stared at each other, pulses pounding. Finally he straightened and skittered down the slope on his bootheels, reaching. His long, sinewy arm extended from a worn denim jacket with the sleeves cut out. His big, calloused hand came closer, within inches. The need to reach for him rose above her pride, but her shaky legs came to the rescue with a face-saving excuse.

"Some muscles I haven't used in a while," she explained. He caught her up off the ground as though she weighed nothing, and she found a precarious balance against his side. The familiar scent and feel of him overwhelmed her with a wild sense that the lost years had been instantly restored.

"Lean on me," he said gruffly. "I'll get you to the top."

She gave in, clutching handfuls of denim as her feet scrabbled along ineffectually next to his. She leaned on him the way she'd longed to years ago.

Toward the top of the hill he set her down carefully, hunkering close, still supporting her in the protective circle of his arm. She looked up and found him studying her with those dark eyes that never betrayed his thoughts the way hers did.

"You never were much of an athlete," he said. She remembered their mock wrestling matches, the way he had enjoyed teaching her to put her arms around him this way, her legs around him that way. He read her mind, and his smile spread slowly.

"I exercise now," she said quickly. "I have to. It's just that I haven't been on a horse in a long time."

He turned, reluctantly releasing her as he directed her attention to the scene beyond the hill. "That's my place." Teri noted the log house, the pole barn and the corrals, then the dirt road and the jumble of vehicles at the end of it. "And my problem is that I've got cops blocking the driveway."

"I see a pile of junk blocking the driveway."

"That's blocking the *gate,* and some of it isn't junk. I still owe six thousand dollars on that hay wagon." Squatting there next to her, one knee planted in a clump of silver sagebrush, he braced his forearm on the other and scrutinized the stack-making machine. "I should be out making hay with it," he said, apparently gaining a new perspective from this vantage point.

"Why aren't you?"

"I saw your picture in the paper." His hooded glance was more intimidating than she remembered. "Did you see mine?"

"No. Lavender told me this has to do with people wanting access to the lake."

"Across my land. They take it for granted that they can come through here. They leave gates open. Their kids ride around on their ATVs and their motorcycles, chasing my cows. They camp, they hunt, they don't care what they do with their garbage." He pivoted, turning his back on the scene below as his fist hammered his thigh with each phrase. "So I said, no more trespassing. I don't care if you have to build a new road. I don't care if you have to drive a few miles out of your way. This road is closed."

"Can you say that?"

"Easy." He flashed her a reckless smile. "They just can't listen. The Corps of Engineers says I'm interfering with their access to the shoreline. The county sheriff says he's got a temporary restraining order, and some guy who owns a cabin down there says his abstracts show he has some kind of a prior agreement."

"Do you have a lawyer?"

"There's no prior agreement. There's no easement." He let one leg slide out from under him as he seated himself on the ground he was claiming. "This is Indian land."

"I thought it was your land, your father's—"

"I know it's been a while, Teri, but in case you've forgotten, I'm an Indian. This is *Indian* land."

"Does that make it different from—"

"You're damn right it does. It's trust land. It's mine—well, mine and my father's other heirs—but it's in federal trust. So they can't just do anything they damn well please."

He sighed as he lifted his face to the sun and the breeze. He hadn't changed so much, she thought. Oh, God, he looked so much like Rachael. His square chin, the shape of his eyes. Even his thick, shiny hair. His features were dominant in the child he'd never met. Teri both loved him and hated him for it.

"I didn't want all this trouble," he told her. "All I wanted to do was lock that gate and go on about my business."

"Why do they want to arrest you?" She didn't want to side with him, but it was happening. Damn her for having mush for brains, it was happening.

"Couple of guys cut the fence and drove right on through. We had to relieve them of their vehicle. A few shots have been fired," he admitted, and he offered an apologetic glance, as though he'd come to the only part she might have to overlook. "They were purely warning shots. At least, ours were. Nobody's gotten hurt. Not yet, anyway."

"Call it off, John." He looked at her as though he had no idea what she meant. "Just call it off and take it to court."

"I moved out here two years ago. I've talked to these people, I've hung up signs, I've called the police, who generally can't figure out whose jurisdiction it is. I'm through asking nicely. They're not using my land anymore."

"Why did you want to see me, John? Why now?" She started to stand up to see if her legs would hold her.

His hand on her shoulder forced her back down with an order to "Stay put. Your hair's flapping in the breeze like a bright yellow flag." But he was admiring it. Half smiling, he recalled again, "I saw your picture."

"You *have* my picture," she reminded as she gave in and sat beside him on the ground. The needlegrass prickled through her jeans.

"I have several. They're all over eight years old. My mom showed me another one from a magazine. I don't see too many women's magazines."

"I sort of stumbled into all that," she said as she gingerly unfolded first one leg, then the other, stretching them out in front of her. "After I graduated from college, I started working for a department store in the

marketing department. They transferred me to Minneapolis. Someone suggested I take a modeling class, and
the whole thing took off from there.''

''Someone,'' he repeated. ''A boyfriend?'' She glared,
and he raised both hands in surrender. ''Just checking. I
need a favor from you, and I'm wondering what my
chances are.'' He gave her the charming smile that always got to her—the one where his eyes said, *I know you
want to.* ''You're here. I know that's a start.''

Teri folded her arms and tossed her hair, letting the
wind sweep it back from her face. ''I came up here
strictly out of curiosity. I wanted to see what you'd gotten yourself into. Lavender says this isn't the first time
you've been involved in a political protest.''

''Is that what I just described to you? Sometimes I
think they put ears on you people just in case you need
glasses.'' The sun rendered her scowl less effective, and
she wished she had her dark glasses right about now. She
caught the echo of the smile that used to linger in his eyes
when he'd succeeded in getting a rise out of her.

I'm not smiling back, John, so be straight with me.

He lifted one shoulder and explained, ''My brother
was involved in the Crimson Eagle demonstration. When
I got out of the army, I joined up with him and the other
protesters. That was about treaty rights. This is about *my*
rights.''

''None of it sounds like you, John. Except the anger.''

''Yeah, well, I'm tired of being angry. All I want now
is—'' He glanced away and thought about it for a moment. ''Peace,'' he said quietly. ''I'd like to live here on
this land the government allotted to my father's family
before they decided to dam up the river. Before this so-
called lake was ever here. I'd like for my neighbors to

show me some respect, so I can return the favor." He turned to her, searching her eyes to measure the extent of her interest. "My grandfather was a rancher. Did I ever tell you?"

"No."

"Not big-time, but he raised cattle on this land. I never knew him. He died before I was born. My dad let it all go, just took the lease money."

"You never said anything about ranching. I thought you wanted to go to college."

"I wanted to be on a wrestling team in college." They both knew the difference. They'd talked about it, argued about it. He'd lost a year of his life—that all-important senior year—and there was no way of replacing it. "I wanted a lot of things back then. Took me a while to figure out what I could actually have."

"What you have right now is a big mess," she insisted, changing the subject before he could name anything. He didn't have the slightest appreciation for what he could have had.

"I really don't see how I can help you, John. I can't make the police disappear, and I can't do anything about the charges against you. Do you want me to be a character witness?" She gripped her legs, digging her nails in deep. Her smile mocked him. "Nice guy, but he shies away from commitment."

"Which was no great setback for you. It worked out better. As for me, I need a way to get to South Dakota. My mom's in a hospital in Sioux Falls. She's had a stroke."

His tone was flat, but he couldn't hide his anguish. For once his eyes gave him away.

The smile dropped from her face. She held tight, resisting the urge to touch him as she whispered, "Oh, John, I'm sorry."

He stared at her, struggling even as she struggled. There was not a wall between them but a gulf. Hollow fears. Empty years. He needed to be touched as desperately as she needed to do the touching. She lifted her hand and tentatively uncurled her perfectly manicured fingers. He allowed himself a moment of anticipation, but he drew away before her hand reached his arm.

It was his move. He grabbed her abruptly and hauled her to her feet, holding her in a half crouch until they'd skidded down a ways from the crest of the hill. "I must have been out of my mind," he muttered, still hauling. She bumped against him, and he steadied her next to his side without missing a step.

"John!" she gasped. "What—?"

"Can you ride?"

"Did somebody see us?"

"Just tell me if you think you can ride."

"John!" She grabbed his arms above the elbows and skittered around him like a tetherball until they were both struggling for balance on the steep slope. They skidded to a stop and stood for a moment, holding each other by the arms, staring into each other's eyes, chests heaving.

"Stop running, John," she demanded, her voice surprisingly strong. "I'm sorry about your mother. I mean that."

"I don't need your sympathy!" he shouted. The cords stood out in his neck as though he were hefting a burden aloft.

"You said you needed something from me. Tell me what it is."

His skin felt hot from the sun. He started to pull away, but she held fast, forgetting his strength, ignoring her own sore muscles. He stared hotly, nostrils flaring like a stallion blowing after a long run. He could have flung her away from him easily and sent her tumbling down the hill, but she stood her ground until she felt his resistance melting.

"I need to be there," he said quietly as the hardness vanished from his eyes. "She might not regain consciousness. It might not make any difference to her whether I get there or not. But it makes a difference to me."

"Maybe if you explained the situation to the police—" He started to shake his head, and she tightened her grip again. "Listen to me, maybe—"

"Maybe they'd let me call time-out? I don't think so."

"Then what?" she implored. "Tell me what."

"I think *you* could get me some time-out."

"I don't see how."

"Come on," he said, then nodded toward the foot of the hill, where the horses stood munching on the bushes. They fell into an easier descent, with John offering assistance as he explained. "From what the paper said, you're gonna be getting your picture taken close by."

"We were going to use the lake as a backdrop. Lavender wants her catalog to play up North Dakota scenery."

"I suppose you'll be driving up here with a bunch of other people."

"A photographer, of course, and an art director. Lavender might come, and maybe..."

When they reached level ground he stopped her, taking her shoulders in his hands as he faced her with his proposition. "Maybe you could figure out a way to get

Lavender to stay home. And maybe you could find an excuse to drive up in a separate vehicle.''

And rescue you, she thought. *As I once hoped you would rescue me.*

''I don't know what excuse I could come up with, and I still don't see what good it would do you.''

''What kind of background do you need? Trees, water, hills, what?''

''All of the above.''

He let his hands slide slowly down her arms, then reluctantly released her. ''I'll tell you where to go. Prettiest spot on the lake. Secluded. A place I can get to without being seen. You'll smuggle me safely out of the area, and I'll take it from there.''

''What if you get caught?''

''I probably won't get sent up for much more than a year.''

''Sent...'' He was smiling now because, damn him, he knew he had her. He knew she couldn't refuse. ''Oh, John, this is so crazy.''

''Nobody's gonna suspect you, Teri. Who'd ever look for a renegade Indian in the company of a classy model?''

''Anybody who knew we...we went to school together.''

''We did a lot more than that together,'' he said quietly.

''Don't, John. It isn't fair.''

''I know. If I could afford to be fair, I wouldn't be asking.''

''Suppose you get away with it this time? Then what? You can't stay here forever, and you can't—''

''I'm only asking you to worry about it just this once.'' His jaw tightened. It was hard for him to ask this way. He would have preferred to tease, to charm, or offer a trade. But he swallowed his pride when asking the first time wasn't enough. He reached for her again. "Help me, Teri."

"Oh, John." She closed her eyes and let his hands warm her shoulders as the sun warmed her face. It felt like summer for the first time in eight years. Eight long years with nothing but winter sun. She could refuse. She had the strength and the good sense. But the wonderful heat made her whisper, "I'll try."

Chapter 2

John dressed in a blue chambray shirt and his least-worn blue jeans. He had to make himself look as ordinary as apple pie for this trip. He liked his hair the way it was—neat but unfashionably long—because it felt right. It contributed to his sense of who he was. But he would have cut it if he'd had a pair of scissors. Probably just as well he didn't. He'd had some pretty bad home haircuts in his time, but a self-inflicted scalping could be disastrous. He was aiming for common, not downright homely.

It wasn't that he felt a need to impress anyone, but neither did he relish the idea that someone might be thanking her lucky stars that she hadn't gotten stuck with him. The straw cowboy hat he took off the hook next to the back door would cover his hair.

Teri was the one who might attract attention. What was he thinking, *might?* She had always turned heads, but now she was hardly homespun North Dakota. Maybe *she* would have to wear the cowboy hat. He yanked open a kitchen drawer, rifled through the assortment of receipts, bent nails and fence staples, and came up with a pair of aviator glasses. On his way out the back door he caught a glimpse of a boxful of paper grocery sacks, and he laughed aloud. Putting one of those over her head might be the only way to make Teri look ordinary.

It was still dark when John led the sorrel out of the barn, and he was still thinking about Teri as he mounted the long-legged horse. It had been good seeing her. The time and distance he'd put between them hadn't changed the way she made him feel—as if he'd die for sure if he didn't get his hands on her, and if he did, as if he were going straight to heaven. He thought he'd outgrown that crazy kind of feeling.

He knew he had no business getting her into this, but he was fresh out of ideas. The cops were watching his friends, but they weren't going to search Teri's car. After all, she was white, and few people knew she'd ever been his friend. All she had to do was clear the reservation, take him a few miles south on the highway, and then he could hitch a ride with an out-of-state truck.

He'd told her one small lie the other day. He knew damn well that if he ended up in federal court, he would wind up in prison for more than a year. A year probably sounded like a lot to Teri, but when they locked an Indian up, they usually threw away the key. A couple of the guys he'd bunked with at the Crimson Eagle protest could attest to that. One of them had probably even deserved it.

They used to call the guy Button Ears, and he'd had a habit of getting into other people's stuff. He'd gotten hold of the small metal box John referred to as his "office," and old Button Ears had ended up with his arm in a sling. Along with John's discharge papers and his GED certificate, the box contained his small collection of photographs. Most of them were pictures of Teri.

Eventually Button Ears had gotten himself convicted of armed robbery, and John figured he was probably guilty as sin. But Paul Broken Pipe had been convicted of murder, and Paul was about as violent as the Little Drummer Boy on Christmas Eve, but he hadn't stood a chance with a plea of self-defense. He was a "known troublemaker," one of those notorious Indian activists. The FBI had enough information on everyone who'd been at Crimson Eagle to fill an encyclopedia. Step out of line just once, as the old tune said, and the man would gladly come and take any one of them away.

Daylight was just beginning to crack a hole in the purple horizon when John met up with Woody at the end of his fence line. Woody opened the barbed-wire gate, and John rode across the line onto federal taken land. He had directed Teri and her entourage to a picturesque inlet where they would find bleached driftwood—remnants of cottonwoods from the recent past—and huge chunks of petrified redwood from a prehistoric forest. Seemed like trees never did have much of a chance in North Dakota.

"I knew you were crazy when you hatched this idea, buddy, but at least now I know how you got that way." Woody flashed a grin over his shoulder as he worked the gatepost into the wire loop at the bottom of the fence. "Now that I've seen your lady."

"She's not my lady," John said as he watched his friend shoulder the top of the post within reach of the wire loop that served as a latch. "Anymore."

"She must wanna be. Otherwise why would she agree to this?"

"For old times' sake, maybe."

"She must be thinkin' back on some damn good old times." Woody grunted with the effort of swinging his ample body into the saddle, but once settled, he grinned again. "There's a whole string of wanna-be's waitin' in line for the Cat. Maybe you wouldn't notice if I just cut one out for myself."

"Guess I wouldn't. Not unless you showed me the line first."

"Well, they all had to step back one, and I can sure see why you've only got eyes for the front-runner."

"I've got eyes for nothing but heifers, Woody." John smiled. "White-faced heifers. They don't give a guy much trouble, except at calving time."

Side by side, they picked up the pace, Woody's belly bouncing with the chestnut gelding's choppy trot. "She's white faced, all right, but she ain't no heifer. What kinda trouble did she give you, if you don't mind my asking?"

"I do mind." But Woody's childlike smile turned sorrowful, softening John some. "Think about it, Woody. How many wanna-be's you think she's got lined up?"

"Plenty." But that solicitous glow in Woody's eyes said he couldn't see any of them edging the Cat out of his rightful position as top choice. "So what? Back in the old days the guys used to line up outside the girls' tipis. The girls would come out, spend a few minutes with a guy under his courting robe, all innocent, 'cause everybody in the whole camp could see. I s'pose the prettier the girl, the longer the lineup of wanna-be's, huh?"

"I suppose." No point in fighting Woody's logic, even if the traditions he used to back it up were ancient history.

"Didn't matter, though. She could only pick one."

"And that one is supposed to stop worrying about the rest of the line?"

"You can't stop 'em from wishing." Woody shrugged. "I did a little wishing myself when I drove her up here." He risked a glance at John, whose icy stare prompted a sly grin. "Just *wishing*. Hell, I'm only human."

"Wish all you want." John stood in his stirrups and set his sights on a scrub pine up ahead. "Hell, grab your courting robe and get in line. It's not my worry anymore."

"She's doing you a big favor, buddy. If she's doing it just for old times' sake, I'd say times haven't changed much." He paused, anticipating a comeback, but John didn't offer one. "She ain't married," Woody pressed.

"She's been too busy getting her picture taken."

"You ain't married."

"I've been too busy raising those heifers." With perverse satisfaction he smiled. "And before that, a whole lotta hell."

"You got all the excuses, and I got all the facts. I got a feelin' after today you're gonna know what's what and which is which."

"Whitestaff, you are so full of it." He slanted Woody a grim look, but the man clearly believed in his own baloney. John had to laugh. "You should have been a politician or a TV preacher, you know that?"

"You think so?" Woody took the comment as a compliment. "Hell, I coulda been cruisin' down Easy Street."

"Or sitting in jail waiting to tell all your 'facts' to the judge."

"With you sittin' in the next cell over." Both men laughed, agreeing on the likelihood. "Difference is," Woody added, "they'd show my trial on cable TV, and I'd be gettin' offers to write my book."

"Hell, you can't even write your damn name."

"Sure I can." With his pinkie delicately crooked, Woody inscribed the morning air. "Right across the back of that million-dollar check."

They shared a belly laugh as they reached the crest of a hill. Still chuckling, John dismounted, flipped the reins over the sorrel's ears and handed them to Woody. "This is about as far as we go, buddy."

"You takin' a hike now?"

"I'm takin' a hike," John said. "I'm countin' on you to watch my place. Turn this guy out and let him graze. Keep him away from that bay mare. She'll kick the hell out of him. And make sure—"

"We've got you covered. You sure you don't want me to mosey down the highway and give you a lift?"

"If they suspect I'm gone, your license plate number becomes the prize in the cops' cereal box, my friend. They wanna talk to me, tell 'em I'm hung over or something. They'll buy that one for a day or so."

"Keep your head down." Woody offered a good-luck handshake.

"You, too."

After a short trek John hid in a shelterbelt, secreting himself in the shiny, deep green foliage of the outside row of chokecherry bushes. Racking his hat on an upraised knee, he leaned back on his elbows and settled in to wait for his ride. The morning sun was a blinding yellow headliner in a cloudless pale blue sky. Woody's talk of old customs made him think of the scouts who would sit for hours in a spot like this, watching and waiting for needed game or dreaded enemy. He'd been feeling restless and eager from the predawn start of today's venture, and he wondered if it had been any easier to keep watch back in those days. He'd never been long on patience. He remembered Teri pointing that out to him on more than one occasion.

High above the straight, scanty line of treetops, a red-tailed hawk spread his wings over a pillow of warm air and coasted lazily. Without warning the bird dived directly for the ground.

John's heart lodged in his throat. He dropped his chin to his chest and closed his eyes, but it was too late to make it stop happening. He'd gone too far. Down, down through the darkness he hurtled, and the earth rose up to meet him.

The squeal of a hapless gopher brought him back into the light of day and the safety of the present, his butt and his bootheels firmly planted on prairie sod. Reassured, he permitted himself to remember the aftermath and the girl who had seen him through it.

"What you did was a mistake," Teri had told him time and time again. "Ally made mistakes, my mom . . . even me. I made a mistake by not questioning Ally about those pills I knew you guys were using. But that's all behind us, John."

She'd spoken of it almost with a sense of relief, as though they had learned their lesson at a tender age and were done with mistakes. And she would always talk around the biggest mistake he'd made. He'd told himself it scared her too much to name it, but he had always suspected it disgusted her, too. So they had never actually talked about the night he'd taken his big nosedive.

In his mind it was largely one drug-induced haze. First he had lost a wrestling match, then he'd completely lost his mind. He and Teri had driven out to an isolated country road. He'd known she was willing to let him talk about his disappointing match without criticizing him. He'd known that if he kissed her, she would put her arms around him and kiss him back. Trusting him, loving him, she would let him put his hand inside her blouse and touch her breasts. Wanting her, loving her, he could indulge his petting artistry until they both ached so badly they could hardly back away from taking the next step.

But that night, when they parked her car in their favorite secluded spot and she turned to him, ready to transform him from loser to winner, he knew something was wrong. He raised his hand to touch her face, and his fingers felt thick and hard. Suddenly his lips were gone, and he had only teeth to kiss her with. His gut churned, and his brain became a pressure cooker. He knew if he laid his hand on her, he would explode.

He'd had the presence of mind to get out of the car and bellow some kind of a warning at her. But that was the last of it. After that he was a loose cannon. He didn't remember exactly how he'd gotten out on that train bridge. To this day he wasn't sure whether he'd fallen or jumped. But he remembered exactly how it felt to kick his heels at heaven on his way to the ground.

"Healing takes time, John."

Such a sweet, sympathetic voice. Such a loving look in her eyes. He had wanted so badly to put his body back together, to be young and strong and whole again, just for her. Leg, hip, back, shoulders, all dislocated or broken, all surgically pinned, sewn and set, all painfully pulled, pushed and prodded day after day, month after month, to make them work again. Just for her, he'd told himself. Be a man again for her.

"Look at this." He'd struggled until his tears blurred the gray thing in his hand. "A stupid little ten-pound dumbbell. Ten pounds, and I can't even press it. God, I used to be able to press—"

"You will again. You have to believe that, John."

He had to believe he was the world's biggest jerk for doing what he'd done. He had wanted so desperately to be the biggest and the best. A champion, like Coach Archer, the man with all the right moves. John had gone to live with his married sister so he could claim a spot on the famous Wyatt Archer's high school wrestling team. He and Archer made up 99 percent of the Indian population in the small rural community of Glover, North Dakota. Like Archer, John had been determined to prove himself, especially once he'd managed to catch the eye of the prettiest girl in school.

Wrestling was generally considered a white man's game. Big, beefy farm boys were good at it. But so was John. He was quick and strong. All he'd needed was a little more muscle. That was his excuse for listening to Teri's brother, Ally, and some of the other seniors who were experimenting with anabolic steroids. The drugs had miraculously bulked up his body while they worked black magic on his brain.

The steroids scandal had blown the whole town apart. John had hated seeing Teri caught in the middle. Her brother had been selling the stuff, and her mother's boyfriend had been the dealer. He was glad all that was behind her now. It was good to see her doing so well—making good money, wearing pretty clothes, getting her picture in the paper. She deserved all those things and more, though what more, he refused to say.

He should have left her alone. That much he had to admit, and he'd atone for it once he'd accomplished his mission. The best way would be to duck back out of her life and stay out. Even now, as he shifted position, his stiffening back muscles reminded him that his body was not equipped with wings. Nobody could assure him that he hadn't done even more damage to himself with the damn drugs.

He'd been laid up for months, and he'd had plenty of time to read. History, English, math—he had tried to keep up with school. And medical journals from the hospital library. He knew all about athletes who had ended up with heart or kidney damage, the tumors that had turned up in others, and the cases of sterility and genetic disorders. How much of it was behind him and how much he was carrying around, he didn't know. He hadn't thought about it much for a long time.

But then Teri Nordstrom had been out of his life for a long time. Now she was back. He sat up slowly and watched her park the small station wagon right where he'd instructed her to, amid the only copse of cottonwoods standing next to the narrow dirt road that led to the lake.

A green panel van pulled up next to her, and a man and a woman got out. He was juggling cameras. She was flipping through a notebook. Teri gestured expansively toward the lake, the hills and finally, stretching her whole body, she reached both arms toward the sky. John smiled to himself and thought, yes, the space here feels good, the air is fresh, and the morning is beautiful. *And so are you.*

He watched the three of them get their heads together on a plan. The photographer rearranged a pile of driftwood, while Teri hopped into the back of the van and emerged wearing a long white coat over a white dress. John recognized Lavender Holland's handwoven fashions. When Teri had worked for Lavender, she'd worn tops and dresses she had made herself on Lavender's looms. He remembered how soft and touchable the fabric was and how nice Teri's gentle curves had felt beneath it. He wondered how those curves had changed since he'd last caressed them. Just wondering forced him to shift his seat again to ease the tightness in his jeans.

The coat was more stylish than anything she'd worn in those days. Suddenly the whole scene seemed to be taking place at much more than a quarter-mile distance. His memories of the shy girl he'd loved didn't jibe with the chic woman to whom the photographer paid homage with all his crouching and kneeling and darting here and there, recording every graceful move she made.

The morning breeze made the white coat billow and flutter around Teri's slender body. She tossed her golden hair, using it to net shards of sunlight as she struck pose after pose. The click and whir of the camera echoed in the gully. Teri shed the coat. Click. She tossed it over a sun-bleached branch and modeled the simple white sheath. Click. She shaded her eyes and pointed toward the lake. Click. Her laughter was bright, like tinkling crystal, much as it had always been. Click, click.

She went to the van and changed into a sleek black dress. As planned, she led the way to a place John had described that was farther up the beach, where he'd promised she would find several stumps of petrified wood too big for scavengers to carry away. Once they were out of sight, he made his way down the hill to the car and climbed into the back seat. She'd left the front windows down a couple of inches, but the sun had already made the car's vinyl interior soft and hot. When Teri and her friends came ambling back from the lake, John crouched behind the front seat and buried himself beneath the pile of clothing she had provided as cover.

By the time he'd heard the panel van's doors open and shut for the third time, John was ready to erupt from the pile and send the fashions flying. Every muscle in his body was screaming to be flexed, and he was sweating so profusely he figured the next person to wear the stuff he was hiding under would be mistaken for John Tiger by the sheriff's best bloodhounds.

The car door finally opened on the driver's side.

"Stay quiet until the car is moving." She had to be leaning over the back seat. She was talking quietly just above his ear. "Mick and Joan are still oogling over the petrified wood they picked up."

"Roll the damn windows—"

"Shh." She settled into the seat in front of him and raised her voice substantially. "Wait just a second, Joan. I have to get some..." The door closed. He heard the chink of keys, then the drone of the power window. "...ah, air in here."

He was still sweating like a racehorse.

"So, when did you say you'd be back in the city?" an unfamiliar female voice asked.

"I didn't," Teri said with what sounded to John like artificial cheer. "Since this job is done, I thought I'd take a couple of days to visit family. It's going to be good, isn't it, Joan? Lavender's catalog?"

"With what we got today, it's going to be great. The line is wonderful, Teri. I've ordered two dresses myself. And this countryside is just beautiful. Isn't it, Mick?" There was a pause. "I said, the countryside..." The woman laughed. "Look at him. He can't stop with the camera. I have to say, I didn't believe it would be worth it to come all the way to North Dakota, but I see what you mean. The farther west you go..."

The groan John had going in his head somehow sounded in his throat. Thrusting her hand between the seats, Teri made matters worse by blindly ramming him in the belly. He stifled a protest.

"I'm sorry, Teri, did you say something?"

"Oh, no, it's just my—" in retaliation John managed to trap her hand in the crevice between the bucket seats "—seat belt. It's twisted."

"Well, anyway, I don't mind going the extra distance to get the right setting," the woman rambled. John squeezed Teri's hand, hoping she'd take it as a hint and pass it on. She squirmed. "Have you lost something?" Joan asked.

John relinquished his hold.

"I've got it. I've got such a mess back there—"

"Are those extra changes? Do you want us to take some of that stuff back for you?"

"No, no..."

"It's no trouble. You don't want to haul all that around with you."

John was ready to blow. *Start the damn car.*

"I wanted to show them to my mother. Family. Cousins and everyone, you know. I really have to get on the road, John—*Joan.*" Teri recovered with a winsome little *tsk.* Despite the pouring sweat, John felt absurdly close to smiling. "I said I'd be there by... Oh, my, look what time it is. I'll see you...." The next sound he heard was a smacking kiss.

"Have a good..."

Another dry smooch. The display made John uncomfortable, even though he couldn't see it.

"And you have a safe trip back." She started the engine and put the car in gear.

"Good God, you think you can tear yourself away?" John grumbled as the tires rolled at last.

"Not unless you keep still," Teri warned, singsonging between clenched teeth. She made a quick U-turn, and they were on their way when she blurted, "What is the matter with you, John? You almost—"

"I'm suffocating back here, and you're taking your sweet time about—"

"I had a job to complete, which is my primary reason for being here."

"Does that make me secondary?"

"You're incidental." It was John's turn to squirm. "And I suggest you keep your head down until I tell you otherwise."

"Does this thing have an air conditioner?"

She was turning on a cold blast, all right. Too bad it wasn't physical. Buried under all her fancy clothes, he would have taken any breath of fresh air he could get. Some sticky, silky thing clung to his damp face, and the way he'd wedged his shoulders between the seats, he couldn't lift his arm high enough to get it off. He felt like a caterpillar all wound up in a cocoon.

"There, it's on," she said. All he got was the *sound* of air, which didn't make him feel any less clammy. "It'll take a few minutes before we get cold air."

"Didn't take any time before I got the cold shoulder from you, though. What happened? Did you have trouble getting past North Dakota's finest?"

"Truthfully the man who directed us around what he called the 'contained area' was quite friendly. He assured us that this land was here for public use and that his job was to see that we had safe access. He warned us to stay off Indian land because—" The car jolted, and he imagined her slender hands working to keep the steering wheel steady as she chuckled. "I believe he actually said the natives were restless."

"He's right." From his position on the floor he could feel the contour of every rut as it buffeted the wheels, and his hip was throbbing to beat hell. He tried to turn a groan into a chortle, but it came up short. "This one damn sure is."

"You . . . you're not hurt or anything, are you?"

Hey, a little concern. He liked the way it softened her voice. "I'm a little cramped back here. Where's the van?"

"They're behind us, so stay down. You were right. That was a beautiful spot for the shoot. We found a gorgeous petrified stump. Joan would have taken it home if we could have lifted it."

It was nice of her to try to distract him from his discomfort, but it wasn't working.

"Teri, can you reach behind the seat and push some of this stuff away from my face? I'm wedged in . . . think I'm gonna lose it any minute now."

"Lose what? Where's your head?"

"Right behind you, bumping against the door." In a moment the layers above him started to move. "Just . . . yeah, get that off my face. . . ."

The sticky silk thing came away as Teri's fingers burrowed into the jumble, letting more light reach him, along with a little cool air. Those fingers wiggled, searching, and he figured the lethal-looking nail tips might be something he'd want to avoid, but he wasn't going to say anything. He'd risk a scratch or two if he could touch his nose to the place where the delicate blue lines crisscrossed her wrist. Small price to pay for a deep breath of the floral scent that teased him now.

In a first tentative encounter she found his hair. He resisted the temptation to move his head and guide her groping. Maybe it was just another bump in the road, but he could have sworn he felt her fingers tremble when they rested lightly against his temple. He closed his eyes as she turned her hand slowly, passed it over his moist face and cupped his cheek in her palm. Here was delicious distraction. He wanted to groan in protest when she took her hand away, but soon she sent it back again, this time with a bit of cloth to blot the sweat from his face.

"Your hand felt cool." He wanted it back, and that was as close as he could come to asking. She finished drying his face, dropped the cloth and touched him again. For a moment he felt utterly calm inside.

Then her hand was gone, and the moment was over.

"Did we just take a left turn?" He'd drifted a little and lost his bearings.

"Yes."

"Should have been a right. We should be headed south by now."

"South is where the police are."

"Yeah, but north is where nothing is." He knew damn well what was what and which was which, Woody's assessment notwithstanding. "I need to get to the highway so I can hitch a ride."

"You have a ride."

He had an *escape.* "All I'm asking you to do is get me past the watchful eye down there. Then I'll hitch a ride with a southbound semi."

"You have a ride, John."

She plowed into another rut, and he bit off the urge to ask how many ten-cent tickets this ride was costing him.

"Did you think I'd go through all this trouble and then just dump you out on the side of the road?" she demanded.

"A truck stop would do nicely." If she would rub the top of his head a little, that would do nicely, too.

"What if you can't find a ride? Then all this was for nothing."

"Just what is 'all this'? I asked you to bring a separate car, and you said you'd have to think of an excuse to rent one. I'll pay for the rental."

"I'm not worried about that. I'm worried about all the policemen around here." The car stopped. Another one whizzed by, and he knew by the sound of it that they'd reached blacktop. "There's another one," Teri said with forced merriment. "He waved. He's my friend."

"You can keep your friends. If we get stopped, you don't know anything about me."

"You're just some guy I picked up and stashed under a pile of clothes in the back seat."

"That's right." A sharp left turn plastered the top of his head against the door. "*That's* wrong. I've gotta get out of here before I explode."

"Hold on just a little longer, John. I told Joan and Mick that I wasn't going back to Bismarck, so we parted company at that last turn. I'm planning on bypassing a big chunk of 83, but you've got to stay down until I get through this little town, okay?" Her tone shifted from soothing to smug. "I don't know why *you* didn't think of this."

Damn half-witted woman. "I don't know what you're thinking. I was going to get past the cops and have you shake your buddies, then drop me off on your way back to Bismarck. Once I'm off the reservation, I'm a fugitive. You know that, don't you?"

"You didn't actually set fire to a government vehicle, did you?"

"Of course I did. The damn . . ." He sighed. He didn't feel like arguing. "Woody lit the thing up. They don't know much about Woody, which is just fine. They know me. I'm the one makin' all the trouble. It's my land."

"Couldn't you think of a better way to—"

"No, but I'm sure you could. You know me. I don't always do things the best way. Or the right way, or the easy way." He allowed half a second for a rejoinder. "You're not gonna disagree there, are you?"

"No, I'm not."

"You've got more options, Teri. You've always had—" Had what? He would be lying if he said *advantages*. All he could come up with was "Other options."

He didn't expect her to understand the mess he was in. He wasn't sure he could explain it to her, even if he wanted to. Explanations always sounded like excuses. It had always seemed better to walk away—or battle it out, if your back was against the wall—rather than try to explain what simply *was*. At the moment it was his head against the wall, and walking away was out of the question, so he was grateful for the stretch of silence in which he was permitted to suffer.

And suffer he did. By the time she pulled over on another gravel road somewhere, his body was awash in aches and pains. The click of a seat belt signaled a shift in her attention, and her voice came from above.

"I think it's safe for you to ride in the front seat now. We're east of 83, and we're . . ." The clothes were lifted completely away from his head now, and there was light, a drift of blond hair, and blue eyes that suddenly filled with alarm. "My God, John, you look—"

"Could you move your seat forward, please?"

"John, why didn't you say something?" She sent tops and skirts flying, muttering as she shoveled him out of his hole. "I've squashed you, smothered you, oh . . . I could've . . ." She disappeared behind the seat, then jiggled and rocked, muttering still. "I should've thought to move this as far . . ."

"It wouldn't have made much difference." The seat finally gave up a couple of inches, which only lost him ground. His back was useless, and his shoulder was shaking. "I can't get up, Teri. You'll have to help me out."

"How?"

"Open the back door and give me a push. My back's stiffened up on me."

She opened the lid on his can and started scooping the clothes onto the back seat of the car. The air felt good, but he was still one sorry sardine. He did take some satisfaction in her continued lamentations, and even more in the way he finally had her hurrying along.

He bit off a curse as her initial efforts forced his rigid back muscles into play, bringing his face within an inch of hers. "My left leg's dead."

"What?"

"Numb. It happens sometimes when I sit too long. It's from that time when I..." They both went still, exchanging haunted looks. Then he offered a small, penitent smile. "Well, since then I've aggravated it a little more, so sometimes I..."

"You have no business trying to turn yourself into a pretzel." He was halfway up, and it occurred to him that she was stronger than she looked. "Can you get up on the seat?" she asked.

The pain made him dizzy. He closed his eyes, and his head fell back against her breast while the car spun around him. In the depths of hell he'd found a heavenly pillow.

"John? If we could get your head down between your knees..."

"It's good where it is." *Between your knees would be even better.* "Can you reach the other door?"

"My God, you're like a sack of..." She reached over him, and the opposite door sprang open.

"Good. I'll pull, you push. Once I get on my feet—"

The first forty-five degrees were rough, and the next were a killer, but once he was upright he had some momentum going for him. He tumbled out and caught himself on the car door. Straightening slowly, he stretched one screaming muscle at a time.

"Are you okay?" Teri stepped out behind him. He gripped the top of the door and rested his forehead on the back of his hand. "Dumb question, huh?"

"I will be, soon as my blood finds my feet." She touched him so gently that he thought his back had been brushed by a bird's wing, and it wasn't until her hand slid away that he realized he'd been holding his breath. He gave himself a mental boot as he squared his shoulders and took a look around. "We're not lost, are we?"

"Of course not. It makes more sense to stick to the back roads, doesn't it?"

Carefully assuming his own weight, John moved away from the car. He surveyed the bend in the road and the wire fence that followed it, the huge grass pasture and the low hills in the distance. "It makes sense if we end up back on the highway pretty soon. I can't catch a ride out here." He took a pack of cigarettes from his shirt pocket and shook one out. It was bent out of shape, just like his body.

"I'll get you back to 83," she promised.

He struck a match on his thumbnail. He couldn't quite steady his hand, and the quivering flame humiliated him. He shook it dead as soon as he'd lit up. "I didn't figure on running you around the countryside like this," he confessed on the tail of a stream of smoke.

"It's for a good cause. I don't know much about what's going on back there." She cast a quick glance down the road they'd put behind them. "But getting you to the hospital to see your mother is a good cause. I remember when you were in the hospital, after..."

"After I took my famous dive," he finished lightly before he took a long, slow pull on his cigarette.

"Yes, after you fell. You asked Wyatt to find your mother for you."

"I was just a kid, and I was scared." He braced his arm on the roof of the car, staring past it at the hills as he shifted his weight off his weaker left side. The smoke worked its calming magic. "I figure, even though she's an old woman, she might be scared, too. I'm not her only son, but I'm the one who knows what it's like to be...that kind of scared."

"It's important that you be there, then. For yourself as well as for her." Teri stepped closer. He turned his head, rested his chin on his shoulder and looked into her eyes. Such a soft shade of blue. She smiled softly, and spoke softly, too. And honestly. "I was a little jealous, as I remember. That you asked for her and not for me."

"I didn't want you to see me bleeding all over the place and whimpering like a baby." He raised his head and glanced away again. "You figure your mother's the one person who's already seen all that, so you ask for her."

"I didn't see much blood that night. It was too dark. But I was scared, too. I saw how badly hurt you were, and I see now—" She stood next to his shoulder, so close he could hear her swallow. "I didn't realize it was still that bad."

He shrugged. "I got to thinking I was some kind of superhero when I was in the army. Tore open a few old wounds."

"That's not a good idea, you know."

"I ought to." He shook his head and sought out her eyes again. "By this time I ought to. But I wanted to see you." She nodded, understanding too well. "Back then, I mean, when Coach brought you to the hospital. I felt like such a jerk, but you didn't seem to notice."

"You weren't the only one who was just a kid then."

He chuckled humorlessly. "Meaning I *was* a jerk."

"Meaning I was naive." He grunted as he sought consolation from his cigarette. "I wanted to see you, too," she said. "I kept coming back, remember? It didn't matter what my mother or my brother said. I kept coming back. I couldn't stop myself. I believed all the wounds would heal."

She explained things too readily, too damn eagerly. Things that would lead to more things, the kind best left undisturbed. He pushed himself away from the car and turned his back, telling himself he needed space to enjoy his smoke.

"But there were more wounds to be inflicted," she persisted.

"Yeah, well, I get along with mine okay, and you were naive, like you said." His hat was still in the back seat. The hell with it. He didn't feel like ducking in there to get it. He heard himself telling her, "It was good to see you again, Teri."

"What are you doing?"

He was walking. "I can get to the highway from here. I figure if I catch a northbound rig into Minot, I can probably—"

"What!" The sudden sharpness brought him up short. "Get yourself back into this car, John Tiger. Look at the way you're limping."

He turned and tried for a little sarcasm. "Am I doing it wrong?"

"John, you're not doing this to me again." With her fists clenched next to her slim hips, she marched up beside him. "This is exactly what happened that night. You got out of the car and started walking."

"Now we're both walking. How far is it to the highway?"

"It'll seem a lot farther on foot than it will by car. Especially to the one of us who's limping."

He took a quick puff on his cigarette as he dragged his bootheel in the gravel and cocked his weight off his temporarily gimpy leg. "Okay. First truck stop we come to, you let me off and be on your way."

She stared up at him, her lips pressed together in a hard, angry line. "You should have cut your hair."

It wasn't one of the hundred retorts he'd expected out of her.

"You got something against long hair? Is that a new wound you're gonna have trouble with, that I let my hair grow?" Her eyes softened. Her mouth followed suit. He tested out a softer tone, a little smile. "Yours is longer than I remember. Lighter, too."

"It's called sunglazing." She wouldn't smile back. She almost looked scared. "They'll recognize you, John."

"You got a pair of scissors on you?"

"No."

"Then I'll hide it under my hat, okay?" She glanced pointedly at his bare head. "I brought a cowboy hat. I gave some thought to using an electric mane trimmer, but, hell . . ." Now, finally, she smiled. "See, that's why. I knew you'd laugh."

And she did, just a little.

His shoulders sagged as the tension dissipated. He was glad for a steady hand when he did his Little Jack Horner pose. "I've done a whole lot of traveling with the help of this thumb. It'll get me to Sioux Falls if you get me across the county line."

"I like your hair."

He wondered if she'd heard what he'd said. "I like yours, too."

Chapter 3

With a couple of extrastrength aspirin under his belt, John had pushed the front passenger seat as far back as it would go, slid down, positioned his straw hat squarely over his face and fallen asleep. They had passed three truck stops and two patrol cars without his notice. Teri was careful to observe the speed limit. She was also watching the fuel gauge, determined not to stop until it was absolutely necessary. When she passed a green sign warning Last Gas for 40 Miles, she knew the time had come.

The minute she slowed for the turn, John snatched the hat away. He came awake almost as quickly as he'd dropped off. He was also quick to realize they'd gone farther than he'd intended, and he whistled softly.

"Lady, you must've been flyin' low."

"Not at all," she said as she steered the car into the shade of the gas-pump portico. "You've been sleeping long."

"Got up pretty early this morning." Stretching, he surveyed the situation, pointedly taking the big diesel pumps and the sign designating Truck Parking into account. "This is good. Don't see anything now, but I should be able to hook up with somebody goin' my way pretty quick."

"I told Lavender I'd give her a call." While he'd slept, she'd thought about his plan and firmly decided she had a better one. Ease in, she told herself, as she aligned her gas tank with the pump. She glanced John's way. "I told her I might not be back today."

"*I* told you you *would* be." He gave her a stern look, but his voice mellowed as he tucked the longest ends of his black hair under the hat. "I appreciate what you've done for me, Teri, but I'm not asking for any more of your time. I'm letting you go on your way now."

"I need gas."

"I'll pump it for you. You go on in and get yourself something cold to drink." He was determined to be stubborn about this and flick her offer away like a piece of grass clinging to his jeans. He was already halfway out of the car. "I'll come in and pay the bill, and then . . ."

It shouldn't have bothered her. If he wanted to get caught, let him. "I'll pay for my own gas."

"You think I'm not going to pay my way?" With one foot on the pavement, he turned to her. "You don't owe me anything, Teri. I'm the one who owes you." He jerked his chin toward the gas pump. "This much, at least."

"Will you call me when you get there?" He shook his head. Foolish as it was, she found herself needing some kind of concession from him, even though it cost her pride to persist. "But how will I know . . . ?"

"I'll be okay." A part of him seemed reluctant to move, even though his feet were ready to take him away.

He leaned a little closer, searched her face, then smiled gently, as though he'd found something at once unexpected and endearing in her eyes. "I'll get there okay."

"I want to know... about your mother."

"I'll tell her you're thinking about her. She told me once that you were a good woman with a strong heart." He chuckled. "I don't know why she thought I was too dumb to figure that out for myself."

"I'm not leaving until I'm sure you have a ride."

"Yes, you are." He used the car door for support as he pushed himself to his feet. "Super unleaded, right?"

"John..."

She watched him through the windshield. The cowboy hat looked wonderful on him, with the brim slightly tipped back as though he'd just completed a hard ride. He walked that way, too, gingerly stretching the kinks out. He'd managed to tuck most of his hair under the straw crown, but the shorter part that swept his forehead made him look boyish, a young broomstick cowboy. He put on a pair of mirrored sunglasses, rapped his knuckles on the hood of the car and grinned at her through the bug-speckled glass.

With a sigh Teri grabbed her purse and got out of the car. They could probably both use something cold to drink, she decided. No matter how reluctant she was to leave him in a situation as uncertain as this, she couldn't make a scene the way she had when they'd been out in the middle of nowhere on an uncharted gravel road. He knew that, and he seemed content with it. He even had the nerve to hum along with the country tune on the radio in the pickup at the next pump as he took hose in hand and flipped a switch.

Being afraid for him was an old habit Teri knew she should have broken a long time ago, but the lump of panic springing in her throat told her that she wasn't there yet. John knew that, too. She could tell by the nonchalance he was affecting now, showing her everything was cool.

He took a turn around the gas pump and approached her with a long-handled squeegee in his hand. "Service with a smile here, lady. How 'bout I clean your windshield for you?"

"You work here, Chief?"

It was the epithet that pulled them both up short. A burly man with bushy blond eyebrows approached. He adjusted the bill of his blue-and-white cap as he glanced at the sign above the pumps. "I don't think so. This here's a self-service island." Shuffling his rubber-soled work boots and trying out a spraddle-legged stance, he turned to Teri.

"You don't have to tip him or nothin', ma'am. He's just tryin' to—"

"We're together," Teri said. She laid her hand on John's arm and felt the tension in the corded muscles beneath his sleeve. Big as the man was, she didn't doubt that John could tear him limb from limb.

The man registered Teri's claim with a frown, made almost comical by his bristly eyebrows. Clearly disgusted, he glanced away from her and scowled at John. "You wanna move it along, then? The pump's shut off, and the other super unleaded ain't workin'."

A jacked-up four-wheeler nosed up behind Teri's station wagon and sat there purring like a Bengal tiger.

"Maybe you oughta grab a place in line," John suggested, gesturing offhandedly. "You mess with me, you might be waitin' in line to use the can."

Teri rubbed John's arm slightly, discreetly. "Let it go," she whispered.

"Hold him back, lady. He's got me scared." The man laughed as he headed for his car, tossing back, "These days, you just never know."

John took off his glasses and wiped his forehead with the back of his hand. "Must be tough, never knowing," he grumbled. Then he looked over his shoulder, a smile in his eyes as he reassured Teri with a confederate wink. "Guess I can let him live to disgrace himself another day."

John moved the car while Teri breathed a sigh of relief and went inside. She picked up a couple of candy bars and the extra can of pop that would give her license to touch his hand again or, more precisely, to make him touch hers. At least this time he would have to say goodbye. She knew too well that the want of goodbye only intensified the pain, dragged it out, kept it alive. It had never seemed to be officially over between them. Maybe that was because she had never officially let it be.

She was on the verge of deciding that the time had come when a state trooper pulled into the gas station. Standing right outside the door, John saw him, too. He dropped the cigarette he'd just lit, snuffed it out on the pavement with his bootheel and started for the men's room. But the man with the bushy eyebrows had already claimed the big metal tag with the key attached.

"Looks like you're the one's gonna be gettin' in line, Chief," the big man with the big mouth bragged, dangling the key as if he'd initiated a game of keep-away. He leered tauntingly as he sauntered past. John stood steadfast. "Hope it ain't some big emergency."

Teri stepped outside quickly and handed John a can of orange pop. "What is that man's problem?" she asked innocently. At a loss for his next move, John looked to her. She hooked her hand in the crook of his elbow and smiled as though she hadn't noticed that the trooper was scrutinizing license plates, but she invented an itinerary for his benefit. "Why don't we just go on? We're not far from my mother's. The sooner we get there, the sooner we can leave."

"Yeah, I..." He looked around. Bushy Brows was having trouble fitting the key into the lock, and the trooper was standing tall now, hands on hips, scanning the lay of the land. "I guess you're right."

John had parked the car at the side of the building, out of the way of the gas pumps. Teri slid behind the wheel, started the car, rolled the windows up and turned the air conditioner on full blast. The noise effectively shut out everyone she wished would go away, which meant everyone but John.

She glanced furtively over her shoulder as she buckled her seat belt. "What do you think he's looking for?"

"Who knows?" He shrugged. "Could be a speeder. Could be me."

"I don't think he recognized you, and there's no reason for anyone to be looking for this car."

"Unless they know I'm gone." They were entering the roadway. He instinctively glanced right while she waited for a car approaching from the left to go by. "And somebody noticed that the van headed back without the car."

"They can't check every vehicle. There are too many ways you can go, and too many—"

"They're not trying to keep me there, Teri. They want me off the reservation, and I'm sure they don't expect me to walk out the front gate."

They were heading down one of the state's few divided highways again, but not for long, Teri decided. It was time to disappear. She felt a little reckless all of a sudden, and her right foot was feeling heavy. "Do they know about your mother?"

"I don't know."

He glanced at the speedometer and raised an eyebrow, but she ignored him. "Are you sure she's really sick?"

"I talked to my sister, Marla. You remember Marla?" Teri nodded. "She gave me hell over my poor timing."

"Does she know you're coming?"

"No." He shrugged again. "Doesn't matter. Marla wouldn't... Where are you going?"

The sign said Baldwin, but more to the point, the condition of the road surface took a turn for the worse. After her quick turn, Teri was forced to slow down.

"I think we need to stay on the back roads, don't you?"

John's groan was decidedly disapproving. "I think if we head south and pick up the interstate, I can hitch—"

"I'm taking you to Sioux Falls." In the blink of an eye they'd already passed Baldwin. "If they're looking for you, you can't be standing along the road hitching a ride."

"We don't know what that guy was looking for, and I don't think there's much chance of this road getting us to Sioux Falls."

"I was thinking we'd stay off the highway until it gets dark."

"If we can even *find* the highway by the time it gets dark. We should've picked up a map back at that pit stop." Dejectedly he examined the soft drink he'd been sipping. "And we should've gotten something to eat. It's nice that you remembered I like orange pop, but this is diet." He turned the can and checked the label, just to be sure. "It doesn't even have any sugar in it."

"I'm sorry." Teri produced two candy bars from the pocket of her pale blue skirt. "Here's the sugar."

"Great." He accepted only one of her offerings, so she dropped the other one in his lap. It disappeared between his denim-clad thighs, and he made a little clucking sound as he shook his head. "We're gonna need real food. I am, anyway."

"There's a map in the glove compartment. Figure out where we are, and we'll find a town with a grocery store."

He tore into a wrapper with his teeth as he popped the button on the glove compartment. The small door fell open and whacked his knee. "Usually you eat pretty good when you ride with a trucker," he grumbled.

"But they don't take you all the way there." She offered a plaintive look. She'd won by default, but that wasn't enough. "Be sensible, John. I'm your surest bet."

"You really want to do this?" Holding off on the candy, he gave her a long, considering look. His dark eyes were deep-set. They had a way of arresting her train of thought and changing its course to suit his own. "You wanna take me all the way, Teri?"

"I've got the car. I have a few days to spare." She returned her attention to the gravel road and the stomach-knocking rise up ahead. Perversely she accelerated, slanting him a pointed glance. "And I don't want you to get caught before you see your mother."

"What about after I see her?"

"I don't want you to get caught, period. Don't ask me why." She nodded, indicating the paper accordion he was shaking open. "What does the map say?"

"It says the governor welcomes us to North Dakota." He smiled as he lifted the lower left-hand corner closer to his face. "And he suggests we take advantage of the great fishing at Lake Sakakawea. 'Drive right across John

Tiger's pasture,' the ol' boy says. 'Just leave the gates open. Tiger's got nothing better to do than to run around checking his gates.'"

"It must be a constant nuisance." As long as she was sticking her neck out, she needed to rack up a host of legitimate reasons to sympathize with him. Reasons that had nothing to do with the fact that she had once loved him.

"You start losing livestock, it's more than a *nuisance.* I've got fifty-six head. That doesn't afford me a lot of slack." He bit off a chunk of chocolate-covered peanuts and caramel, which momentarily gummed up his storytelling.

Teri smiled. "Neither does that caramel."

"This other one's all yours."

"I think I'll pass on it for now." Just the smell of chocolate nauseated her empty stomach, and she wondered why she'd picked candy, of all things, which she had diligently trained herself to detest. "Exercising my right to refuse," she added with a wan smile.

"I can support that." He tossed the extra candy into the glove compartment. "My brother Chuck, he's been active with the Indian movement for quite a while. After I got discharged, I hooked up with him for a time, and I kinda got used to the idea that Indians have rights, too. Can't seem to shake it."

"You don't have to shake it. You do have rights." She wondered at his skeptical look. "I mean, you're supposed to. We're all supposed to have the same rights."

"Sounds good to me." Case closed, he leaned closer to show her what he'd found on the map. "I figure this little gray line must be the road we're on, so if we turn here, there should be a fork coming up right about..."

The road forked directly ahead. "Which way?"

John glanced up from the map. "Left. If there's a grocery store in the next dot on this map, I'll buy lunch. Then we'll lie low till it gets dark." He chuckled. "How bad does that sound?"

"It sounds like something I've heard before. *Bonnie and Clyde?*"

"Never saw it."

"I did. Let's not rob any banks."

The comment echoed in her head and made her smile as she watched him pay for their purchases at a small-town variety store. She wondered about the pack of cigarettes he'd tossed in last. How much had he changed in eight years? He hadn't been a smoker when she'd known him before. He hadn't been a cowboy then, either. He hadn't been a rabble-rouser or a protester or a fugitive—except, possibly, from her.

He had picked a bad time to run away from her. She had to remember that in order to keep a clear head. She had to watch herself. She was still drawn to him. She was naturally curious about who he was now. There would always be a link between them, whether he knew it or not. And he needed her help, whether or not he would admit it.

He needed *her* help this time. She liked that.

Deciding on a picnic, they found a quiet spot in a windbreak planted thick with wild plum bushes and silver-green Russian-olive trees. Nearby a narrow creek slipped sluggishly through the notch it had carved in the clay, but the broken-down fence on the opposite bank was evidence of the high torrent of an earlier spring run-off.

Tall slough grass made a springy cushion beneath earth-tone-fringed ponchos. The weaver would approve, Teri mused as she spread out a third long wrap. Lavender loved to boast of the many practical uses for her simple designs. She also loved to share natural foods in natural settings, so she would have been pleased that Teri had made John put the white bread back and take the whole wheat. He'd won out on the ring bologna, but Teri had slipped in a wedge of Muenster cheese and a carton of yogurt along with the apples, bananas and oranges they'd both agreed on.

Since there was no hurrying the sun down, they took their time with their food. John defied tradition and tempted Teri with a bite of his apple, but he refused to share her yogurt. It felt so much like old times that she almost expected her brother, Ally, to pop in and swipe an orange while he teased John about catching him in the act. Even if they were just looking at each other, Ally would say he'd caught them in *the* act.

But when stretching his back made John wince, Teri remembered just how far behind them those innocent times were.

"Still hurts?"

She saw herself massaging his back and shoulders, the way Lavender had taught her to do, and she had to busy herself taking her shoes off and setting them neatly beside their handwoven pallet.

He shook his head, not to deny the pain, but to dismiss its significance. "I act like an old man sometimes."

"You're lucky to be alive."

"See? Old men feel like that, too. Aches and pains are good for reminding you that you're not dead." Munching on his second apple, he leaned back, resting on his elbow and his hip—the good side—and inclined his chin toward the car. "That wasn't too smart, getting myself wedged in there like that. Maybe by the time I'm an old man I'll wise up."

"You said you'd aggravated the injuries," she recalled. "How did you manage that?"

"Lifting weights. I got on a bodybuilding team when I was in the army." He detected something more than surprise in her eyes. "Strictly natural. No steroids, I swear." He held up the apple, as though it had something to do with his claim. "After all the physical therapy I'd had, weight training was a breeze."

"I'm surprised the army would even take you with your medical history."

"You think I told them about any medical history?" With another gesture he dismissed that, too. She heard a note of male pride as he recalled, "I passed my physical, no problem. They ignored the scars, and the only thing they X-rayed was my lungs. I was in good shape, and after I got into bodybuilding, I was in *great* shape. I was almost convinced I could get back into wrestling."

"Was that what you wanted?"

"I guess I wanted to prove I could do it right, without the drugs."

"Prove it to yourself?"

"Yeah, maybe." He took one more bite, then pitched the apple core across the creek. It smacked a fence post and sent a black-winged magpie fluttering from its perch. "Anyway, I started out real careful, but after a while I decided I was so solid, nothing could break me. So I kept pushing it until I screwed up my back again. After I got out of traction, they handed me a medical discharge."

She had watched him suffer for so long, but he'd gotten better. Damn him, he'd clawed his way back, only to put everything in jeopardy again. Served him right, she told herself. He deserved traction. Oh, God, the way it had hurt him at first just to move a single...

She set her jaw and forced herself to wonder casually, "Why would the army have a bodybuilding team?"

"We competed in amateur contests. Mainly the recruiters liked to show us off at high school assemblies, where we'd make the principal happy by talking down drugs while we dazzled the kids with our amazing biceps." He turned on the charm, smiling for her as he flexed one shoulder. "Especially the girls. The recruiters swore up and down that the army had truckloads of soldiers built just like us, and the girls couldn't wait to sign on."

"I'm sure. What did you wear for these assemblies?"

"Not much," he teased. "Just a little bikini sort of thing. And lots of oil."

"Really?" She sighed and offered a coy smile. "That's what I hate about a swimsuit shoot. All that oil." Two could play at this game. "And the inevitable argument over who gets to help put it on."

His smile faded as he took a sudden interest in the magpie, who had come back to investigate the apple core.

"I was teasing, too, John," she said quietly.

The magpie chattered noisily as he pecked at his find.

John shook his head. "I never could take a joke when it came to—" They both remembered. It had been the subject of nearly every argument they'd ever had, including the last one. His eyes held the apology he'd never quite brought himself to express. "Guess I haven't changed. I've got nothing to say about it anymore, but I still get this god-awful feeling...."

"You never understood that it worked both ways." With the force of reason on her side, she elevated her chin a notch. "The difference was that I trusted you."

"Is that the only difference between us?"

His dark gaze riveted hers, but she refused to flinch. Not even when he ran his forefinger lightly along the point of her chin. Especially not when the light of a smile softened his eyes and the corner of his generous mouth twitched. Most certainly not when he sighed.

"We both know it's a damn good thing I got out of your life when I did. All you did was get prettier. If we had stayed together, I would have been a basket case by now."

He drew his hand away, slowly at first, and then it went to his breast pocket as he sat up smiling. "Remember that song about not making a pretty woman your wife?" She nodded, watching him pull out his cigarettes. "It makes a lot of sense. Soon as I get some time, I'm gonna find me a real ugly one, like the song says."

She gave him the smile he was angling for, but the cigarettes drew her attention. "Did you start smoking in the army?"

He grunted, a sound of reluctant assent. He went to his front jeans pocket for matches.

"Why?"

"Kill time, I guess. Relax. Keep my hands busy." He drew out a cigarette, watching it emerge from the pack as though there might be a prize at the end of it. "Funny, isn't it? You watch what you eat, exercise, build your body up one way, break it down another."

"You're not broken-down." She laid her hand on his sleeve, and he looked up, surprised. "Your friend, Woody, would be horrified to hear you say that. He calls you the Cat, and it's pretty obvious he thinks the Tiger is the real king of the jungle."

"What jungle?" He gestured with the book of matches between his fingers. Across the creek a patch of yellow sweet-clover blossoms nodded in the breeze. "We've got prairie here."

Smiling now, she conceded, "King of the prairie, then."

"Woody's the kind of guy who needs a hero. He picked me back when we were kids." He tucked the pack of cigarettes back into his pocket and draped his forearms over his knees. "I'm not trying to be a hero, Teri. I'm just trying to make a living. I've got one brother who's always trying to make some kind of statement and another one who can't stay away from the bottle long enough to get his act together. My sister left the reservation and married a white guy. This land is what was left to us, and I'm the only one who's interested in using it. So they all said, 'Sure, John, give it a shot.' And that's what I'm doing."

"But you *are* making a statement, whether you set out to or not."

"I'm just saying, 'Back off and give us half a chance.'"

"*Us,*" she repeated. "Not you."

"Yeah, well, maybe some of Chuck's philosophy rubbed off on me. But it's *my* rights I'm claiming. I'm talking about *my* land, *my* fences, *my* gates."

"I understand that. Otherwise I wouldn't be here."

The significance of her claim seemed to escape him as he leaned forward and gestured with the unlit cigarette. "You look at that road map you've got in the car. You look at how much of the reservation land is covered by water now, since they built these dams. Who do you think all that 'taken land' was taken from? Some money was paid, but the money doesn't mean much to most people. It gets spent."

"Isn't that what you bought your cattle with? Isn't that where the 'per cap' payments come from?"

"Yeah, it is. But I'd rather have the bottomland where my grandmother's garden used to be." He gazed across the creek, as though he could see the garden plot behind the broken fence. "My dad was from up here. His ancestry was Arikara and Mandan. They were farmers from way back, ancient times. My mother is from South Dakota. She's Sioux. Back in the old days, the Sioux used to steal corn and squash from the Mandan. The Arikara used to scout for the army because they hated the Sioux so much." He shook his head, remembering with a smile. "You talk about opposites attracting. I was pretty young when my dad died, but I can still hear them. Man, they used to argue sometimes. They always ended up calling a truce before they went to bed. So I've got both farmer's blood and hunter's blood in my veins."

Teri was fascinated. "You've never told me much about these things before."

"Back then I wasn't sure you wanted to know." He leaned back again, gesturing offhandedly as he braced one elbow on the ground. "Hell, I wasn't sure *I* wanted to know. Or remember. But now that you've got no reason to be interested anymore...well, you've got no reason to be offended by it, either."

"Offended?" The word came at her like a blast of cool air. "Did you ever think—?"

"No," he said quickly, then shrugged. "You never seemed to be. And I never talked about my background much because...I guess because if you were going to be offended, I didn't want to know. It was *me,* Teri, *my* problem. Okay?"

"Okay," she agreed. If he wanted it, he could have it.

"I'm talking about it now." He sat up again, facing her. "So I wanna hear some talk back. You said if it didn't involve my rights, you wouldn't be here. What did you mean by that?"

"I'm here because you need a ride to the hospital where your mother's gravely ill. You should be with her." She smoothed her skirt over her knees, a scant inch away from one of his, and drew her bare feet up closer to her hip, settling in. "That's why I'm here."

"You're helping me duck the authorities, sweetheart."

"The authorities would prevent you from getting to your mother's bedside."

"Simple as that, huh?"

"That much of it is clear to me." She sighed, seeking some hint of understanding in his eyes. "I grew up in this state, John, but I know very little about the politics you're talking about. I know that the Indians have been treated badly, but I have to admit, for me, the reservations have just been places to drive past. When you were in the hospital there, I would visit you. Just you. You're my only—" She caught the expectant glimmer in his eyes first, caught herself second. "You *were* my only connection to any of this."

The light dimmed. The look in his eyes acknowledged her amendment without comment, but now without sadness.

"It isn't that I'm not interested." She looked for the light again, but it was gone, along with the fleeting glimpse of disappointment. Just as well. "It's just that I don't know enough about it to rally around any flags."

"It's pretty simple. The government said, 'Here, take this little chunk of land. We want the rest.' And then a little while later, they said, 'Wait, we want some of that back. Here's some money.'" He pointed toward the car again. "You can look at that map. See where the dams are, where the backwater is. Even the shoreline isn't Indian land anymore. That belongs to the Corps of Engineers."

"But the Indians have a resort there, don't they? A vacation lodge or something?"

"Yeah, but it's not exactly conveniently located, and besides..." He shook his head. "That's not my problem. All I want to do is close my gate. That's all."

"I don't think that's unreasonable. Don't..." He'd just remembered the cigarette, but she caught his hand before he got it to his mouth. Their eyes met, his questioning her move. "You're not broken-down, but you are showing a little wear and tear around the edges. You can reverse this kind of damage, John. All you have to do is quit."

"Is that all I have to do?" He smiled indulgently. "I'm supposed to ask first. Isn't that the way it's done? Do you mind if I have a cigarette?"

"Yes, I do."

"Then I'll wait," he said easily, pocketing both matches and cigarette. "Since you were willing to listen to me plead my case just now, I'll wait. Are you going to be up to driving through the night, or will you trust me behind the wheel of your rental car?"

"If we got stopped for any reason, I'd rather be the one to produce the driver's license."

"Then it's time you got some sleep."

"Sleep?" She glanced away briefly. "Right now?"

"You look as though you could use about twelve hours." He cupped his hand lightly around her cheek and grazed her cheekbone with his thumb. "You seem a little worn around the edges, too. A little...I don't know, fragile, maybe.''

"Don't be silly—I'm fine. I can't just..." Her eyes drifted closed for a moment. His hands, at once powerful and tender, had always made her stomach flutter this way. ''...fall asleep right here, right now.''

"Would you be more comfortable in the car?''

"No, but I—''

At her words he put his arm around her and drew her down on the pallet with him. "Put your head on my shoulder, then. You used to be able to fall asleep easily in my arms, especially after...''

"Oh, John, that was a long time ago," she said with a sigh, but she stretched her legs alongside his and gave in, just for a moment, she told herself. He pressed her head to his chest and held her, accommodating himself to her as she relaxed, muscle by muscle. Resting was a flimsy excuse, but she found it was enough.

"I still think about it," he confessed after a long, sweet, settling-back silence. "Do you?''

"Sometimes." *Often.* The lub-dub of his heart next to her ear echoed the beat of her own. She wanted to slide her arm around him, but she kept her elbow close to her side and rested her hand on his chest. "I never understood—''

"Shh." He brushed a wisp of hair back from her face, then rubbed her shoulder soothingly. "Don't try. Not now, when all you need to do is relax and let sleep come.''

"You'll get stiff and sore from having my weight on you.''

"What weight?" He lifted her with a slight shrug. "This little bit?''

"Nice biceps," she said, smiling as she snuggled closer. "I can see why it would be a fine recruiting tool.''

"Just think of it as a fine pillow. Are your eyes closed?"

The leaves rattled overhead. Hoppers and winged insects whispered in the grass.

"Mmm-hmm."

"You want me to tell you a story or sing or something? What puts you to sleep?"

Complete sexual satisfaction, she thought.

"Besides that," he said softly, and she knew he was smiling right along with her. "But if that's what it takes, all you have to do is say the word."

"I'm almost asleep now, so just be quiet." He was. The sound of his breathing was a soothing intimacy. "Are you going to sleep, too?"

"I've already slept," he said, his voice as smooth and mellow as blended whiskey. "I'm going to watch over you."

"Oh. That's nice." She felt too good about where she was now to question it anymore. "John?"

"Hmm?"

"Nothing about you has ever offended me."

"I'm glad."

"And I think you have every right to do what you're doing."

"Thank you."

"And I'm very interested in—"

"Shh, rest now." He stroked her arm and turned his cheek against her forehead. "Go to sleep in my arms, pretty woman."

Chapter 4

The lights of Sioux Falls glimmered softly beneath pale daybreak. Teri had driven through the night, with John serving as copilot most of the way. He had kept her awake by exchanging stories with her, two for one. He'd talked about the army and about his days with the Crimson Eagle protesters, and she'd told him what there was to tell about her modeling career.

His exploits were far more interesting, she thought, full of colorful characters and risky business. He was curious about the places she'd been, but the designer names she might have dazzled him with meant nothing to him. She wasn't surprised, of course. She was glad he wasn't a man to be impressed by such things. But some part of her wanted him to say, "Well done." And he had, after a fashion. He'd said, "You've sure moved up in the world." She wasn't sure she was comfortable with whatever that meant.

She knew he was tired now. After their picnic she had surprised herself by sleeping most of the afternoon away, while John had kept his vigil, as he'd promised. As the night drew on he'd worked hard to stay awake and keep her company, but he'd lost the struggle and dozed off half an hour ago.

In that time she had sorted back over all that they had said, then considered the topics they had not discussed. Other men. Other women. The last time they had seen each other, the last tears, the final slamming of the door. She hadn't mentioned her futile attempts to contact him, nor his subsequent attempts to find her, which had been too little too late. And there was so much more to be evaded, so many things she had schooled herself not to think about. Much to Teri's relief, they had both found it easier to avoid the looming closet full of dreams gone bad. If the rest of the trip went as planned, maybe the closet would stay closed and they would part friends.

The moment they walked through the hospital door, John's whole body tensed. Teri knew that he had done enough hospital time to last him a lifetime, but there was something ominous about the clinical sterility of the place. Teri felt it, too. At first she was afraid the police had tracked John down, that maybe they were waiting at the end of one of the white corridors or behind one of the gray doors. From the moment John asked to see Della Tiger, responses were guarded. He and Teri were directed to the fourth floor, where a nurse made sure John was a member of the family before showing the way to his mother's room.

"The doctor just left. I'm sorry. At least your brother was with her," the cherub-faced woman in white said. As though she were hosting a tour, she took a post next to the door, which stood slightly ajar.

Teri saw the alarm in John's eyes. He stared at the door, but he made no move to open it farther. The silence was cast in black. Finally the nurse made the move for him, stepping inside to announce quietly, "Your brother is here, Mr. Tiger."

"My brother? Jeez, I sure didn't think..."

The sound of the man's voice drew John closer, and the nurse stepped back to hold the door for him.

"Chuck?"

"She's gone, John."

Teri stood awkwardly in the doorway. She had never met John's brother, but if she had seen him on the street, she would have known they were related. John was the larger man, but Chuck was the senior brother. It was he who muttered something both cryptic and sad as he initiated what must have been a rare embrace. When the two men stepped apart and turned toward the white bed, Teri glimpsed Della Tiger's ashen face.

"When?" John's voice was steady, but so low that Teri could hardly hear him.

"Just a little bit ago. It happened peacefully, just that quick," Chuck explained, snapping his fingers.

"Didn't you have a priest?" John took a step closer to his mother, speaking as though he wasn't convinced she could no longer hear him. "She would have wanted a priest."

"The priest was here late last night."

John started to turn, but he couldn't pull himself away. His eyes never left his mother's face. "She...she never woke up?"

"No." Chuck laid his hand on his brother's shoulder.

Teri wanted to touch John, too. She had taken it upon herself to bring him here, and now she felt as though they had just watched his train leave the station without him.

She hurt for him as she surveyed the apparatus that had been pushed aside—the monitor, the glucose bottle and its tubing, the ventilator—all of it useless now.

"I should have gotten here sooner," she heard John say.

"I don't think she knew who was here. It was better this way. She didn't suffer." Chuck patted John's shoulder. "You wanna sit by her for a little while?

"Teri..." John turned, searching. There was a vacancy in his eyes until they met hers, and then she could have sworn she saw something in them akin to relief, maybe even thankfulness. "Teri's with me."

Her heart fell a notch when Chuck said, "I'll take care of Teri."

With a pointed look the nurse invited Chuck to take care of John, too, presumably so that the staff could get on with its job, but Chuck was an able intercessor. "Give him a minute, okay? He's my kid brother. He just got here."

Teri glanced over her shoulder as she allowed Chuck to lead her back to the hallway. She saw John touch his mother's gray hair as he lowered one knee to the floor beside her bed. Tears stung her throat. For a moment she lost track of everything but John's grief.

"So you're Teri. John's old shoe, huh?" Teri turned to the man, trying to make sense of his remark and to put his older, rounder, John-like face into clearer focus. "His high school sweetheart. I'm Chuck."

"I'm really sorry about your mother." The handshake they shared was oddly unsatisfactory. Teri felt an urge to put her arms around Chuck the way John had. Resisting, she busied one hand with her hair. "We drove all night, but we stuck mostly to the back roads. I know he was hoping..."

"If he'd seen the way she was, he would have known there wasn't much hope."

"I think he still would have tried."

They had left the door slightly open. Teri was drawn to the vertical crack of light. She didn't realize she was actually leaning in that direction until Chuck put his hand on her shoulder.

"He needs a little time alone with her. We'll stand here and see that he gets it." Chuck shoved his hands in the pockets of his jeans and leaned back against the wall. "Did he cut a deal with the cops to let him come?"

"You mean, call time-out?" With a dispirited smile she remembered John's words and shook her head. "No."

"Crazy kid. He should have stayed put."

"It all seems so unfair. He should have been able to come sooner, to be..."

The door opened slowly, and John stepped out. Clearly he had not shed tears, but pain haunted his dark eyes. He was carrying a stout diamond-willow walking stick. The bark had been peeled away, leaving a random pattern of dark, diamond-shaped knots in the light wood.

"I'd like to keep this," he said, holding it across his palms like an offering. "I know it was passed around to whoever needed it—from Grandma to Uncle Titus to Mom." He stroked the polished stick as though it were a beloved pet. When he looked up, the memories glistened in his eyes, and he smiled. "I could have used it yesterday when my back seized up on me like a rusty gear. Right, Teri?"

Teri nodded quickly, certain the only sound she could make would be some sort of a croak.

"It's yours," Chuck said. "Same old trouble?"

It was John's turn to answer with a nod. "Is there someplace we can go?" He glanced down the hall, then at Chuck, who led the way to a small lounge across from the nurses' station. He said something about the coffee there being "rugged," but Teri wasn't listening. She was watching two men who were wheeling an empty stretcher out of the elevator.

The lounge was empty. Chuck headed for the coffee-pot. John closed the door and turned to Teri. "You okay?"

"That's my line." She was okay, but she was crying. She put her arms around his waist and pressed her face to the side of his neck. "I'm sorry," she whispered.

"Thanks."

For so many things, he thought as he held her close to his side. For still being Teri after all this time, for being both stronghearted and softhearted, and for being there. His one glimmering spot of brightness was the mere fact that she *was* there. He laid his cheek against her hair and closed his eyes, wishing away everything and everyone but Teri. He didn't want anyone else around him at this moment, not even his brother.

"So how did you get here?" Chuck asked, breaking into John's illusory bit of privacy. "Did you just drive right past—?"

"No. Not exactly."

With a sigh, John pulled back from Teri and accepted the steaming cup Chuck handed him. He offered it to Teri, but she shook it off, so he sipped the coffee and re-counted his story. He knew it was an adventure after his politically minded brother's own heart, which was exactly why he had refused to let Chuck join in. Chuck's name was synonymous with Indian activism. John had done his time doing things Chuck's way. He was taking his own stand now, and all he hoped to get out of it was the right to make a life for himself on what was left of the land that had been allotted to his forebears. And part of that was the right to keep his gate closed.

But he'd gotten Teri mixed up in something she had no stake in. She had helped him, and in return he had brought sadness to her heart. He looked her way, and she dabbed at the corner of her eye and smiled at him. He felt disgusted with himself for wanting her to hold him again.

He turned away from her smile. "I don't want Teri taking any more chances. I need a way back."

"John, I have to go back that way anyway. We've got our system all worked out now. It'll be fine." She put her hand on his arm and drew him back. Her gentle smile was still there, gleaming in her eyes like soft blue silk. "Let me do this. I've come this far."

"Too far," he said, more brusquely than he'd intended.

Chuck intervened. "I think you're safer with her, brother. Besides, I have to make some arrangements. I'm going to take Mom home, and you're going to be there waiting for us. You think they'll let us through the gate?"

"They wouldn't dare interfere with an old woman's final journey." It was the first thought he'd given to the funeral. Of course it would have to take place at home. "We've got to tell the others. You call Marla yet?"

"You can do that." Chuck took a key from his pocket and put it into John's hand. "I've got a room at the Red Carpet Motel, just down the street. You can use the phone there, the shower, borrow a change of clothes, whatever you need. 'Course, you outgrew my shirts a long time ago with those shoulders of yours." He clapped his square, beefy hand on John's shoulder as he smiled at Teri. "You believe this guy's the baby of the family?"

"I'll take your word for it," she said.

John pictured a bed as he stared at the brass key lying in his palm. "Marla's back in Glover now?" he wondered absently, thinking the other stuff sounded good, too, but this was the key to a bed big enough to stretch out on, even if it was only for a little while.

"She had to get back to her kids. But you tell her I was there, and Mom went peacefully." Chuck pounded John's shoulder affectionately. "Marla's been worrying about you. Guess it's an old habit from all the time she spent looking after you."

"What kind of arrangements have to be made?"

"I'll take care of things on this end. Get some rest. Then go on back home and prepare the place next to Dad."

Following Chuck's directions they drove the three blocks to the motel in silence. Teri remembered another time when they had rented a motel room, in the fall of her sophomore year in college, after John had hauled a truckload of fall calves to Fargo. The trucking company ended up firing him for laying over that night, but he'd soon had another job. It was one of the things they had argued about. She'd said it was the perfect time for him to enroll in school, and he'd said he was making good money driving a truck. But they hadn't argued that night. She'd been nervous, and he'd been risking his job, but nothing could have stopped them from spending that night together.

The Red Carpet reminded her of the motel in Fargo. It probably wasn't recommended in any guidebook, but it was clean. It didn't look as though Chuck had gotten much use out of the room. His duffel bag was perched on the black straps of a folding luggage stand, and two shirts hung on the clothes rack. The bed, which looked inviting after a night on the road, was neatly covered with a white chenille bedspread. Teri would have been happy to close her eyes and fall across it, but John directed her toward the shower.

"You go ahead. I'll make this call, and then we'll decide what to do next."

She was inclined to do whatever he wanted, anything that might ease the strain.

This was the first time during the whole escapade that he had said, "*We'll* decide."

The motel had provided soap, shampoo and a wall-mounted hair dryer. The pile of woven samples Teri had supplied for John's camouflage yielded a handy change of clothing. Teri emerged from the shower wearing a sleeveless white shift.

John was sitting on the bed with his head in his hands. He straightened quickly, as though she'd caught him in some unseemly act. She wanted to cry for him. Instead, she sat beside him, challenging his restraint.

"Did you talk to Marla?"

He nodded. "She was here last week, but she had to go back. It's been hard for her, with kids at home and a husband who won't even make his own sandwich."

"I'm sure she feels just the way you do about not being here." Teri rubbed John's back as she had in times past, comforting him, comforting herself with the feel of soft cotton covering the contours of his muscular body. "You both did what you could."

"She's already got the star quilt made to put on the casket." He stood up abruptly, distancing himself even as he turned and offered a wistful smile to accompany a compliment. "She's almost as good as you are at sewing, making pretty things like . . . like that dress. It looks like one you used to wear. I remember, you made it."

"Not this one," she said, glancing down at the simple garment. "Some styles never change." She looked up. "Like so many of the things that really count for something. You can talk to me, John."

"I was just about to swipe some of Chuck's stuff," he said, snatching a green shirt form the rack. "After I get cleaned up, we'll...maybe we'll get something to eat. You hungry?" She shook her head, and he did the same. "You're never hungry. You need to eat. I need to make sure you get something to eat before you disappear on me."

"John..."

"I'll be out in a minute, okay?" He took socks and underwear from the duffel bag and brandished them in her direction. "Just give me a minute."

She didn't count the number of minutes she sat listening to the water run. It was probably cold by now, and he was still standing under it. She felt as though he'd shut her out again, which hardly seemed fair. She was mourning his mother's death, too, even though she'd hardly known the woman who had once credited her with a strong heart. Her own mother had never paid her such a compliment. Marge Nordstrom had never understood who Teri was or who she wanted to be. But Della Tiger might have, had she known her.

Teri remembered her as an old woman—seemingly too old to be John's mother. It seemed that he had been farmed out a lot, but whenever she had asked John about that, he had shared very little. His mother was old, he'd said. She was often sick. She had moved in with her sister, just as he'd moved in with his. In his world, that was what families were for.

The bathroom door opened, and John padded across the floor on bare feet, returning the green shirt to its hanger. "Chuck was right. He's got skimpy shoulders, that guy."

John's shoulders, bare and broad and bronze, were stunning. He'd draped a white towel over one of them, and his wet, seal black hair brushed the other. He moved to the mirror and took a long look, ruffling his hair with his fingers before he finally jerked impatiently at the towel. "If I'd cut this, it wouldn't take it so damn long to dry."

Teri pushed a chair across the floor and parked it behind him. "Sit," she ordered as she reached for the hair dryer. It took a firm hand on his shoulder to persuade him, but finally he dropped into the chair. "I'm good with hair now, too. It's part of my business."

The dryer hummed as she directed warm air over and under his luxuriously thick hair. Damp, it felt cool between her fingers, but as it dried it became soft and warm. She massaged his scalp with her fingertips. He closed his eyes and gave himself over to her ministrations. When at last he drew a long, deep breath, she could almost see his hard casing fall away. His chest quivered, and the mirror reflected the single tear that slipped to his cheek.

He turned and hooked his arm around her hips, drawing her into the cove between his thighs as he pressed his face against her belly. She turned the dryer off and set it on the counter. She'd yet to have close dealings with death, but in the past she had seen John through days, weeks, months of pain. In all that time he had shed tears in her presence only once—the first time they'd been allowed to see each other after his accident. She had been there for him unconditionally, just as she was now. She held his head close, stroked his hair and let her own tears fall.

For long moments he sat with his warm face rooted fast. Finally he lifted it, his eyes red, his cheeks damp. His hands went to her face as he came to his feet slowly, awkwardly trying to brush her tears away after he had hidden his own in her dress. With a trembling hand she touched the damp spot he had left behind.

"I didn't mean to make you cry," he professed as he swept a bit of fine hair back from her temple.

"It's all right," she assured him. "For both of us."

"No, I feel like a fool now. I should be—" He shook his head as though clearing away cobwebs and tried to retreat from her. "I *am* done with this."

"John." She stopped him, gripping his thick upper arms in her small hands. "I let you hold me yesterday, and it didn't hurt a bit. Now let me hold you."

He looked down at her for a moment, searching the depths of her glistening eyes, astounded by the way they dominated her face. She had offered to hold him, and yet it was he who towered over her. He was the one who could wrap his arms around her slight body and engulf her completely. With no effort at all he could lift her off the floor and set her out of his way. But she was asking to hold him in her arms, little realizing that she already held him fast with a tender look.

He wasn't going to kiss her, no matter how badly he wanted to, but her eyes drifted closed as though she felt it coming, and he gave in. Maybe she was never hungry, but he was—had been since he'd watched that photographer steal pieces of her that belonged to him. All the images were his. He had recreated them time after time in his dreams. He could hardly believe it was real this time, that the taste of her sweet mouth was no illusion. Her lips parted for him, and his tongue sought its rightful reunion with hers. He kissed her deeply, eagerly, indulging himself until they both came away gasping for air.

"Oh, God, I've missed you." Eyes closed, he pressed his forehead to hers, touched noses with her and clutched her to him as though she were all he had. "Teri, I've missed you every day."

"I've missed you, too."

"Every damned day." He kissed her eyelid, her cheek, the corner of her mouth, as he moved her toward the bed, muttering, "Every miserable night."

He took her face in his hands and kissed her mouth again. "Let me back inside you. Please let me back inside you, where everything feels good and nothing hurts and I can't be alone, because I'm..." He lifted his head to see, to make sure, because he had dreamed deeply and come up empty and aching too often. "Because I'm with you."

He followed his heart as he lowered Teri to the chenille spread. The bedsprings received her weight silently, but they squeaked beneath the pressure of his knee. Like a bird of prey he hovered over her, assessing her for delectable spots—her lips, her neck, her shell-like ears. It was she who lacked patience. Her hands were in his hair, and then his were in hers as he made his descent, yearning after her luscious mouth. His fingers fumbled over a few small buttons before he laid the yoke of her dress open and found warm, dewy skin. Her breast barely filled his hand, but her nipple made an impression that connected the hollow of his palm directly with the fever that was spiking deep in his belly.

"You're so small," he whispered, awed anew by her. He caught the flash of emotion in her eyes, and he knew he'd struck a chord of some kind. He turned his hand, caught her nipple between his fingers and plucked it gently with his thumb. Bittersweet music. Her breath fluttered like a sparrow's wing as she closed her eyes to listen. He wanted desperately to play the tune with the tip of his tongue.

He ached in so many places, but the pain in his heart was the most acute. Deep down he knew he held the keys that would bind her to him again. And God help him, he wanted to use them.

He laid his face in the cool valley between her breasts and fought hard to steady his breathing. "I'm sorry, Teri," he said when he found voice.

She went very still. It scared him for a moment, until she said softly, "It's all right, John."

"No," he groaned as he slid the cloth back in place to cover her breast. He kept his hand there, cupping her protectively. The challenge was to protect her from himself. "I have no right. I gave that up when I..."

"Shh." She combed her fingers through his hair. The kiss she bestowed on his head made his scalp tingle. "It's been eight years. I don't want to think about what we gave up. I want...so much to be..."

"I'm feeling a little crazy," he said. "I'm afraid I'll hurt you."

"You couldn't."

"I wouldn't do it on purpose." He lifted his head and told her solemnly, "I never meant to."

"Oh, John."

"It might hurt you if I did what's in my head right now." He wondered if it was similar to what was in hers. He touched her temple as if to touch her thoughts, his fingertips sliding over fine beads of moisture, which he spread to her hairline, and he smiled apologetically. "If I got inside you, the way I want to. Deep inside. So deep that I could just live there, with your heart beating close to my ear, always, never stopping. If I did that now . . ."

"You'd never leave me?"

"I'd never want to leave you."

He couldn't leave her just now, either, since his bones had turned to putty. He rested his cheek in her cool, sweetly scented valley once again. "Can I sleep here, just for a little while?"

"As long as you like," she said, stroking his hair. "As long as you want me this way."

They slept together. Teri was still sleeping in his arms when he woke, and he realized it felt even better than it had the day before—and worse. He felt good because he needed her, and, for the first time in eight years, she was there. He felt bad because he needed her, and he had let her see for herself just how strong his need still was.

And how weak he was. That was the part that was beginning to work on him, now that he'd had a little rest. He had behaved shamefully, letting her do things for him, things no self-respecting man would let a woman do. Gazing down at her sweet, fine-featured face, he thought about the way he had sat there letting her mess with his hair. That was what had started it all. It had been easier to accept her gesture than to put up a fight just then, with his head swimming and his whole body doing a slow burn beneath the surface of his skin. Something about the way her fingertips stirred against his scalp must have triggered the unmanly outpouring. He had to admit it; those tears had cooled that choking fire, but, damn, they were an embarrassment. And they had left him wanting her in the worst way.

Right now he wanted a cigarette in the worst way, but he didn't want to move away from her. Wanting was another bad weakness in him. But she had seemed willing— God, he couldn't believe it! This beautiful woman was not only willing to take the risk of aiding a wanted man, but she wanted him, too, and in the best way. Too bad he'd done just about everything a man could do to make sure he didn't deserve any of the good things she might give him.

Still, he was going to have to let her do him one more service, and in the process maybe he could come up with something he could do for her, though he couldn't imagine what. His former small-town girl had been to a lot of fancy places, had seen plenty of pretty sights. But in the time he had left with her, he hoped to find some way to treat her well, and maybe this time, since she would be the one to go, she would take a few kind thoughts of him along with her.

He smoothed her hair back, touched his nose to it and inhaled the fresh scent of the shampoo they'd both used. It smelled fresher on her. Lighter. Sweeter. He raised his head and found her blinking sleep away.

"Are you going to be ready to make another run for it pretty soon?"

"A run for what?" she asked groggily.

"Indian country, sweetheart, where you can drop off your renegade friend."

"I don't know about the renegade part." Her neckline gaped open as she shifted to her side. He fixed it for her, and she propped her head on her arm and smiled at him. "We are friends again, aren't we?" She sounded hopeful.

He swallowed hard, so unexpected was the thought. "I could always talk to you, Teri. I never realized how important that was until—" the soft sheen of her pale, spun-gold hair invited his touch "—you weren't there anymore."

"*You* weren't there anymore."

"I couldn't keep up with you. You went to college. I got a job driving a truck. Every time I went to Fargo for a weekend, I felt more and more out of place in your life."

"You *were* my life." She lay back on the bed, staring at a water stain on the ceiling. "And that was something *I* didn't realize until you weren't there anymore."

"So it's a good thing I left."

"No. But it's a good thing I realized that I needed a life of my own, with or without you." She turned her head, seeking contact with him again. "You must have realized that, too. You've explored other avenues. You've become a cowboy." She smiled. "You look wonderful on a horse."

"I used to ride a lot when I was a kid. One of the things I remember about my dad was that he always liked to have a horse or two around."

"And your grandfather who used to ranch—he must have been a horseman, too."

"I didn't know him," John said with a sigh, which she took as a bid for more of her attention. She scooted closer to his side, and he slipped his arm beneath her head. He loved the way it felt when she draped her hair over his shoulder.

"I knew my grandma," he told her, "but she died when I was pretty young, too. They're all buried on a little hill out at my place."

He remembered the last time he'd been up there on horseback. A gray boulder served as a marker, completely natural but for the name TIGER chiseled in the side. He'd thought about replacing a couple of the weathered white crosses, trimming the needlegrass and maybe scattering some wildflower seeds over the knoll.

Another time, he'd decided, and now that time would come soon.

"It's my place now. So it's up to me to take care of them. See that they aren't disturbed. We had to move my grandfather's grave when they flooded the bottom-land." It was a chore that lived in the family's memory more than in his own, but he related it the way it was always told, in the first-person plural that stood for family.

"I see." Teri laid her hand on his chest. "It's probably unusual for the baby of the family to take on that legacy." He chuckled, and she added quickly, "That's what your brother called you."

"I was the baby, all right. The one my mother thought she was too old to have." He covered her hand with his. "When I got to be about twelve, she couldn't handle me anymore, so I stayed with Chuck a while, and then my other brother, Buckshot. You don't know him—he's kind of a wild man. And then Marla. Buckshot had enough problems, and Marla had her own kids. And Chuck had his own life, too, you know. He was young." Much as he and Teri had their own lives now, he thought. But he laced their fingers together and continued to share his story. "Being the baby meant not being a kid for very long."

"Did you feel cheated?"

"Sometimes," he admitted. "My mom was good to me. She took care of me when I was little, but I know it was hard. I was lucky the older ones were willing to help out. I didn't see much of her in the last few years, so I guess I cheated her some, too. I'm going to miss her. I feel like I've lost my footing, you know?"

"I think I do."

"You're still a good listener, Teri." He kissed her forehead, which brought her chin up. He kissed her lips quickly, then lingeringly. "You're still a good..."

Good everything, and he would prove it if they lay there together much longer. Summoning some shred of willpower, he sat up, taking her with him. "I've gotta get you something to eat. I know you're hungry, and you just don't wanna say so. And then we'll take a look at the map. You're probably anxious to get back to Bismarck. I thought we'd head west first, and then—"

"John." She took his chin in her hand and spoke instructively. "If I'm hungry, I'll say so. And if I'm in a hurry to get back, I'll tell you that, too."

"Okay." He smiled. "You gonna teach me to be a good listener?"

"I've tried that before."

"Give it another shot." He wished he could remember what she might have tried to tell him that he hadn't heard. Probably a hundred things. "I've got a little more age on me now. A little more experience. That's gotta count for something."

She smiled, too, but it was the wistfulness in her eyes that jarred him slightly. "We'll see," she said.

Chapter 5

When Teri said she wanted to make a phone call before they left the motel, John took the cue to head for the car and give her some privacy. He put the station wagon's back seat down. Neither of them had had any real sleep, and at some point he figured somebody, namely Teri, might need to stretch out back there. She thought she had to do all the driving, but it was beginning to wear on her. He could see it in the dark circles that were taking shape under her eyes. He folded the colorful array of woven clothing she'd brought and arranged it in the back in neat piles. Then he had a smoke while he waited for her to come out.

They had a long drive ahead of them. The trip would be shorter if they took the interstate, but John wasn't willing to take that chancy route, not with Teri along. He had decided to stick to the back roads and head for patches of Indian land, where it would be safe for him to take over the driving. They could puddle-jump from reservation to reservation through most of South Dakota, though if the dark clouds that were piling up overhead brought rain, he would have to stay on the blacktop. There was nothing worse than sinking up to your axles in South Dakota gumbo.

Teri emerged from the room wearing a tight smile. At first John wasn't going to ask her anything about her call. He trusted her. He left the key at the desk with a message for Chuck telling him to send word when their mother was ready to come home. Then he suggested a stop at a fast-food restaurant, where he watched Teri pick at a wilted chef salad in a plastic box while he devoured two deluxe burgers.

"You want something else?" He couldn't stand these fussy new eating habits of hers. "That lettuce looks like cellophane."

"This is fine," she assured him, and she ate a bite of hard-boiled egg just to prove it. By the time they left the place, she'd managed to put away almost half her salad, which John considered to be a remarkable feat, considering how unappetizing it looked.

They left town with Teri behind the wheel. John figured it would take a couple of hours to reach the Crow Creek reservation, and then he could take over for a while. But she hadn't talked much since they'd left the motel, and it bothered him. Even though it was none of his damn business, he finally had to ask.

"Was that your mother you were calling back at the room, or Lavender?"

"Lavender." Her tone disallowed any other choice. "My mother and I have a greeting-card correspondence, and I do most of the greeting."

It was the first multiword answer he'd gotten from her in the last hour, so he knew he'd tapped the right vein.

"Besides, my mother would have called the police by now, asking if they were offering a reward for your..."

He hiked an eyebrow in her direction. "For my what?"

"Capture."

He chuckled as he pictured the frowsy woman in skin-tight jeans who simply didn't fit as Teri's mother. "Your mother never did think much of me, did she?"

"She never knew you. She never gave you a chance." Teri sighed and stared hard at the road ahead. "Or Lavender."

"I remember how she was always bad-mouthing Lavender. Telling around that she practiced some kind of witchcraft." Half the town of Glover had believed it, or wanted to. But the kids—his friends and Teri's—had known better. "She sure had Lavender figured wrong."

"My mother had a lot of people figured wrong, including Ally and me. All she cares about is having a man around. By the time I was a sophomore in college, she'd gone through three boyfriends since Starky."

Starky had been dealing drugs out of Marge Nordstrom's home and using Ally to deliver them. Teri sighed, wishing her mother had learned something from the experience. "None of those three was much of an improvement over that dumb Starky." She lifted one shoulder and shook her head indignantly. "*I* certainly never thought much of *her* boyfriends."

"So I guess that made you even."

Even, maybe, but it was hardly the same. Teri hoped John realized that. Her mother's unkind and unenlightened bias was more than a discomfort, just as the woman's life-style was more than an embarrassment.

"What did Lavender say about us?" He smiled knowingly when Teri did a double take. "You did tell her you're with me."

"Yes, I did." She didn't know whether to apologize or justify herself. She was inclined to do both, but because of the mental rounds she'd been having with herself, she was better prepared for the latter. "I hated not telling her the truth in the first place. When I rented the car, I told myself, well, maybe I *will* go to Glover and visit my mother after I bust John through this roadblock thing. And I kept that thought in the back of my mind, because Lavender isn't somebody you feel like you have to lie to. You can always trust her, and she won't—"

"She did once. She told Coach about the steroids."

"That was for our own good. Yours and mine and Ally's." She glanced at him, looking for a nod that wasn't forthcoming. She gave a little shrug. "Anyway, the doctors already knew you were on them. Your accident—" She cut herself off with a gesture of dismissal. "Wyatt and Lavender were there for both of us."

"What did Lavender say about you being with me now?"

"She said to be careful."

There was more to it than taking care of herself. There were all the wrinkles in the arrangements, all the bumps in the road they'd traveled that were too ticklish to talk about. Between Lavender and Teri, those things were acknowledged with a look or a sigh, then passed over. The news that she was with John, no matter what the reason, had caused tension to crackle on the telephone line, and the words *just be careful* had said it all.

"She asked me to give you their love and tell you how sorry they were to hear about your mother's death." Teri paused when John shifted uncomfortably. He couldn't sit easily in the company of sympathy. "Wyatt would like to tell you himself. He still talks about you, John. I mean, he still thinks of you as . . ."

"The kid who threw it all away. Every time he looked at me, he must have been thinking that." He looked out the window, and she knew better than to argue with his assumption.

"I almost called him once," he recalled distantly, "when I was competing as a bodybuilder. I'd just won a trophy, and I thought about sending it to him, so he'd have something from me. Something to prove—" He slid down in his seat and tipped his head back against the headrest. "But then I thought, nah, it's not the same. He was a wrestler. He wouldn't be impressed."

"You were a wrestler, too. You looked great out there on the mat." He turned his head, surprised, and she flashed him a warm smile. "Now you look great on a horse. Did I mention that?"

"I think you did."

"And you're happy with what you're doing now?"

"I like being where I am and doing what I'm doing." She could tell by his upbeat tone that he welcomed the shift in the conversation. "How about you? Are you happy with your life?"

"That's not exactly the same question I asked you," she said. She was hard-pressed to avoid too much speculation about the details of his present life, while her own wasn't much more than her job. "I like being part of the fashion industry. It's exciting."

"So is the cattle industry," he assured her, teasing with a deadpan echo. "Exciting." Her smile gave him leave to continue candidly. "I like having my own place. I like working with livestock. I feel like I've missed something, but I've found something else."

"I think Wyatt has learned to put the sport of wrestling into perspective," she said, speaking of what she assumed John felt he'd missed. "He teaches Native

American studies at the University of Mary in Bismarck.''

"He also coaches wrestling. I follow his team in the newspaper. He's still a great coach." He sounded like the hero-worshiping boy she remembered, but her smile faded when he asked, "They got any kids yet?"

"They have a little girl."

Her own voice sounded reedy to her, maybe because it was abruptly outstripped by her pulse pounding on her eardrums.

"Oh, yeah? Just one?"

The note of innocence in John's deep chuckle made Teri's cheeks burn. She concentrated on the broken yellow line in the road ahead.

"Sounds like the coach is letting some grass grow under his feet," John quipped. "He needs a little wrestler."

"Wyatt loves . . . his *daughter* very much."

"Don't go getting your female hackles up on me, now. Girls are fine, too. I'd want both if I could have . . ." She glanced his way reflexively, and it was his turn to falter and fumble. "I mean, if I had kids, I'd want—" He risked a look of his own. She wondered what he saw in her face, because he turned just enough to meet her head-on. "Both," he said solemnly. Then a twinkle flashed in his eyes. "But I wouldn't let my daughter wrestle. I don't care what you women say about equal rights. I wouldn't let *my* little girl get in there and grapple with some horny teenage octopus. No way in hell."

"Is that what *you* were? A horny teenage octopus?" It was a dumb question, but her noisy heartbeat was going to give her away unless she got him off this talk of *his* little girl.

He bit with a racy grin. "You'd be the best judge of that."

"I guess I never thought of you in those terms."

"Mostly you thought of me as crazy jealous." He paused to reassess. "Or just plain crazy."

"Jealous, yes. Crazy, no."

"That night we ran into that college friend of yours—that football jock who said he was some kind of partner of yours in one of your classes..."

She wished she could forget the incident and others like it. But it had been a weighty straw, that stupid argument. "We were working on a market-research project together, and that was all." She'd offered similar words in a like tone the first time around, but she couldn't seem to stop herself from doing it again. Then she realized there was one thing that hadn't stayed with her. "I don't ever remember his name."

The passage of time, if nothing else, had cooled John's response. "Whoever he was, he thought he was pretty hot stuff. He expected you to ditch me for him that night."

"You should have given me the chance to prove him wrong. It might have settled a more critical question than whether you could humiliate him in a fight." She offered a reproving glance. "Which you did, but it's a wonder you didn't hurt yourself that night."

"The guy had it coming. He had a big mouth."

"He didn't interest me, John. Why wouldn't you believe that?"

He sighed deeply. "It was me, Teri. *My* shortcomings. I was beginning to realize just how bad I'd screwed up, and I couldn't see how *I* could interest you. I left you because I was madder than hell at myself." He paused, then quietly confessed, "I left you so you wouldn't have a chance to leave me."

Teri's double take left the car nipping the shoulder of the road. "I tried to find you."

"I know. Marla said you called her. She didn't know where I was at first, either, so she wasn't holding out on you. I didn't tell anybody. I walked into the recruiter's office and signed my name. Once I got past the physical, I put everything I had into basic training, thinking I was gonna do something right for a change." He glanced away as he offered his single consolation. "I wrote to you."

"Months later," she said indignantly.

"I know, but I thought you would at least read my letter." Half to himself he grumbled, "I didn't much like getting the damn thing back."

"Didn't you?" She was glad. The sparse scattering of raindrops on the windshield was welcome, too. They expressed her feelings perfectly. "It was too late, John. By then it didn't matter what the letter said, and . . . and I couldn't deal with it."

"Was there somebody else?" She met his question with a sharp look. He held his hands up in swift surrender. "Okay, it's none of my business."

"It *was* your business. You should have made it your business, John. You were always so ready to get in there and fight for me, but when I needed you the most . . ." Oh, God, her throat was getting tight. If she had any sense, she would grip the wheel, grit her teeth and drive.

But sense eluded her, and there was water sheeting across her field of vision. The million things she'd wanted to say to him crowded into her head all over again. She was slipping into a place she wanted to avoid, uttering words she wanted to hold back.

"Where were you? The time when you should have been there for me. . . ."

"Pull over, Teri."

She took a deep breath and shook her head. "No, I'm fine. I'll be fine." But she couldn't see very well, and she couldn't find the damn switch for the windshield wipers.

"You need a break. Come on, I'll drive for a while."

"No, it's daylight. It's too dangerous. No, I'll be fine."

"Pull over at this next approach." He leaned closer. "Slow down now, Teri. You have to stop the car," he said calmly as he put his hand next to hers on the steering wheel. "It's raining outside, raining inside. You can't even see the road."

She took a swipe at her tears with the back of her hand while he located the wiper switch and talked her over to the side of the road. She struggled with the gearshift. He helped her find Park, and she resented his steadiness.

"That's fine," he said softly. "I'm here for you now, okay?"

His hand felt warm on her shoulder, and she closed her eyes, because she resented that, too. "No, it's too late. It's much, much..."

"No, it's not. Come here," he said, and she offered little resistance as he took her in his arms. There were her tears to deal with, after all, and his assurances sounded exactly the way she'd so often dreamed them. "It's not too late. I'm here for you now."

"Oh, John, we were so young," she said, sobbing uncontrollably.

"I know. And I was so crazy about you it made me act like a fool sometimes." The way he rubbed her back was soothing, but his question was not. "There was somebody else, wasn't there? After I left, I mean. That's why you sent my letter back." She shuddered in his arms and tried to pull away, but he held her and whispered, "It's okay, Teri. You deserved to be happy, and I didn't make you very happy."

"Yes, you did. Most of the time, except when you left me." She had uncorked a terrible sadness. She looked to John to help her plug it back up, but, much to her horror, some half-wit had taken over her tongue. "And then . . . there *was* someone," she confided. His eyes glazed over. "But not the kind of someone you're thinking."

"Did he hurt you?" His arms tightened around her, and the look in his eyes demanded the truth. "It's not too late for me to pay him a visit, you know, if . . ."

"No, no, John, it wasn't like that. I kept hoping you'd come back and we could work things out." She closed her eyes as she whispered the first and foremost truth. "I loved you so much."

He kissed her then, while the sweet affirmation still clung to her lips. He kissed her tearful shuddering away and freed her for quiverings far more subtle, more exquisite. All it took was the familiar taste of him, the deeply drawn scent of him, the brawny feel of him, to give her that quicksilver shiver that sent all doubts flying. She put her arms around his neck and parted her lips for his redeeming kiss.

Soaking up those heartbreaking sobs gave him power. Whatever plagued her, he would drive it back. He would draw off her demons and let her breathe easy. His first kiss calmed her. She melted against him as smoothly as a pat of butter set in a sunny window, and he felt favored. His next kiss quickened her breath again. He felt her hands in his hair and the brush of her thigh against his as he tried to pull her into his lap.

John glanced up when a car swished past. The window defogger was losing ground, and the wipers were beating ineffectively against a curtain of rain.

"I'm going to move the car," he said, cupping her cheek in his hand. His kiss promised more of the same, with only a short delay. "Come over here. No—" He slid his hand down her arm, stopping her before she opened the door on her side. "Don't get out. You'll get wet."

He jumped into the driving rain, circled the front of the car and hopped into the seat Teri had obligingly vacated. In a matter of seconds the rain had darkened his blue shirt and plastered it to his back.

"Let's hope we don't get stuck," he said as he shifted into gear. He checked the road, not for clearance, but for witnesses to the unexpected turn he was taking through an open fence. A set of overgrown tire tracks led to an old gray barn, which listed to one side like the ark set afloat by the deluge.

"What are we doing?" Teri asked shyly.

"We're putting this abandoned barn to good use." He drove around it, looking for a way in. The sliding door stood open, and the car's headlights illuminated puddles, rotting wood and empty space. "It looks like a fugitive's hideout, doesn't it?"

"How do you know it's abandoned?" she asked as he eased the car through the doorway.

"No gate on the fence, no cattle guard across the road, no house in sight. Nobody's using this barn," he assured her. "Except us."

"How...how do you know it's safe?" Her voice came hushed and hollow, now that the old structure had swallowed them up and John had shut the engine off.

He rolled his window halfway down, and Teri followed suit. The place smelled earthy and damp, but not unpleasant. Missing planks and shingles admitted not only the rain but a diffusion of gray afternoon light, casting them in soft shadows.

"Nobody's going to bother us here," John promised. "Not as long as the rain keeps up." He leaned closer, tucking his nose into her hair. "Do you want me to close the barn door?"

She glanced toward the light that glowed in the back window. "I like being inside looking out at the rain."

"Do you want to talk now?"

Eyes closed, she shook her head and whispered, "No." The word had barely escaped her lips before he kissed them.

Talk was the last thing on her mind when the tip of his tongue slid across the roof of her mouth. It was out of the question when his lips touched and teased, taking delicate sips of her, the way a hummingbird might approach an open bloom. She had no words, only sighs, soft as the swish of wet cottonwood leaves.

"I'll listen," he promised on the cusp between kisses feathered across her face. "Show me the way you want me to listen."

She kissed him, harder than he'd kissed her, more urgently. She wanted to get closer, to be in his lap, but the steering wheel boxed him away from her.

"Like that?" No shadows could shroud the smile that glistened in his eyes.

She nipped at his chin, then ducked coyly beneath it. "Yes, like that."

He lifted her chin and traded nibbles with her. The backs of his fingers slipped along the curve of her neck, then down a path that took them skimming over the crest of her breast. He heard the quick catch in her breath, and he smiled. "Like this?" She gave a small nod, and he closed his eyes and saw a flash of green light as he took her in his arms. "Tell me more, Teri. Tell me again how you used to feel about me."

And she did, in the breathless way she whispered, "Oh, John..."

"This is the way I used to feel," he said, letting his hands wander slowly over her dress, tracing curve after curve. "Remember?"

"Yes, but it isn't the only..." Before she could suggest alternatives, he had her front buttons undone and was slipping his hand inside for a more personal touch. "Yes, that way," she allowed with a wistful smile.

"The way we would usually start." Her nipple puckered in the hollow of his palm. Sharing her smile, he nuzzled close to her ear and whispered, "I'm listening, Teri. Just say the word."

"You always knew. You always—"

"Tell me," he said hotly.

"I want... I want you."

"To make love to you?" With her cheek against his, she nodded, but that wasn't enough. "Say it," he insisted.

"Make love to me, John."

"In back," he told her, and he kissed her again before they moved.

It was more space than they had had the first time, in the back seat of her Aunt Janine's old Buick. John left the station wagon's tailgate open, adding a feel of more space and a flow of cool, damp air. The neat piles of woven garments were quickly thrown into disarray as they made their nest from whatever was handy, just the way the swallows in the rafters had done. They fluttered a bit, too, undressing each other with eager hands and greeting bare skin with appreciative lips.

His body was more beautiful than ever, she thought. His smooth chest and brawny shoulders belonged to a working man. His rich brown skin proved that he worked in the sun. He was sweet dessert for the eyes, and this was one feast she actually craved. There was a brief interruption when he swept her dress over her head. Once her arms were free she retaliated by slipping her hands behind him and squeezing his buttocks. He laughed and went so tight that her fingers made little impression.

She enjoyed a fleeting fantasy of him riding the crest of a grassy hill, the wind spreading his hair, the sun blazing down on his bare back and steely thighs. He was sitting his blaze-faced stud as naked as he soon would be in her arms. The brassy reverie set her cheeks aflame, but she, too, laughed as she rubbed her palms over his muscle-bound backside.

And John thought he would surely die of the driving need to be inside her. She was both bold and shy. The combination was compelling. She was lovelier than she'd ever been, but seemingly ten times more fragile. He wanted to take the time to kiss her everywhere, to let the day tick by while he made every inch of her wet with his tongue and every nerve sizzle with his touch. But he needed now, right now, to permeate every part of her, to penetrate all her soft, silky places with his questing, blood-throbbing body. Every mewling sound she made drove him harder, but he took the time to taste her, to touch her, to drive her as exquisitely mad as he was.

It was a prophetic reunion, marked by glad cries and blissful sighs, by whispered words of care and conciliation. He was unprepared to protect her by any means other than to spill his seed on her belly. They held each other tight and shared a shuddering moment, a close cousin to real contentment, and he apologized and thanked her, both in the same breath.

She could only close her eyes, kiss his neck and return his embrace.

Through the open tailgate they watched the rain tumble down like poured salt, obscuring the stand of cottonwoods that grew not forty yards beyond the barn door. Touched only by the mist, they felt cleansed. Naked and newborn, they lay wrapped in each other's arms, intent upon the wonderful rise and fall of each other's breath. The hardy thumping of John's heart so close to her ear gave Teri a full-length quiver. John pulled a blue shawl around her shoulders and briskly rubbed her, making her shiver again.

"Are you sure you're okay?"

"I'm fine." She smiled and caught a lock of his hair between her fingers. "It's been a long time since I've been this fine."

He turned her and pulled her back against him as he crossed his arms over her chest and lovingly took her breasts in his hands. "One of your breasts is still smaller than the other." He massaged the left one. "I have a real soft spot when it comes to this little guy," he whispered close to her ear. "The bigger one is nice, but this little one needs special care."

Teri giggled deliciously. "How can you call a woman's breast a 'little guy'?"

"I don't know. Just an expression, I guess. It's like a little baby." He smiled as he ducked down to nuzzle her. "A little guy that needs my personal attention."

"It does. I can feel it smiling when you do that."

"You're right. He is. But this big girl over here—" He peeked over her shoulder and admired the beads he'd made of both nipples. "Oh, yeah, she knows. She smiles because she just *knows* how pretty she is."

"Are you trying to get me going again?"

"I'm just taking care of my babies. My *un*identical twins." He shifted her in his arms again. Leaning over her, he rubbed his cheek over the crest of the smaller breast, then bumped the larger one with his nose, like a seal playing with a beach ball. "They've been away from me too long."

"They've missed you. They haven't smiled since..." His head went still as he hung on the last word. "Since you went away," she assured him softly.

"I'm sorry, Teri. I've been such a sorry bastard for such a long, long time." He scooted up, bracing himself on his forearm, seeking her eyes. "I couldn't tell you that before. Not to your face. I tried to tell you in that letter I sent you. I didn't want to mess up your life again, but I wanted you to know how I felt." He paused, then added, "I guess I thought you'd want to know."

"I did," she told him. "I wanted to read the letter. But I was afraid of what it might say."

"What did you think I was capable of saying that would be so bad?"

"I already knew what you were capable of *doing.*" She covered her breasts with the shawl and reminded him quietly, "You left me without a word."

"We had words before I left." He rolled over and lay on his back, studying the close ceiling, listening to the rain. It reminded him of her tears. "Too many words."

"There was no one else, John. There was never anyone else."

"After I left, there should have been someone else. If there was, I hope he was good to you, even if he didn't make your breasts—" He turned to her and laid a possessive arm across her chest, groaning miserably as he drew her close. "God help me, I hope he's out of your life and out of your head. I don't want to know his name. I don't want to know anything about—"

"John." She stopped him with a thumb against his lips, his smooth cheek in her smoother palm. "John, don't. It was a bad time for me after you left."

"I'm sorry." For the hundred-thousandth time, he thought. He'd spawned a legion of sorries, most of them heartaches rather than spoken words.

"But I got through it, and now I'm okay. Now, right now, I'm better than okay."

"You're thinner than you used to be." He played his hand lightly up and down her arm. "You're as beautiful as ever, but I'd hate to see you lose any more weight." His hand continued to stir solicitously, gradually brushing back the shawl to expose her breasts. He smiled when the small one peeked out to greet him. "This little guy might disappear altogether."

"No, he won't. Now that he's got so much to smile about, maybe..." He tongued her nipple, and her voice was gone for a moment. She swallowed and reclaimed it. "Maybe we'll be able to put him to good use, with you taking such special care—"

"To bring you pleasure," he said as he took her in his arms again and pillowed her head on his chest. "That's the best I can do."

"What do you mean? The best is yet to come." She kissed her pillow, then glanced up. "Isn't it?"

"Depends on how much time I have. How much time you can give me." He raised a warning finger when she opened her mouth to speak. "Before you say anything, I want to tell you what was in the letter, okay? I want to tell you some of the things ... some of the reasons...."

"It doesn't matter anymore."

"Yes, it does," he contended. "I ran away."

"Why? You didn't..." Teri frowned and finished the sentence silently. *You didn't know.* How could he have known?

"You were growing away from me, Teri. You were going to college, and I was driving a truck."

"You were planning to go to college, too. You always said—"

"I always said I was going to be another Wyatt Archer. Only I *wasn't* Wyatt Archer. I wasn't even close. I had damaged my body so bad that I had to fight for every muscle. I got so I couldn't see past the end of my nose, and inside my head I was always slogging around in a swamp of doubt and suspicion. And the future..." He shook his head, regretfully pondering the word as he remembered what it had meant to him then. "The future was a big, blindingly bright place that scared the hell out of me. It was all I could do to get that GED."

"What you did was remarkable, John. It was an uphill climb. Everybody admired the way—"

"It took me almost a year to get back on my feet and another six months to get that damn certificate. By that time you were at the university, and I felt like I'd been running on a treadmill for a year and a half. There wasn't going to be any wrestling scholarship. I had to get a job so I could start paying my own way."

"All I had was a student loan. I had to work, too. And you could have applied for—"

"I know." He tucked her hair behind her ear, smoothing it at the temple with the backs of his fingers. "You just got ahead of me, that's all. And I couldn't handle it. I didn't fit in with your friends. I didn't know if I could cut it academically. There were too many unknowns, too many doubts."

"You doubted me."

"I doubted *me*. I read a lot about all the effects that steroids could have on a person. I was obviously pretty susceptible. They turned me into a madman."

"But you stopped taking them."

"Yeah, I know." He remembered trying to figure out where he might fit into what he had read. Dosage levels. Age. State of his health. State of his mind. "I didn't know what kind of damage had already been done. I read about people coming up with liver and kidney problems, tumors, and worse."

"What's worse?" She looked up, and he saw that terrier tenacity of hers. She wouldn't let the list go on unchecked. "We both know you haven't suffered from impotency, if that's what you think is worse," she said, and her bull's-eye brought him short. "That's something *I* read about."

"Did you read about sterility, about genetic damage?"

"You weren't taking the stuff that long."

"Who knows how long it takes, or how much? It made me jump off a bridge, Teri." Her eyes widened, and she glanced away. "Yes, jump," he repeated firmly. "I was jumping out of my skin, but I happened to be standing on a train bridge at the time."

He wouldn't let her close her eyes to it anymore. He took her chin in his hand and waited until she looked him in the eye again. "I wanted to be your man, but I didn't know how much man was left."

"More than enough."

"Well, more than I thought back then." She was right. He wasn't impotent, and he hadn't been sick. He'd gone almost ten years, but, damn it, he still wasn't sure. There was always the big wild card. "But maybe not enough. I don't know if I can—"

"If you can produce one healthy child, you can have more," she said, so softly he wasn't sure he'd heard her right. She looked up, and he saw something more unsettling than uncertainty in her eyes. She persisted. "Right?"

"What do you mean?"

"I mean..." She drew back from him, covering herself with the shawl as though she were cinching herself into a drawstring sack. "I mean, you did."

"I did what?"

"You... We had a child."

He jackknifed, propping himself on his elbows as his jaw dropped.

Whatever he might have said—and he had no idea what it would have been—Teri cut him off with a tumbling of incredible words, senseless chatter in his ears. "Lavender can't have children, John. They wanted a child. They were wonderful to me...there the whole time. They helped me stay in school. They...they...their little girl..." Her voice went soft again. "Lavender and Wyatt adopted our baby."

"Our baby?"

"I was pregnant when you left me."

Pregnant? "Why didn't you tell me?"

"I didn't know. When I found out, I tried to reach you. I wanted...at least to talk to you about it before I agreed—"

"When you got my letter, did you know then?" She didn't answer him fast enough. He grabbed her shoulders. "When you returned my letter unopened, did you know you were going to have my baby then?"

"By that time..." She shook her head quickly. Her eyes were filling, and she was blinking furiously. "By that time I knew I was going to have Lavender and Wyatt's baby. It was decided."

"Who decided?"

"I did." She looked him straight in the eye, and her chin was nearly steady when she insisted, "It was my decision."

"What do you mean, it was your—?" His hands dropped away from her, but he didn't know where to put them, what to feel, what to think. "For God's sake, Teri, it was my kid, too. Why didn't you open my letter? Why didn't you write back, or call, or...?"

"Because you had left me, John. Not just to get away for a little while to cool off or to think." A deep breath steadied her. "You *left* me. You joined the army without consulting me."

"So you gave our baby away without consulting me," he concluded. That was it. That was all she wrote, only she *didn't* write. Not one damn word.

He snatched up his jeans and scooted into them on his way out the back of the car.

"John, where are you going?"

Trembling hard on the inside, Teri took a two-handed swipe at her tears. The crazy man was leaving again, barely getting his pants fastened as he stalked out into the rain. She tossed a poncho over her head and followed him, clutching the garment around her.

"John, come back here," she demanded. "John!"

He spun around, shouting, "How could you just give our baby away like that?"

"How could you just leave me like that? What was I supposed to do?"

"You were supposed to tell me. Did you think I wouldn't come back?"

"I didn't know if I *wanted* you back!"

There, she'd said it. And that was the truth of it. The rest was all just as much foolishness as the two of them standing barefoot and bareheaded in the mud and the rain. He hadn't known what he'd wanted, and what she'd wanted suddenly hadn't existed. The plans she had made, the love she had counted on, the dreams she had lived by, had turned out to be one-sided, and she'd found herself standing in boiling water on one stilt. None of that foolishness had been good enough for their baby.

"I did the best I could, John. She has a good home with parents who couldn't love her any more than—"

"Any more than I could?" In desperation he grabbed her arms and hauled her close, wet body to wet body. "You could have given me the chance. I didn't think I could—" He was trembling now, as violently as she was. "I didn't dare think about having kids. Don't you understand? I was—"

"She's perfectly healthy, John." She looked up at him and watched the rain stream down his face like heaven's tears. The pain in his eyes had come so swiftly, so unexpectedly, that she was unprepared to say whatever it was he needed to hear. But she gave it a try. "She's happy. I promise you, she has everything—"

"You can't just give my kid away!" He shook her, and she slipped on her heel as she tried to back away, but he caught her and shouted into her face, "If you didn't want me back, and you didn't want her, why didn't you—"

"Not *want* her!" She grabbed his forearms and tried to shake him, but he was unshakable. Water sluiced down his nose, dripped from his hair and clung to his lashes.

She met his scowl with outrage. "You weren't there, John. How dare you suggest that I—"

"How dare you give my baby away!"

"I did what I thought was best," she insisted. "And by the time I got that letter, nothing it said would have made any difference. I was pregnant, and I was very young and very scared, and I had been deserted by the father of my baby."

He let go of her and took a step back, but she followed, shouting, "Look at you! You're trying to run away again!" She caught him by the arm and refused to let him turn away. "But you *are* going to listen. I gave that baby life. *I* did, because *I* carried her to term and went through labor and delivered her into the hands of loving parents. *You* did nothing but plant a seed."

"That's all a man gets to do, at least in the beginning."

"Well, I just finished letting you have at it again, didn't I?" she said sarcastically, gesturing toward the barn. "What a dummy I am!"

"I pulled out. I didn't—"

"That's exactly what you did eight years ago! You pulled out!" His eyes were blazing, but she wasn't about to back down, rain or no rain. "It doesn't always work, John. Haven't you learned that yet? Sometimes you leave something important behind."

"Part of myself."

"That's right."

He scrutinized her from head to foot, standing up to him in the rain with the thin poncho plastered to her slight body. She reminded him of a fancy miniature pup that looked even smaller when it was wet but sounded no less feisty. He looked down at himself, standing shirtless, brainless, ankle deep in mud.

He had a child. He had a little daughter who called another man "Daddy."

He put his arm around his child's mother and led her back inside the barn. "You should have stayed in the car," he said, realizing how unfit he was to play the voice of reason at this point. "Now you're shivering."

He stood her next to the car, removed the drenched poncho and dried her off briskly with the first piece of clothing that came to hand when he reached inside the back door.

She hugged herself as she stood there, shivering. "I d-didn't know what you m-might do, John."

Chagrined, he made a clucking sound in his cheek. "I haven't jumped off a bridge in years."

"I wasn't worried about j-jumping."

"And I'm not about to walk back to North Dakota," he assured her as he went down on one knee to dry her legs. "I just needed to, uh . . ."

"G-get away from me?"

"For a minute or two, yeah. But you had to come after me, just the way you always did." His ministrations slowed, then halted. He tipped his head back and looked into her eyes as he amended softly, "*Almost* always. You finally gave up on me, didn't you?"

"Only after you'd given up on me." With that, he hung his head. She laid her hand on his wet hair as though she were blessing him. "It's done, John. I only told you because I thought . . . I thought it would help you to know that she's a healthy child."

It's done. He mulled the words over in his head as he finished his job. *It's all over and done with.* But the idea didn't sit right with him. He helped Teri back into her dress and absently watched a feral tabby cat chase a mouse into the corner shadows as he wrapped a wool shawl around her shoulders.

"What are you thinking?" she asked finally, lifting an unsteady hand to push his wet hair back from his face.

"That maybe in your mind it's all settled. You've known about it all along." His actions mirrored hers, rearranging wet hair, assessing the look in her eyes. "It's all new to me. All of a sudden I have a child."

"No, you don't. Lavender and Wyatt have a child."

"I'm her father, right? Biologically, I'm her father."

"Biologically, yes, but—"

He turned to toss his makeshift towel back into the car, and he caught a glimpse of the two of them reflected in the window. Night and day, he thought. They were opposites in every way he could see, but together they had made something good. It had damn sure taken both of them.

"Then I have a child."

Chapter 6

She hadn't expected to drive him all the way to his front door, but pulling over to the side of the road and letting him off in the middle of nowhere had unnerved her. She remembered the terrible time so many years past, yet so fresh in her mind, when she had watched him get out of her car and disappear into the night. Even so, she had complied with his wishes again, leaving him to his own devices and following his directions to get to the highway. The radio was better company than a brooding man, she'd told herself on the way back to Bismarck, but she kept thinking about him, wondering whether he was still walking, still angry, still thinking about her.

She tried to sleep late the next morning, but her eyes wouldn't cooperate, and neither would Rachael. The persistent child wanted to know where Teri had been and why her car was so muddy and why she'd come home looking like "Becky Snustad's Afghan hound." Teri evaded Rachael's questions by agreeing to make a guest appearance at Brownie camp, which filled what would have otherwise been an empty afternoon with a bevy of seven-year-old girls and their attentive mothers.

More than once Rachael said cheerily, "We're like sisters."

I could agree with you, Teri thought, if it weren't for the fact that I've just been with John.

After a day of canoeing and firewood gathering, Rachael went to bed willingly without her usual hour of television. Wyatt claimed that this was finally his chance to watch a Twins game from beginning to end, and Teri knew from the moment he left her alone in the kitchen with Lavender that the time of reckoning had finally come. It was understood that the herbal tea was being offered in trade for straight talk.

"Nothing's changed, has it?" Lavender asked as she set a cup on the table. Sweet-scented steam curled beneath Teri's nose.

"For John and me?" It was unnecessary clarification. Teri knew that Lavender had been tuned in to her thoughts since she'd straggled in the door in the wee hours of the morning. Lavender never pounced. She waited for a mellower time, so that Teri could answer calmly, matter-of-factly, "Everything's changed."

"I mean *between* John and you. You're still in love with him. Whatever the changes, they're not that important to you right now."

"Yes, they are." Teri looked at her friend across the table. Her friend, her mentor, the woman whose instincts she trusted more than her own. It was the kind of trust most women gave their mothers. With her eyes Teri begged Lavender's indulgence. "Very important."

"Rachael?"

Teri nodded.

"You told him?"

She nodded again. They ignored the phone, which rang twice before Teri said quietly, "How could I not tell him? Every time I looked at him, I saw Rachael's eyes, Rachael's chin...." The phone gave another half ring. Teri sighed and shook her head. "One of the disadvantages of our arrangement has always been the fact that we all shared so much. John and Wyatt. You and me. Maybe I should have stayed away, the way John did. Clean break."

From across the table came Lavender's hand, reaching for Teri's. "Would you really have preferred it that way?"

"No."

"Neither would we." Lavender squeezed Teri's hand, then retreated back across the table, seeking the handle of her cup. "Honey, John factored himself out of the picture. I wouldn't call it a *clean* break, but it was a break, and it looked pretty final after a while."

"He didn't know." No matter how often she ran the whole mess through her mind, she always came back to that fact. "Oh, *he's* the one I should have stayed away from," she lamented. "I know that. Because you're right. I still love him. But I love Rachael, too, and I know who her parents are."

"She has—"

"She's had you and Wyatt since the day she was born—even before that. My regrets are for my sake, not for hers."

"Thank you," Lavender said, almost reverently.

"John was running scared when he left. Among other things, he thought the drugs he used might have ruined his chances of fathering a healthy child." Teri wrapped both hands around the warm cup and leaned forward.

"You read about so many possible side effects from steroids, and you just don't know what to think."

"Rachael *is* healthy."

"Yes." Teri nodded and studied the pale pink tea she had yet to taste. "Yes, I told him that."

"How did he take the news?"

"Not well." Alarm rose in Lavender's eyes, and Teri hastened to add, "But that's my problem, not yours."

"Why do you say that? We've stood together, you and—"

"Rachael is legally your daughter. John can't change that." She took a sip of tea. Tangy rose hips and lemon revitalized her tongue. "And if he's been wronged in any way, it was my fault."

"Don't you say that." Lavender came out of her chair and circled the table. "Don't you dare start thinking that way, Teri. You're always trying to hoist such big, heavy loads onto your slight shoulders." Slender hands kneaded those slight shoulders, and there was no frailty on either side. "If somebody's hurting, it's not necessarily *any-one* else's fault."

The phone rang again.

"Wyatt got it," Lavender said as she pulled up the chair adjacent to Teri's and sat next to her, knee to knee. "Now, did you hear what I said, and do you know what I'm talking about?"

"Yes." She had to remind herself that she was no longer a teenager seeking this woman's advice. "You make it sound so simple, Lavender, but it isn't."

"Of course it isn't simple. None of this was ever simple. But you are not responsible for the pain John feels right now."

"It doesn't matter whether I caused it or he brought it on himself or *nobody* caused it. It's there. He lost so much in the space of a few short hours yesterday, and I can't help feeling—''

Wyatt appeared in the kitchen doorway, stocking footed and scowling. "What's all this about John wanting Rachael to come to his mother's funeral?''

Lavender and Teri exchanged wary glances. Wyatt Archer was not a man who took unpleasant surprises in stride, even though he'd mellowed out some since he'd married Lavender. He looked like an older, more conservative version of John—athletic build, angular features and dark, penetrating eyes.

"He's called twice now," Wyatt explained. "I told him I was planning to be there, and then he started talking about Rachael. I tried to talk some sense into him, but, hell, I haven't seen the guy in years, and I wasn't quite prepared for—" He paused for a more considered look at Teri's face, then another at his wife's. He saw that it was time to *get* prepared. "This is gonna be a tough one, isn't it?''

Teri glanced away. "I'm sorry.''

"I'm sorry, too." He joined them at the table, sitting on the edge of the chair across from Teri as though he didn't plan to be there long, and he folded his big brown hands in front of him. "I have to protect Rachael, Teri. You know that. I'm Rachael's father. No matter how I feel about you or John . . .'' He turned to Lavender. "*We* have to protect our daughter. She's only seven years old.''

"I didn't expect him to...'' Teri felt trapped. They had agreed to tell Rachael when she was older. John's name would have been part of the information, to do with as she pleased in her own good time. But Teri had blown the plan. "I thought, knowing both of you, and given the circumstances, he would appreciate—''

"Indians are kinda touchy about adoption, especially nowadays. There was a time when the courts were adopting Indian kids out wholesale, but times have changed." He jerked his chin in the direction of the white wall phone. "Do you want to talk to him? He's still on the phone, and he asked for you. I can tell him . . ."

Teri went to the phone, cueing Lavender and Wyatt to leave the room.

"John?" The line was open, but he gave no immediate answer. "John, please don't—"

"I want her here, Teri. You want the Archers to raise her, fine. But she's got more family, and she ought to—"

Teri closed her eyes and rested her forehead against the side of the cupboard. "She's too young, and this isn't the time."

"What do you mean, it isn't the time? Her grandmother just died. We didn't get to pick the time. It just happened."

"I know," Teri said quietly. "I can be there."

"And you can bring our daughter. The whole family goes to this old woman's funeral. You understand? That's the way it's done."

"This is a special circumstance."

"You're damn right, it's a special circumstance. All the grandchildren will be there. It's her right."

"Whose right?

"My mother's *and* my daughter's. They both have that right. You ask Wyatt. It's an honor due. It's an honor that must be given in person."

"Wyatt won't let her go, John. She doesn't know she's adopted. She's only seven. She doesn't know about you *or* your family."

"*Her* family." He gave a deep, distant sigh at the other end of the line. "All right, I won't tell her anything. I just want her to be here, okay?"

"You and I have nothing to say about it." That was the point he didn't seem to understand, the point she had to get through to him somehow. "Someday she'll be told, and, of course, when that day comes..."

"She can meet the cousins she never played with and the aunts and uncles who won't seem like family to her because they're Tigers, not Archers."

"John, please. She's just a little girl. If you knew how innocent she is, how completely happy..."

"I can't know that, can I? Not unless I'm allowed to see for myself."

"You can take my word for it." She closed her eyes, wishing for the link that continued to elude her. "You can *trust* me, John."

"The funeral's tomorrow at ten."

"I'd like to be there," she offered. "Would that be all right?"

"Suit yourself. Nobody gets turned away except cops."

The Indian police were not turned away. A Bureau of Indian Affairs patrol car preceded the funeral cortege on the dirt road that ended at the foot of the hill. At the top, surrounded by woven wire and marked by a great granite boulder, was the Tigers' burial ground.

Teri's car was the last one in line. She had gone to the church alone and sat on one of the folding chairs that lined the back wall to accommodate the overflow of mourners. She didn't know whether John saw her at the end of the service when he passed, following the casket with the rest of his family. He carried his mother's diamond-willow walking stick as a symbol rather than a crutch. He was favoring his right leg a little, but he walked tall. He held his head high, eyes straight ahead. Whether he cared or not, Teri wanted him to know that she had come, as she'd promised, to pay her respects.

She parked her rental car with the other vehicles, changed her shoes and followed the column of people up the little trail. John stood at the top, watching, waiting. The warm summer breeze unfurled his hair like a black curtain fluttering in an open window. She remembered her erotic vision of him on horseback, and her cheeks flamed at the impropriety of such thoughts at a time like this.

He looked handsome, surely, if a bit uncomfortable in his black Western-cut sports jacket, crisp white shirt and beaded black-and-white bolo tie. His shoulders looked impossibly broad, his hips unbelievably narrow and his eyes achingly dispirited. He watched her scale the hill. With every step she was sadly aware that it was not her presence he had requested, but that of a little girl he had never seen. She wondered whether he was angry with her now, or whether he watched with complete dispassion as she climbed toward him.

Teri remembered the woman whose body rested in the star-quilt-draped box, and she recognized Marla, whose brood had grown by at least two since Teri had last seen her. She also recognized Chuck, who acknowledged her with a nod. Beyond that, Teri knew nothing about the mourners.

Time and place seemed a little disjointed. Parts of the ceremony were familiar. Other aspects of it were foreign to Teri, and she felt like an outsider. John was her touchstone, but she was witnessing the part of his life that he had not shared with her, the quiet neighboring world she'd known about but never really seen.

It felt strange, observing John as an Indian among Indians, watching him participate in strange rites. When an old man offered a smoking coffee can among the mourners, John waved the sweetly scented cloud toward his face, smudging himself with the dark smoke as the others did. The blue-and-white quilt was smudged, too, and then John stepped forward, along with his brother and four other men, to man the ropes. The women wailed in a mournful tremolo as the casket was lowered. After that, friends filed past family members, offering solemn handshakes.

Chuck surprised Teri when he slid from his place and plucked her from the fringe of the gathering. "If you're here for John, you should not hesitate to stand with him," he muttered as he gestured toward the family.

"I'm here to...to pay my respects," she said under her breath. "I'm not hesitating...." But her feet had gone clumsy as she stubbed one toe on the sod.

"Show *him* your respect," Chuck said. "He's made you one of us."

She wondered how and when this had come to pass. What had John done to make her one of them, besides making her pregnant?

John turned to her as she approached him, and her resentment melted. When she saw the raw sadness in his eyes, it didn't matter what he had told them. Whatever it was, it was true. She was one with him today, and she stood with him while he accepted his neighbors' condolences. When only the family was left, he entrusted her with his jacket and his mother's walking stick. Then, with the help of his brothers, he shoveled dirt into his mother's grave.

Teri's heart tagged after the wailing voices of the women. Her chest fairly burst with the need to cry out with them, but she clutched John's jacket to her bosom and held her sorrowful song inside.

She gripped the diamond-willow cane so tightly in her other hand that her nails dug deeply into her palm as she watched John pour his passion into his work. She remembered him putting his shoulder to another laborious task recently, after they'd pulled out of the barn and mired the car up to the tire rims in soggy clay. He had been angry with her then, and on the strength of that anger, he'd pushed the car out of the mud. Once it was free, he'd braced himself on the trunk while the rain washed over him and the paroxysm of back strain washed through him.

This man would not give up. Teri admired him for it, but she shuddered to think what the limits of his dogged persistence might be. Where Rachael was concerned, there were limits that Teri had promised to observe.

"There's food down at the house," he told her when he came to get his jacket. They were the last ones left inside the fence. At the foot of the hill the vehicles were peeling off one by one and trailing one another across the flat. "It's not a big house," he said, shifting his gaze to the collection of buildings at the end of the dirt road as he tossed his jacket over his shoulder. The hair close to his face was damp with the sweat from the last chore he had done for his mother. "We put up a shade for the feed," he said, pointing out the pole shelter thatched with leafy cottonwood cuttings. "Some people call them 'squaw coolers.' Ever seen one?"

Teri shook her head. She had seen little of this world, and she felt distanced by her ignorance. She wished they could be alone for just a moment. She wanted to be closer to him now. She thought of cooling him, of mopping his brow, quenching his thirst, offering him anything that might bring him comfort.

He scowled as he tried to read her thoughts. "Don't tell me you're not hungry."

"I could eat a little something."

The frown gave way to a slow smile. "I'd like to see you eat a big something, you know that? Just for a change."

Teri handed him the knot-studded cane, and he put it to use as they walked down the hill together. She could almost feel the pain in his back and hip. She could almost hear his thoughts, his disappointment in her failure to grant his single request.

"John." She wanted to explain, but his detached glance had her fumbling to find words that would gain ready acceptance. "I'm sorry I couldn't . . ." His expression would not change for a meaningless apology. She shook her head and swallowed the rest of her sentence. "No, I'm not. It would be too confusing for her. It wouldn't be right." Softly, sincerely, she added, "But I understand how you feel."

"No, you don't. But maybe you will." A stone, loosened by his bootheel, skittered down the path in front of them. "Maybe after you've eaten with us and met some more people, you will."

"It won't change anything." Her heel slipped, too, and her arm flew up for balance. The cane clattered to the ground as he caught her by the elbow. Why was she so graceless around him? she wondered. So unsteady at every turn?

She looked up at him, lifting her free hand to shade her eyes. She wished she could dispel the shadows that clouded his mind. "You understand that, don't you? I can't change it now."

"Would you, if you could?"

"It's not good to ask questions like that." In time he would accept that, but he had had so little time to make his peace, while she... "Believe me, I know."

"Then we won't talk about it now," he said. She sighed and started to move on, but he stopped her, tightening his grip on her arm. She looked up again, waiting. "We won't talk about your answers. We'll talk about mine. I told Chuck and Marla."

"Oh, John..."

"You see? You don't understand." Releasing her, he started down the hill, muttering, "But maybe you will."

The traditional feed had already started by the time they reached the yard. Folding chairs and tables were on loan from the community center, and there were pots of soup and white dishpans full of potato salad, along with sandwich meats, frybread, sheetcakes with three kinds of frosting. The older people sat beneath the leafy bower of the shade, the women bowing their scarf-covered heads over their plates and the men sipping their coffee. The younger people chased flies away from the food, and the children chased after a playful black pup or a third piece of cake.

Teri pitched in to help with the food. She refilled plates and refereed a tug-of-war over the last piece of cherry-chip cake, offering a fat square of strawberry with double-fudge frosting as a consolation prize.

While she was manning the coffee urn she overheard a good deal of speculation about how long the standoff over the access road might last. One older man told John that the tribe's attorneys had differing views on the matter, but that he should "hang tough." Chuck grumbled about the never-ending "Indian-country legal hassles."

Someone pointed to the black pup, who was chasing his tail. Heads turned and nodded, people chuckling. "Sanderson gets paid for doing that," the older man said, gaining a round of belly laughs.

"Sanderson is one of the tribe's lawyers."

Teri turned her head quickly toward the man who'd offered the clarification. She'd been so absorbed in her eavesdropping that she hadn't noticed him, but he was standing right next to her elbow. He handed her a cup and nodded for a refill. Another Tiger, she was certain, for she could see the resemblance to John and Chuck.

"I'm the one they call Buckshot," he explained as she returned his cup, now full. "The one you haven't heard anything good about."

Teri smiled and offered her hand. He hardly looked like a "wild man," as John had described him. In fact, he looked more like John than Chuck did. "I haven't heard anything all that *bad,* either."

"This is my daughter, Missy." He indicated the little dark-eyed moppet who was clinging to his pant leg. "Say hello to Teri."

The little girl's eyes brightened with her shy smile as she hugged her dad's leg tighter. Another unmistakable resemblance pierced Teri's heart. The child reminded her of Rachael.

"How old are you, Missy?" Teri asked.

"Thix" was the answer.

"Do you go to school?"

Missy nodded, then giggled as she pressed her nose against the side seam of Buckshot's jeans.

"First grade next year," Buckshot said proudly.

Teri caught herself before she responded that Rachael would be in second. The instinct to relate Rachael's status came out of the blue. She *never* spoke of Rachael to anyone but Lavender and Wyatt. And now John. She had unwittingly opened the door to a whole family of Tigers. Somehow she would have to keep them standing outside until Rachael was old enough to come to the door herself. What grade, she wondered, would her cousin Missy be in then?

"She wants cake," Buckshot explained as he allowed himself to be pulled along by his daughter's small hand. "I've been wanting to meet you. Everything I ever heard about you was pretty damn good."

Buckshot went away smiling, and Chuck took his place in line for coffee. Chuck, the serious one. He could get his own coffee, Teri thought, but she took his cup and filled it anyway. Finding ways to be useful made her feel more comfortable among so many new faces.

"Missy must be about the same age, huh?" Chuck smiled knowingly above the rim of his steaming cup. "Same age as John's little girl."

There was nothing Teri could say. She owed this man no explanations, no apologies, but his dark eyes seemed to accuse her of some kind of betrayal. She wanted to tell him that it was none of his business, but the words wouldn't come. This was not the time, she decided. Not on the day of his mother's funeral. If he continued to stalk her, she would show him she had claws of her own, but for now...

"How many deputies they got down at the gate?"

Marla's interruption, directed at Chuck, took them both by surprise.

"Two," came the answer.

"Take them a plate," the older sister ordered. Chuck took one sip of coffee before, much to Teri's surprise, he retreated to do as he was told.

Marla lifted the urn to see how the coffee was holding out. "John told me you had a baby for him," Marla said, avoiding Teri's eyes. "I know it's hard."

"Yes, it is," Teri said quietly. "Very hard."

"He cares for you." Marla gathered a few empty cups, then wiped a small spill off the laminated tabletop with a napkin. Finally she looked at Teri. "He always has."

Marla's observation was offered in a comforting vein, but it felt like a lead weight lodged in Teri's chest. If he had always cared for her, they wouldn't have been in this mess. Which wasn't a mess at all, Teri amended. Good things had come of it. Rachael was a wonderful child, and she was a joy to her parents. Wonderful parents, Lavender and Wyatt. Ideal parents. It *wasn't* a mess.

But the desolation Teri felt when a guitar trio led in the singing of several doleful hymns went beyond paying respects. In silence she mourned her own losses.

As the last light of day cast the hills in silhouette against the streaking purple sky, the family members began stacking the folding chairs and flipping the long tables over to collapse the legs. One of the older boys tossed two big green garbage bags full of paper plates into the back of a pickup, then slapped the back of his neck. The mosquitoes were out. It was time to head home.

"I think I'd better go now," Teri told John between visitors' goodbyes. He gave her a quick, questioning look. "Back to Bismarck, back to Minneapolis. I'm scheduled for something next week. Jeans, I think." She smiled at him warmly. The bolo tie was gone, and he had rolled back the cuffs of his white shirt. He looked bright and beautiful in the twilight. "They should use you instead. You're the perfect jeans man. The perfect..."

She shook her head and stepped back. "I have to go."

"Not yet. We have to talk."

"I don't think it'll do any good." Buckshot was approaching, assisting one of John's elderly aunts, and Teri hastened to make way for them. But the riveting look in John's eyes kept her hanging in the balance, unable to take her leave altogether. "I can't think of anything else to say," she protested softly.

"Shake hands with these people. You don't have to say anything."

After everyone was gone he took her inside and offered, of all things, more coffee. She leaned back against the small piece of wall next to the kitchen door and closed her eyes. "John, I'm really tired."

"I only have one bed, but you're welcome to it."

"I can't stay," she insisted.

"You can't leave." She opened her eyes and found him standing closer, the expression in his eyes unreadable in the dim light. "Your car won't start."

"You tried it?"

"Didn't have to. I took the distributor cap off. If you left now, I might never see you again." Cupping her cheek in his hand, he spoke to her tenderly, as though he were speaking to a child. "And we're going to talk after you get some rest."

"John, I understand." She wanted to touch him, to hold him, to make him believe that what she said was true. But she put her hands behind her back, touching her palms to the wall for support. "I understand that you have a wonderful family and you want Rachael to be part of it somehow."

"Is that her name? Rachael?" He brushed her hair back from her shoulder and searched her eyes in an achingly needy way. "You never told me."

"Lavender and Wyatt chose...chose her name."

"It's a pretty name. Rachael." He smiled when he heard himself say it. "Do you have a picture of her?"

"Oh, John, please don't do this to me." His small request seemed to squeeze the air from Teri's lungs. Wearily she dropped her chin to her chest. "I think of her as a little sister. At least, I've tried to think of her that way. And I've succeeded, mostly. Up until now." She looked up, searching his eyes for help. "Seeing you makes it so hard."

"We can get her back, Teri." Eagerly he took her shoulders in his hands and lifted her away from the wall. "I've talked to Chuck about it, and he talked to a tribal judge. You know that old guy who talked about the lawyers working on—" he jerked his chin in the direction of the disputed access road "—this other deal? He's a judge. The tribal courts have their own jurisdiction. As long as I'm her father—"

"No," Teri groaned, shaking her head so vigorously it made her dizzy. "No, no, no, John."

"What do you mean, no?" He adjusted his grip and waited until she looked into his eyes again. "You said I was her father."

"You are. *We* are her biological parents, but..." Bracing her hands on his chest, she took a deep breath, trying to find strength for a losing battle against the heartbreaking look in his eyes. He wanted the child they'd conceived together, and Teri wished she could think of a way to ease the disappointment for him. Tears burned in her throat, because she knew that no such way existed. Tears formed and brimmed and spilled over because she had known from the beginning, and she had made the choice, and she had lived with it. Now the man she loved would have to do the same.

"We can't take her back." She closed her eyes and wept, pleading, "Don't even let yourself think about it, because it can't happen."

"Don't cry, honey. Anything can happen." He pulled her into his arms and moved her away from the door. "I want you to rest now. Come on. You're not going anywhere right now except to bed."

Chapter 7

Teri wasn't quite sure where she was when she first awoke. The room was small, but the open windows admitted cool night air that gave the feel of spaciousness. Moonlight cast a white glow over the bare walls and sparse furnishings. There was a dresser but no mirror, a small but comfortable bed with no headboard, a window with a half-drawn shade but no curtain. There was a single pillow, smooth white sheets, and a quilt, neatly folded across the foot of the bed. Her navy-and-white coatdress was draped over the back of a wooden chair. Her slip lay across the seat.

She sat up slowly, feeling heavy all over, her head miserably sleep logged. It dawned on her that she had behaved like a child, wearing herself out emotionally, forgetting to make herself eat something, forgetting what a mistake it was to fall asleep on a pillow full of tears. It had all made for one of those dull headaches that were so hard to shake. But she told herself that she deserved it, because she was not a child.

She tossed the sheet back and headed for the dresser, hoping to find a clock. She was wearing only her bra and panties, and she remembered John helping her unbutton her dress. He'd told her how pretty she looked in her satin slip, and she had thought he was taking her to bed with him. When he had left the room without closing the door all the way, she'd thought he was coming back. She'd wanted him back. Oh, Lord, how many times had she berated herself for wanting him back? And how many times had she faced the day with one of these dumb cried-herself-to-sleep headaches?

Obviously she was a slow learner.

The windup clock on the dresser said eight-twenty, but it wasn't ticking. Teri set the clock down, thinking that if she asked John, he would say it was nighttime, unless he'd come up with a new comeback. Wondering when he'd last wound the clock, she noticed the picture frame that stood in the shadows beside it. She turned the frame toward the window and studied it in the moonlight. Not one picture, but several. Half a dozen images of her own face stared up at her through the glass.

She remembered giving John her high school picture when he was recovering from one of the several painful operations it had taken to put him back together after his fall. There was also a snapshot Lavender had taken of Teri in her cap and gown, and one taken of Teri and John climbing into the cab of the eighteen-wheel rig he'd driven before he joined the army. He wasn't smiling. He'd been self-conscious about his body after his long convalescence, and he'd hated having his picture taken. Funny he kept that one on display.

Teri had always photographed well, and she didn't mind posing for the camera. She looked better in pictures than she did in the flesh. Proof positive was the small clipping that rounded out John's montage of memories. It was a shot that had appeared in *Woman's Day*. She wondered whether his mother or his sister had given him the magazine, or maybe sent him the clipping. She also wondered why he had kept any of these pictures after he'd walked out on her, and she decided it was yet another testimony to the photogenic Teri Nordstrom. Take her or leave her in person, but she was great in print!

She set the picture frame back exactly as she'd found it, then eyed the clothes on the chair. Dress clothes. Uptown chic clothes. Not the kind of thing you'd want to wear if you were sneaking around the outbuildings looking for a distributor cap, whatever that was. Maybe she would find the keys to John's pickup, in which case she'd just *take* the damn thing. Then again, maybe she'd run into John.

In her search through his dresser she ran into his underwear. She decided that a pair of thermal long johns would probably fit her better than his jeans. She topped those with a white T-shirt that almost reached her knees, covering the baggiest part of the long johns. Fortunately she'd had the foresight to bring tennis shoes. She found her purse beside the dresser, felt around inside for her pillbox, then went looking for a glass of water.

The house was dark and quiet. John had done some cleaning while Teri slept. The tiny kitchen was remarkably immaculate after the day's use. The small dining table had been cleared of leftovers, and the few pieces of living room furniture had been moved around, probably back to their normal places. Teri had expected to find

John asleep on the sofa, but he was not there. While she was taking her aspirin, she noticed that the back door was open.

The screen door creaked as she let herself outside, where the black-velvet Dakota sky was still generously salted with bright stars. Teri's rented station wagon sat next to John's pickup in the gravel driveway. Beyond them stood an empty corral and a dark barn. The night was filled with the chirping of crickets and the rattling of leaves stirred by the breeze, but there were no human sounds.

Good time to make a search, Teri told herself, and then she almost laughed aloud. Even if she found something that looked like a car part—she imagined some kind of a cap that had some sort of distributing things on it—she wouldn't know where to put it. But at least she would *have* it, and she'd be able to say, *See, John. You can't keep my distributor cap from me.*

She stopped kidding herself when she saw him leaning against one of the poles that held up the roof of the squaw cooler. He took no notice of her. Gazing across the dusky flat toward the hill where he'd buried his mother hours before, he raised a cigarette to his mouth and took a long, slow drag. The ash flamed briefly, like a red warning light, becoming a beacon in the night, along with his white T-shirt. His hair was a shadow touching shoulders so broad she imagined him as Samson, about to shove a pillar aside and send the whole structure crashing to the ground.

He heard her coming, but he didn't turn around. He waited, fancifully imagining that she was still dressed the way she had been when he'd put her to bed, or that maybe she was wearing the satin slip that was the color of winter grass, and maybe she was barefoot, and maybe he would sweep her up in his arms when she reached his side so her feet wouldn't get pricked on the stubble that was his yard.

But it was the hair on the back of his own neck that prickled when he sensed the nearness of her. No matter what she wore, he could not be disappointed, and when it turned out to be *his* underwear, his chest swelled.

"I like your outfit."

"Thank you." She smoothed the long T-shirt over her hips, but what amused him were the thick folds at her ankles. "It's too late to make anybody's fall collection, which is a shame. I think it might catch on."

"I think you could wear a flour sack and make it catch on. Come here," he invited with an outstretched arm. "Let me catch on." He needed one last drag on his cigarette before he buried it under his bootheel and tucked her under his arm. "Did it help to sleep?"

"Not really. I woke up to find you gone."

"And you were thinkin', *damn* that John Tiger. He'll never change."

"I was thinking, I wonder where he put that distributor cap."

John chuckled ominously. "Wouldn't you like to know?"

"I'd like to know where to put it if I found it." She tipped her chin up and offered a coy smile. "Actually, I have a couple of ideas. Does it have any sharp edges?"

"Ouch." He touched his lips to her hair and smiled against it.

"When do you sleep?"

"Usually at night, like most people. But I have a guest, and I didn't want her to get up and see a messy house." He straightened, flexing his shoulders as she stepped aside. "I went down to the barricade and found out both sides had taken the night off, I suppose because of the funeral. I could skip out the front door and nobody would ever know.''

"I don't see why they don't back down and build a road somewhere else."

"It's all a matter of precedent setting." He mentioned the term surprisingly easily. It was one of Chuck's favorite topics. "There are right-of-way disputes, water-rights battles and jurisdiction hassles on every reservation in the country," he explained, ticking off the list with his fingers just as efficiently as Chuck would have. "Every concession sets a precedent. So one little fence across one little dirt road can have one hell of a big ripple effect."

He sensed the intensity of Teri's attention, and his arm froze, mid-gesture. She wanted a revelation, and he did, to his surprise, have one for her. "They want to take it all away. Did you know that? They want what's left."

"Who does?"

"I don't know." He shook his head. He had to stick with the basics, with his own beef and his own resolve. "I don't know. I guess that was something Chuck would say, and lately I've had this gut feeling he's right." He sighed. "They're not taking this piece. That's all I know. What's mine is mine."

"You said it belonged to all of you. You and your family."

"It's not ours if we don't take care of it. I'm taking care of it now, and it'll take care of me in return." His eyes were drawn to the hilltop again, and to the inky rock that stood like a hole in the predawn horizon. "The land will take me, too. Not a truck or a tank or a damn train bridge. But this land, where my mother lies."

He felt Teri's quick shiver, and he slipped his arms around her shoulders and pulled her back against him.

"When I'm at least as old as she was," he muttered close to her ear. "Maybe a lot older."

He wanted his time with her first, whatever time she had to give him. Likewise, he wanted his time to sow and reap, his time to fashion his legacy and let it take root, as those who'd come before him had done. He wanted those things here, in a country where studios and houses of fashion would never flourish.

So there it was—the long and short of contentment. He had learned to take it as it came. He smiled as he turned Teri toward him. "I have a guest who hasn't been fed. My mother would have my hide for being so rude."

"What time is it?"

He shrugged. "Middle of the night."

She chuckled. "Can't you tell by the stars?"

"What do you want, a frontier guide?" She was smiling, teasing, her head tipped back and her cool, silky hair lying across the back of his hand. "My guess is three-thirty, four o'clock, but don't quote me."

He tucked her under his arm and walked her to the house. He had to walk fast, talk even faster, to contain the urge to kiss her sassy smile away.

"All I know is you're awake, and I'm awake, and you did your usual dainty nibbling yesterday. There's not much food left, but I can always put a bowl of soup on the table."

"I'm not really—"

"—hungry, I know." He opened the kitchen door and ushered her inside. "You don't eat, Teri."

"Maybe not the way you do, but I eat. I remember when you used to starve yourself to make weight for a wrestling meet."

"Yeah, but I never got down to..." He took a small pot from the refrigerator and set it on a gas burner. Once he'd adjusted the blue flame, he turned and took quick inventory of Teri, head to foot. Between the extremes—and her fine-featured face was a heart-stopping extreme—his clothes all but swallowed up her slight frame. "Do you have to make weight for modeling? If you do, whatever it is, I think you're there. You're thin enough."

"Thin enough? Or too thin?" Abruptly distancing herself, she laid one hand on her breast, the other on her hip and eyed him coolly. "Or maybe too thin here and not thin enough here. Some people want—"

"I want you to eat something." And nobody else had any say in the matter. He dipped a spoon into the soup and tested the temperature with his lips. Satisfied, he grabbed a bowl from the cupboard. "This might not be fancy, but it'll fill the hollows."

She folded her arms across her chest and rested her shoulder against the refrigerator door, thoroughly charmed, he could tell, by his domesticity.

"If you'll have some, too," she said. "Remember how I used to sneak candy bars to you in class to keep you going when you were trying to lose a few pounds before a meet?"

"Then you switched to Lavender's homemade trail mix," he recalled. He handed her a bowl of soup, then set about fixing his own. "I shouldn't have let you tempt me either way, but I wasn't about to refuse any sweet thing you offered."

"This is better than candy," she assured him between spoonfuls. He slid his chair up to the table. The beef broth was actually rather bland, but bland was good for everybody.

"You gave me many sweet things," he told her.

"And when will you..." She gave him a smile, meaning it to be one of them, "...give my distributor cap back?"

"In good time." He tore into a chunk of Marla's crusty yeast bread and handed the smaller half across the table to Teri. "Can't give you an exact time. Don't have a clock around here that works."

"I noticed."

"Tomorrow, when the sun's directly overhead..."

"You'll put my car back together?"

"We'll know it's noon, or thereabouts," he said without looking up from his soup. "Then you'll feel better, 'cause you'll know the time."

"Will that be in *good* time? Will I be free to leave?"

"Who knows?"

Okay, so he was playing a little keep-away with her now, but he had his reasons. He needed some time with her. He wasn't going to let her waltz into his life, tell him they had a kid, then waltz out again. But it bothered him when she stopped smiling and methodically dragged her spoon through her soup.

"Tell me again how sorry Coach Archer is about my mother's death," he challenged, annoyed by the way she managed to make sharing a meal with him seem like such a strenuous task. "Why didn't he come to her funeral? Why wasn't he here to shake my hand?"

"He wasn't sure you'd want him here under the circumstances." She looked up at him. "He was always good to you, John. I wanted our baby to have..." Her voice became distant as she glanced away again. "I thought you'd approve of the parents I chose for her."

"You gave me many sweet things," he said again. Sitting across the table in his big white T-shirt, she looked like a golden-haired angel in the Christmas pageant who had missed her cue.

But she was not a little girl. She had given birth to one, to *his* little girl. "Do you know how often I dreamed of being able to give you...?" He shook off the phrase, amending softly, "Of you and me having a baby?"

"Whenever we talked about it, it was always a future dream. Marriage and children," she said wistfully, as though the dream was lost to her.

"You don't know how glad I am to know she's healthy." He looked to her for more reassurance, and she nodded. For a brief moment they were mother and father, belatedly sharing delivery-room anxiety and relief. Unexpectedly shaken, he went back to his soup. "She's also half-Indian," he muttered.

Teri's brow creased slightly. "If Lavender and Wyatt could have children, they would be half-Indian."

"He can't get her enrolled as a tribal member." The look on Teri's face didn't change. John slid his bowl aside as he leaned into his explanation. "Getting adopted into the tribe is only for tourists. You have to be able to claim the legal blood quantum, which she can only do through me."

"Then maybe that's something you can do for her, John. I don't know what the requirements are, but maybe you and Wyatt can work out some—"

"I'm working on it now, with Judge Shelltrack." She scowled, and he knew he was treading on thin ice. But he could have sworn he'd heard the echo of his own heart's yearning when she'd spoken of marriage and children. They'd both done what they thought they had to do, but maybe he could facilitate a miracle and undo the past. "That's how I know we can get her back. Or I can. I wasn't just blowing steam when I started to tell you—"

Her eyes widened instantly. "You can't. John, adoption is as binding as—"

"The judge can invoke the Indian Child Protection Act and order Rachael to be returned to the reservation as long as everyone agrees that I'm her real father."

"She doesn't need any protection," Teri insisted.

"Tribal courts have a legal right to protect Indian children from being taken from their people."

"Legal right? *Legal*..." She pressed her palms against her temples and shook her head. "I refuse to listen to this. You're talking about turning a small child's whole world upside down."

"No," he said, following her lead as she pushed herself away from the table. He had to make her understand. "Right-side up. I'm talking about making things right. Making it all up to her." He caught her by the shoulders, turning her to face him. "And to you, if you'll let me."

"This is not the way to—"

"Ask them to let me see her," he implored. Maybe that was the place to start, he thought. A small enough request. But Teri shook her head. "You see her all the time," he insisted. "You saw her when she was a baby, from the first moment she was born. Hell, she's already going to school, and I've missed—"

"So have I," she returned heatedly. "I knew her *before* she was born. She was all mine then. But when the Archers took her from the hospital, they became her parents." She looked him in the eye and added pointedly, "They never deserted me."

"And I did." Deflated by guilt, he released her and turned away. "Okay. I know it was my own fault. What I did was—"

"It doesn't matter whose fault it was anymore."

He had never begged for anything, and he cursed the need to do it now. His stomach twisted on itself like wrung-out laundry, but he found a piece of his voice. "Then don't shut me out, Teri. Ask them to let me see my little girl."

"She's not..." It was her turn to reach out, to take his arm in her hands, her turn to plead. "John, you must stop this. You can't take her back—*we* can't take her back. *Please!*" She closed her eyes briefly, gathering strength. "Let's not talk about it anymore."

"Okay." He laid his hand over both of hers. He was not without recourse, the judge had told him. He didn't want to hurt anyone, and he'd hoped Teri would be his ally. But there was time yet. "We won't talk about it."

"I have to go back."

He stared at her, wordlessly rejecting the notion.

"John, you can't keep me here like this. It's not good for either of us. One minute you're threatening to do things that would be..." She shook her head quickly, as though naming the hazards might make them come to pass. "And I just want to scream in your ears and pound on your head, but the next minute I look at you and I want..." Her hands slid down his arm as she stepped back. "I have to go."

"The next minute?" He turned his hand and caught hers before it slid away. "What else do you want to do to me, Teri?" She closed her eyes, but he would not let her shut him out. "What else do you want from me?"

"Why won't you listen?" she said, bristling.

"Why won't you look at me and tell me—?"

"Because you already *know!*" She tried to pull her hand from his, but he held on fast. "I'll ask the police for a ride when they come back." She squared her shoulders, the look in her eyes fiercely defiant. "If they're still interested in you, I suppose they'll be back."

"Sooner or later," he agreed as he reeled her closer. "But you're with *me,* so you're not gonna ask them for the time of day." Touching her hair helped him to quell some senseless apprehension that lurked in the back of his mind whenever he thought of her turning to another man for *anything.* "You need to know the time, you wear a damn watch."

She met his gaze unflinchingly, but her eyes were unreadable.

"Am I right? You're on my side."

"I might be, if I weren't a prisoner," she answered calmly.

"You're not a prisoner. I would never do anything to hurt you. You know that."

"I've always felt safe with you, but as for the hurting part..."

"I need to know where I stand," he insisted. "What my rights are where my daughter is concerned. I'm not letting you run off to Minneapolis until I find out. I know that might not seem fair, considering *I* ran off on *you* once, but I'm not running anymore.

"And I don't know much about *fair.* I've heard a lot about what's fair and what's right lately. And what's *good* for me—everybody seems to have an opinion on that, too." His gut was tightening, and he made a conscious effort to keep his hands, resting on her shoulders, from doing the same. "But I've got my own opinions. Maybe even a few rights, if I've got guts enough to claim them."

"Where Rachael is concerned, your rights and my rights aren't important. It takes guts to admit that we gave them up. Both of us did."

"Except that you're permitted to see her, and I'm not." Her icy stare granted no quarter, and he found himself backing down, hoping she would look at him tenderly again and give him something—some small concession. "Okay, we'll set that aside for now. Where the cops are concerned, you're on my side, right?"

"How can I be on your side when you stole my—?" He gave her a wounded look, and she returned a piece of a smile. "Yes, I'm on your side."

Sweet words of reprieve. "You know, I could use some help with the chores, but that outfit..."

She clutched two handfuls of fabric at her waist and wiggled her hips in a hiking-up dance. "I'm having a little trouble holding up both my pants and my end of the argument."

"My nephew left a pair of jeans the last time he was here. You just might be able to squeeze into them." She looked doubtful. "Jason's twelve," he told her as he led the way to the bedroom.

"Oh, I could never fit into boys' jeans...."

But she could.

John watched her knot his T-shirt over one slim hip. He'd washed up, changed his shirt, found her a pair of thick socks to protect her ankles, and now he wanted to claim the brush she was taking to her long, straight hair and groom her until she crackled.

Couldn't do that right now, he scolded himself as he hustled her along. He held out his hand for the brush, which she surrendered after a few last strokes. He took a couple of swipes at his own long mane before tossing the brush on the kitchen counter on his way out the door. It was good to shake off heavy thoughts and get moving.

Teri had to skip along quickly to keep pace with his stride. Shades of night were fast fading into daylight, and the cool air smelled newly washed. And, thank God, John had stopped pushing the talk about Rachael. He would think about it now, and he would see. He would come to understand. There was time. There would be good feelings again. Her feet were light, and her heart was getting there.

"Do we have animals to feed?"

"We've had a few night visitors lately, since the newspaper ran a story on us. Woody had to fix some fence while I was gone." He pivoted and walked backward while he enlightened her. "So we're gonna check fence this morning."

"On foot?"

"'Course not." He hadn't buttoned his shirt, and he was rolling up his cuffs as he flashed her a grin. He knew darn well what a great chest he had. "Cowboys don't check fence on foot."

She didn't see any horses in the corral, and when they passed through the barn, she didn't see any there, either. "What are we going to ride?"

John dipped some oats from a bin into a galvanized bucket, took a hackamore and bridle off a wall peg and led Teri to his grandstand seating on top of the corral. "You just watch," he said with a wink, his eyes twinkling at her like morning stars.

He headed across the flat toward a shadowy slope that stood like a dark wave against the orangy edge of sunrise. His blue chambray shirttail flapped against his lean hips as he strolled through dew-tipped wild wheatgrass, shaking the oats in the bucket like a blind man seeking alms. Teri sat in hushed anticipation, listening to his swishing footfalls and his swishing bait, watching the Cat stalk his territory. From the shelterbelt near the barn came a mourning dove's melancholy counsel, *Don't mooove, oh, don't mooove.*

The blaze-faced stud appeared suddenly on the hilltop. His sorrel coat glistened with the rays of the rising sun. The oats continued to rustle as John kept a steady pace, signaling with his free hand for Teri to stay where she was. The big stud sniffed the air, and Teri held her breath.

The trust was there. The horse trotted down to claim his treat and allowed himself to be haltered. John fed him the rest of the oats from his hand, then set the bucket aside and vaulted onto the sorrel's back.

"Be right back. He'll tell his girlfriend we're goin' for a ride."

She lifted her hand to shade her eyes from the brilliant sunrise. "And I suppose she'll say, 'Yes sir.'"

"This guy don't get nooo back talk from his women." He patted the animal's heavily muscled neck as he cut a tight circle in the grass. The horse was ready to move out.

"Maybe you should ask him for some pointers," Teri called out.

John laughed. "I already did. That quick, he shamed me out. Then he said, 'Don't feel bad. They gave you a bigger brain.'"

"John!" she scolded in mock horror. Then she laughed. "Trouble is, where did they put it?"

"Trouble is, they gave *you* one that doesn't work the same as mine." His hair and his shirt both fluttered, but he sat the prancing horse effortlessly. He cocked his hand at her, mock-pistol-style. "You stay put."

"Yes, sir!"

He cued the sorrel with a soft cluck, and they fairly lunged over the hill. But they were back in no time with a sleek black mare for Teri. The stud wanted to make things difficult by sniffing around the mare while they were trying to saddle up. She kicked at him to let him know that this was not the time, and Teri laughed as the big brute jumped out of the way.

"Does this mean the male mystique is somewhat over-rated?" Teri tested the mare's acceptance of her by rubbing her velvet nose. "You don't *always* say, 'Yes, sir,' do you, pretty lady?"

"He got her to come along, no problem." John swung into his saddle, then nodded toward the mare. "You wanna mount up there, *pretty lady?* We've got a job to do."

It felt good to be in the saddle again. It didn't matter that she would probably be stiff again that night. The trill of the meadowlark, the early-morning air and the cotton-candy-colored sky were prairie gifts, best enjoyed from the back of a horse. She didn't have to say a word, and neither did John. Approving looks and reaffirming smiles delivered their messages. On this day and in this place it felt good to be together.

The sky had become baby-blanket blue when the black wings of trouble appeared in the distance. John urged the sorrel into a ground-eating lope, and Teri's mare jogged along behind. Beyond the ridge they could see the vulture gliding in circles with a partner, and it wasn't long before the object of their interest came into view. The brown mound of hide lying in the grass was the telltale sign of a dead cow.

"Stay here," John ordered when the stench hit them. Teri reined in the mare, content to keep her distance while he investigated.

"Waste of good beef," he said as he circled the carcass on horseback. "I was feeling guilty because I didn't have anything to butcher for the feed. Whoever shot her should at least have taken the meat while they were at it. I would've gotten the point if they'd just left the head and tail.''

"What possible point . . . ?''

"They're hell-bent on opening up that road.'' He rode the few yards back to her. He'd seen all there was to see, and the message was clear to him. "They can't stand being inconvenienced, driving out of their way to get to the lake that flooded *my* land. My grandfather's land. My grandfather's grave, for God's sake.''

Teri's mount fell into step next to his as John expounded, gesturing in frustration with his free hand. "I can spend half a day running my cows back in, but they have to have *that* access road open, and if I know what's good for me . . .''

"You can't afford to lose a cow like that,'' she observed supportively.

"No, I can't. They don't come cheap. But I can't afford to give in, either. They've taken enough.''

Teri wasn't sure who *they* were, but she was glad he couldn't get his hands on them right now. She helped John fix a section of fence that had been snipped. He was so strong that he didn't need a wire stretcher. Tossing his shirt aside, he poured his anger into the chore. The muscles in his neck and shoulders bulged as impressively as the sorrel stud's as he pulled the ends of the wire taut and held them with gloved hands while Teri worked with a pair of pliers to weave the repair.

They rode the fence line down to the barricade. Sheriff Carl Wickery had stopped to exchange words with Woody Whitestaff, who had assumed the access road standoff as his full-time job. Woody grinned when he saw that Teri was with John, but John ignored the congratulatory signal. He was busy staring the lawman down.

"Somebody cut my fence and shot one of my cows last night, Wickery."

"Sorry to hear that. Can't do nothin' about it, though." Wickery adjusted the brim of his brown cowboy hat. "Federal property."

"It's my property. I want you to keep your people off my property."

"My people?" Wickery squinted up at John and postured, hands on ample hips. "I'm just a county sheriff. I'm no big chief or anything." He glanced askance at Woody, who was perched on the wheel housing on the shady side of the big green haystack machine. "Maybe it was one of your people. Maybe they're tired of all this ruckus you got goin' here."

"I'm tired of it, too. I'd like to take my stacker and go put up some hay."

"Why don't you?"

John draped his forearm over the saddle horn and leaned forward. "I will, soon as you guys leave me the hell alone and let me lock my gates."

"Aw, it's not up to us, John. You know that." Wickery adjusted his hat again and shuffled his boots in the grass. "It'll be up to some judge. Meanwhile, you step on my side of the line, I gotta arrest you." He shrugged off any vestige of blame. "Sorry to hear about your mother."

"Thanks," John said quietly.

"Who's the pretty lady?"

"None of your damn business."

It was hard to tell whether Wickery grimaced or smiled as he squinted into the sun. "I can see why. Those reporters come back, they'll wanna get a picture of *her* this time."

John glanced over his shoulder, offering Teri an unspoken guarantee that they would have to get past him first. But he tossed Wickery an offhand response. "She's an old friend. Came for the funeral."

"Oh." With a doubting snort the sheriff started backing toward his car, but he couldn't resist passing on some wisdom in parting. "It's a sad time for your family. You oughta give it up, John. You know, just back off and get your hay put up."

"The Cat don't have to worry about getting his hay up," Woody put in. Three heads turned in his direction. "It'll get done. He's got his people lookin' out for him." He looked up at John, squinted one eye and grinned proudly. "They might be a little tired, but they ain't *too* tired."

Chapter 8

They went back to the house and spent the rest of the day winding themselves in the cocoon of things once shared. John almost blushed when Teri mentioned his small collection of photographs. When she made the bed, he recalled their first stay in a motel and how he had laughed and told her that even *he* knew that a guest wasn't expected to make the bed in a motel. It was Teri's turn to blush. They played with the black pup, who reminded Teri of one she'd seen at Marla's when John had lived there. Same breeding, John told her, then added with a shrug, "Same neighborhood, anyway."

They spent the day stealing kisses the way they had done in simpler times, before they had erected any barricades, before they had conceived anything but dreams. Reveling in isolation, awash in summer sunshine, they tumbled through the day merely enjoying each other.

John made bologna sandwiches for lunch—"Crimson Eagle burgers," he called them, fondly recalling his protest-camp days. By suppertime he realized that the cupboards were even barer than he'd thought. Undaunted, he cheerfully whipped up two plates of fried macaroni and canned peas.

Teri stared at hers while John dug in eagerly. It was hot, she told herself as she assembled a pea and an elbow together for a wary bite.

"It's not that great, is it?"

Teri lifted her chin and smiled bravely. She would clean her plate no matter what, just to put the sparkle back John's eyes.

"Used up most of what I had in the house for the funeral feed," he said as he stabbed at the pasta, racking it up on his fork like a string of beads. "Chuck's bringing groceries over as soon as he—" He glanced up from his plate, suddenly uneasy, then lopped off his news while he went back to chasing peas. "Next time he comes by."

"I thought you said he lived in South Dakota."

"Did I say?" He enlisted a slice of bread as a pea pusher. "It's not always easy to pin Chuck's residence down. Right now he's trying to take care of some business for me." Another quick glance told Teri that the business might be hard to pin down, too.

John dismissed the matter, gesturing with his bread hand. "He'd like to be sitting up there on top of my hay wagon aiming down the barrel of a thirty-aught-six at Wickery's right front tire, which is why it's better to have him looking into the legal stuff. I'm sitting on a powder keg, and my brother is a walking flamethrower."

"What about Buckshot?" she asked. "You said he was a wild man, but he seems very nice. I didn't meet his wife, though. Was she here?"

"He isn't married."

"Oh." He'd said it too quickly, too quietly. She knew why. "I met his daughter."

"Missy lives with her mother and her stepdad." His explanation seemed to echo with some long-held frustration with his older brother. "Buckshot took too damn long deciding what was good for him, and Sarah—Missy's mom—well, she just got tired of waiting."

"How long did she wait?"

"Couple of years, I guess." He glanced from his plate to hers, and she immediately got her fork moving. "I've gotta find you something else to eat. I can tell you've never eaten hard-times." He pushed the loaf of bread across the table, turning the open end toward her. "Which means you've never stayed with somebody like Buckshot."

"What was that like?"

"Didn't work out real well. I needed a father, and Buckshot..." When she didn't go for the bread, he pulled out a slice and started buttering it. "Back in those days, Buckshot needed somebody to lock him up and hide the key."

Her heart went as soft as the butter on his knife. "Did he hurt you?"

John turned his mouth down and shook his head. "He never got close enough. Too busy running from God knows what, just like..." The knife stilled in his hand, and he looked at Teri. "But he loves his daughter. And she knows who he is, even though Sarah's husband is Missy's dad, too."

"Those things happen. Breakups, divorces...." She tried to shrug it off with worldly indifference. "My father wasn't around very long, either. My mother had her... her boyfriends. You remember."

"Starky's the only one I knew." He offered her the buttered bread.

"You think you're going to do things differently." She shook her head once, and he let the bread drop. She knew she'd missed worldliness by a mile. "You promise yourself you won't make the same mistakes, that your own children will have what you missed out on, but somehow..."

His knife clattered to his plate. "This stuff tastes like cardboard." Reaching across the table, he piled her plate on top of his and shoved his chair back. "I know I've got some peanut butter and jelly around here somewhere. I'll make you a peanut butter..."

She looked up at him and loved him dearly for the thought. Her eyes were locked with his as she claimed the bread he'd buttered for her. Her mouth was dry, but she ate anyway, while he stood there watching. She sipped the glass of milk he'd set out for her, too, and he swallowed.

Abruptly he tore himself away. She wondered if the plates cracked as he tossed them into the sink. Like a chipmunk pausing for a bite on the run, she quickly ate more bread and drank more milk.

"Let me do something," he said quietly when he came back to stand beside the table.

"Do what?"

"Hold you."

It was more demand than request, and he stood there, watching with the eyes of a cat, waiting for her to decide how to move. She licked a drop of milk from her upper lip and watched him swallow again. She wondered what he tasted. She knew what he intended to taste, and she made up her mind to be as good as his eyes said she would be as she bobbed into his arms like the last bubble at the bottom of a glass.

He caught her lips with his and drank greedily. On the tip of his tongue she discovered a touch of spice that made milk taste like ambrosia. She pressed against him as he turned his head, changing the angle of their kiss and sweetening its flavor.

"Oh, God, let me hold you," he whispered against her lips. Strong hands kneaded her shoulders, her back, her buttocks, complicating his modest pleas. "Let me just hold you."

Between kisses she felt compelled to give notice. "I can't stay, John." But she had already forgotten why.

"You're staying with me tonight," he insisted. "One more night."

"Yes," she agreed on the soft tail of another kiss. Her heart was made up, if not her mind. "One more night in your bed." The bed, she remembered, was way back in the bedroom. Way, way back there. "But last night you weren't there."

"Where do you want me to be?" He slid his hands over her buttocks, lifted and pulled her tightly against him. "Tell me, Teri. Where do you want me to be?"

"With me." She buried her fingers in his long, thick hair and pulled his head down. Her neck strained, her lips hungering after him, as she whispered, "All over me."

They got as far as the big, thick black sheepskin in the middle of the living room floor. John had her jeans off and Teri had his shirt unbuttoned by the time he lowered her back against the plush fur.

He straddled her and bunched his T-shirt over her breasts, searching for the clasp that would free her breasts into his hands. His fingers stroked surely, while hers, fumbling with fastenings, went in search of him, too. She found him. When she had him in her hands, he hollowed out his belly with a sharp, quick breath. She knew her power. She, too, stroked surely.

The tables turned quickly as they exchanged gifts of pleasure. He suckled her breast, drawing the nipple between his teeth to tease it with the tip of his tongue. She caressed him until her efforts brought forth John's agonized groan. He lifted his head. "You want me all over you, or inside you?"

"Both." She relaxed her fingers and let the back of her hands play over his abdomen, up and down, testing his limits. She felt deliciously sassy. "I'll take you any way I can."

"Reach inside my left pocket," he whispered urgently as he feathered kisses over her face. "Got a present for you."

She braced one hand on his hip and found a foil packet with the other.

"Ready for you this time," he muttered, his breath warm against her neck. "You know how these work?" When she didn't answer, he raised his head again, smoothed her hair back and found his answer in her eyes. "I never showed you, did I?"

"No."

"Long overdue." He braced himself on his elbow and reached down between their bodies, searching. "Will you give me a hand?" Damp, dark tendrils of hair fell over his forehead, shadowing the carnal smile in his eyes. "Again?"

The pouch passed from her hand to his. "Yes, sir."

"Yes, John," he corrected.

"Yes, John."

Basking in sweet, sensual afterglow, they lay on the sofa, bathed in moonlight, counting stars through the picture window. The bed was still too far away. John had tossed the three back cushions aside to give them more space, wedged her bottom between his thighs and pillowed her head on his chest. He wore his briefs. She wore his T-shirt. It was about the most comfortable she'd ever been in her life.

Until he brought up that damn topic again.

"You never answered me when I asked you if you have to weigh in for your job." He ran his hands down her arms, then slid them from her wrists to her protruding pelvic bones. "Seems like there's less of you than there used to be. I could be wrong, but this part here..."

"Don't."

"You wanted me all over you, so here I am."

"I mean, don't..." She turned her head and pressed her cheek against his chest. "Don't tease me about that."

"I'm not kidding, honey." His hands stirred, caressing her comfortingly. "I don't want you to disappear."

"You're a fine one to talk."

"I mean melt away. You used to worry about me dieting for wrestling. Now I'm worrying about you."

"There's nothing to worry about. It used to be hard for me to watch my weight, but it's gotten a lot easier. I'm not that interested in eating."

"I noticed. But I figured fried macaroni wasn't a fair test." She covered his hands with hers and held them still. "I'm not testing you," he said. "I swear."

"Then let's not talk about food."

"O-kaay," he said with a sigh. "One more thing we can't talk about." He paused. "So how does this modeling work? Do the magazines hire you, the photographers, what?"

"I'm booked through a modeling agency." She smiled. He was making little circles on the top of her head with his chin. "I never thought I would get this far with it. I was working for a department store, and that job led to a print ad, and then another and another." She tipped her head back to look up at him, and his chin plowed a furrow in her hair. "I guess I photograph well."

"You're beautiful. Anybody can see that." He was smiling at her upside down. "Everybody does. That's what used to drive me crazy."

"Not beautiful enough." She lowered her chin again.

"How beautiful do you have to be?" He waited briefly for an answer, while she tried to decide whether one existed. "Is there a rating system or something?"

"I don't know. Is there?" Again she looked up. "Do you have one, John?"

His hands stirred over her pelvis again. "I know beauty when I see it. When it touches me and speaks my name."

"I used to wonder what I could have done differently, how I could have pleased you more." She recalled that when she'd realized she was pregnant—or when she'd actually faced the fact—she'd flirted with the notion that maybe the news wouldn't really scare the hell out of him. It had been a brief flirtation. She was smarter than that. "I couldn't think of anything except that I wasn't pretty enough."

"My God, Teri, if you only knew the kind of pleasure and pain I got from just looking at you. I used to think, 'God, she's mine. Damn, she can't be mine.' Round and round I'd go." He put his arms around her shoulders, hugging her as if to stabilize himself. "Got so I was as dizzy as a tail-chasing pup. The only way I could see to get myself straightened out was to take off." Incredulous, she looked up. He raised his eyebrows expectantly. "Make any sense to you?"

"No."

"Me, neither," he agreed, deflated. "Now you're so beautiful you make my eyes hurt."

"Beautiful but thin."

"No buts." He grinned as he scooped his hands underneath her. "Well, one nice little—"

"Skinny one, right?" Her hand fluttered back and forth, up and down, as though blessing her flawed self. "One big breast, one little breast. Stringy hair, knobby knees, big—"

"Hey, wait a minute." He caught her hand and gave it a quick squeeze. "What is this? I can't tease you anymore?"

He kissed her palm, then lovingly spoke of other parts. "I love your knees and your hair..." His free hand slipped from her shoulder, trekking downward. "And your breasts are like part of my family, which is why I like—" he located a cotton-covered nipple "—to tease them a little bit."

"Oh, John..."

"See? 'Cause it makes you say my name like that." It was as though he had found a piece of soft clay. He shaped it into a ball, compacting it, making it hard and tight. She moaned. "Like you were just dreaming something good about me."

"I often do."

"Still?"

"Still."

He smothered both nipples with his thumbs, and she felt his shape growing and changing against the small of her back. He cupped her breasts in his hands and held them, held the tide back, savored the tangy ebb and flow of need mixed with the cordial balm of repose.

"I dream of you, too," he said. "You're my favorite pleasant dream."

"In your dreams, am I beautiful?"

A cool night breeze drifted across the room from the window above the kitchen table. He shifted his shoulder and his leg, sheltering her. "Here in my arms you're even more beautiful."

"It's the kind of beauty you feel, isn't it?" She could feel the vibration of the deep, pleasured, affirmative sound that came from his throat. "My mother used to say, 'Do something with yourself, Teri. Look at your hair. Put some makeup on. You look like death warmed over.'" She sighed, closing her eyes as she rolled her head slowly from side to side. "I guess that means I look sick without makeup."

"You look great without makeup. You look like Teri."

"She didn't like me without makeup," she recalled matter-of-factly. "I was about eleven years old, going out to a birthday party for a bunch of other eleven-year-olds, the first time she told me to put some color in my cheeks and try a little lipstick. She said I looked too plain."

"Eleven years old?"

"I believed her. She used a lot of makeup and wore ruffled blouses. Low cut. She got all the cleavage." She touched the back of his left hand. "It's no wonder the genes petered out on this side."

He trapped her nipple between his fingers and scissored them gently. "Aw, you're makin' the little guy pout now, see?"

"*You're* making him—*her* . . . oh, John . . ."

"Dreaming again?"

"Mmmm."

"I want you to tell me about the stuff your mother said, but I don't want you to feel bad about it anymore." He smoothed her hair back from her temple, and she turned her cheek into his palm. "Do you feel how beautiful you are?"

"Yes," she whispered, and she kissed the hard heel of his hand.

"What else did she say?"

"That boys didn't like girls with legs longer than theirs. She said I'd never get a boyfriend. At the time, I said I didn't want one." She looked up to assure him, "I changed my mind when I met you."

"Did I count for her?"

"You counted with me."

"Same here." He cleared his throat. "I didn't always know how to show it. Maybe your mom had the same problem. Maybe she couldn't believe how pretty you were, either, and maybe she was scared, maybe jealous...." She wanted to protest, but he was on an apologist's roll. "And maybe she was right not to want a bum like me hangin' around you."

"You were never—"

"I made you pregnant. I should have been more careful."

"*I* should have..." She twisted around, turning on her hip to face him. "We're not going to—"

"Talk about that, I know." He bobbed his head once to reassure her. "Anyway, I was listening." He smiled. "I *was* listening, wasn't I? You were telling me how you thought you had to be prettier, and my heart was breaking over how beautiful you are, but I was listening."

"For a change," she conceded as she struggled to sit up, forcing him to do the same. She fussed with the T-shirt, which had corkscrewed around her.

"You see your picture in magazines all the time. Doesn't that tell you something?"

"The people you love tell you something." She jerked on the long shirt and tucked it beneath her bare bottom. "When they don't try to change you. When they stick by you."

"The only person I wanted to change was me." Her sudden show of propriety had him smiling. "Can I tell you something now? Will you believe me?"

"I've always believed you," she insisted. "Haven't I? I've always trusted you."

"Trust me now." His smile faded. He gazed at her intently, more insistent even than she was. Shaken, she was the first to turn away, but he took her face in his hands and made her look at him again. "Believe me now. I started loving you the first time I saw you, and I've never stopped."

"You must have...."

"I didn't. I swear to you, Teri, I didn't. Look at me." He gave her no choice. He slid off the seat and knelt in front of her, so that they were eye to eye. "No, that's not enough. I want to show you more." He pushed the band of elastic off his hip, down to his thigh. "Everything. All my scars, all my..." Taking hold of her hand, he pressed it against him, drawing her palm over the terrain of surgical scars from the repair of his damaged organs. "There. Remember? Remember how bad it was?"

"Yes."

"Did it make you love me less?"

"No." Her hand tightened protectively over a puckering track in his warm, smooth skin. "Never."

"I've got a lot of scars. A lot of flaws. Here's another one." He slid her hand to his shoulder, and she leaned over to kiss another healed wound.

"The ones on the inside are worse," he said.

She drew back, swept her fingers through his hair, then touched his cheek. "I can't kiss you inside."

"You do," he said solemnly. "Every time you look at me like that." Moonlight softened the angles of his face but not the intensity of his dark gaze. He took her hand from his cheek and drew it down between his legs. "Touch me here. I thought . . . for a long time I thought I might be scarred—" he closed his eyes as he pressed her to make an intimate claim on him "—scarred there, on the inside. That I might ruin your life with my . . ." Her hand trembled, and his tongue tripped over the catch in his breath. " . . . my mistakes."

With a quick groan he took her hand away and drew her arms around him as he insinuated himself between her thighs and buried his face in the warm vale between her breasts.

"Oh, God, I want to kiss you. Tell me where to kiss you. Wherever you feel the least beautiful, that's where I want to kiss you. Here?" Through the cotton shirt he nuzzled the smaller of her breasts like a hungry newborn. His mouth's gentle tugging sent a rush of sweet-stinging darts deep into her womb.

"Oh, John . . ."

"Pleasant dreams, baby. Here, too." He laid her back on the sofa again, lifting the shirt above her navel. He dipped his tongue like a pointed brush into a tiny paint-pot, even as his fingers traced over arches and valleys, seeking sensitive secrets within moist folds. She shivered. "So beautiful. I'm going to kiss you here, too," he whispered hotly into the downy arrow that pointed the way. "On the inside."

"No, John, I'm not—"

"Yes, you are, you're beautiful. Let me show you."

His tongue ignited her and brought her swiftly to a shuddering, flashing climax. He let her drift, but he would not let her sink. Explicit words, whispered in her ear, kept her juices simmering while he found another condom in the jeans he'd left on the floor. Teetering in some far place, she pleaded for him, dimly aware that his hands were trembling as he prepared himself.

"Kiss deep inside me, John," she entreated him.

His sweat-slick body slid over her easily, his breath quickening. He plunged home to meet her need and satisfy his own. Lifting, welcoming, she pitched herself high against him until she cried out, nearly shattering what little control he had left. "I don't want to hurt you," he whispered.

She clutched the backs of his thighs and pulled him deeper. "Just love me."

His own climax took him as his kiss found her deepest mark.

Later, after he'd taken her to bed and they'd exchanged soft, sleepy kisses, she whispered, "You're right, John, I must be...very beautiful...."

John woke to the sound of a motor humming not far off. Getting closer, in fact. Sunlight streamed in through the bedroom window, warming his back. He pushed himself away from the mattress, looking for his pillow, and he discovered it was slipcovered in blond hair. Smiling, he scooted over to her, molding his nude body to her back as he lifted the silky, sun-streaked curtain of hair from her face.

"Good morning, sunshine lady," he whispered against her cheek. "It'd be even better, except I think we've got company."

She uncurled her body, mewling softly as she turned to snuggle into his embrace, running the inside of her thigh straight up the outside of his. He decided that if there were a shred of justice in life, all movement beyond the walls of his room would cease for one hour. The rumpled sheets carried the scent of two become one, and the long leg hooking itself over his lean hip suggested making it happen again. He groaned. Some damned early bird was about to meet one inhospitable worm.

"I've gotta get up, sweetheart." He patted Teri's bottom as he nosed her hair out of his way and kissed her eyelid. "Wish to hell I didn't."

Teri moaned contentedly. "Tell them to come back later."

"It's probably Chuck," he said, rolling to his feet. This early he could easily tell Chuck to go to hell. Unless he was bringing groceries. Then he would ask him to leave the food and have a nice day elsewhere.

But when John peeked out the kitchen window he saw two men approaching his back door. Chuck had brought Judge Shelltrack, the man with the answers. John raked his fingers through his hair, and he was still stuffing his shirttail into his jeans as he answered the door.

"Thought you'd be up by now," the leather-faced old man announced by way of greeting. "I always start the day at sunrise. Best time to get moving."

"I see your guest hasn't left," Chuck muttered as he brushed past John on his way to the kitchen counter. He plunked down two grocery sacks and started unloading them as if he owned the place. "Brought you some chow. Got some milk, got some potatoes. Does she like donuts? Got you some powdered donuts."

"Coffee, Judge?" John asked, remembering his manners.

"Is the woman here or not?" Shelltrack demanded loudly.

John glanced at his brother, then back at the old man. "She's here."

"I get to see her sometime today?"

John hoped to set an example with a quieter tone. "Listen, Judge, all I want is a chance to—"

"I know." Shelltrack waved a gnarled hand. "You'll get your chance." He chuckled as he dragged a chair away from the kitchen table and lowered his stiff body into the seat. "You've sure got things stirred up at the tribal office, Johnny boy. Chairman got a call from the governor himself. He wants this easement thing resolved. Says it's puttin' a damper on people's fishin'."

"They better find another access, then." John took a can of coffee from Chuck's hand and went to the drawer for the can opener.

"Well, they got their noses out of joint over these charges you've racked up. But we're going into court with a petition for an injunction." The old man wagged a finger. "You just sit tight a while longer. You set foot off tribal land, we can't protect you."

"I know."

"Now, about your daughter," Shelltrack continued as though he was moving down a list. "You've never even seen her?"

"I didn't know about her until..."

Soft footfalls sounded in the sudden hush, drawing John's attention toward the hallway. The other two men turned out of curiosity.

There stood Teri, immaculately dressed in her own clothes, staring through John as though she didn't know him anymore. He couldn't believe she'd fixed her hair already, while he still looked like something the dog had been dragging around the yard. Her face, without a trace of makeup, was full of youth, innocence and fear of betrayal.

They had talked about this, John told himself. He had told her about getting advice from the judge, about his need to find out where he stood. Rachael was *their* child, after all, Teri's and his, and there were laws....

But the look in her eyes tied his gut into a knot.

"...just the other day," John finished quietly. "Teri, you met Judge Shelltrack—"

"Good morning, Judge." She stepped closer, her high heels clicking against the wood floor as she eyed each man in turn. "You're talking about Rachael."

The judge swiveled in his seat, studying her in return. "Are you her mother?"

"I'm her birth mother." John was pleased that she stepped over to offer a respectful handshake. "Rachael was adopted right after she was born. She's seven years old now."

"John here claims to be her father. I want to know what you say. Is he the child's father?"

She threw John a scorching glance, then turned her gaze toward the window above the table. "John is Rachael's biological father, yes."

"You have no doubt."

"No," she said without hesitation. "John is..." She stared at him fiercely again, her glistening eyes calling him every name in the book, but still she would not deny him. "There is no doubt."

"He says he never knew you were pregnant."

"He..." She blinked hard and swallowed fast, fighting for composure.

He didn't stick around long enough to find out.

John didn't want to hear her say it, didn't want her to *have to* say it. He wanted desperately to touch her in some comforting way. He longed to apologize, to confess his terrible shortcomings and plunge headlong into promises to do better, with his brother and his tribal elder as solemn witnesses.

He couldn't do any of those things. He had to let her tell her side.

"He left...to enlist in the service. No, he didn't know," she said quietly. "He had no way of knowing."

John stared dumbly.

"So you gave her up for adoption. An Indian baby."

"She was *my* baby, and I did what I thought best."

"But now you want her back," the judge assumed.

"No," Teri insisted. "We don't want to interfere in her life."

Shelltrack looked at John. He had a choice to make. Teri had made hers, and now it was his turn. He glanced at Chuck, who'd lit up a cigarette and was studying the scuffed toes of his boots. He knew what Chuck was thinking, what the judge was thinking, what his mother would have said.

She has a right to know her family.

"I've never even seen her. She's the only kid I've ever..." His explanation was for Teri, but she had already turned away. "I want to know if I have any rights," he told Judge Shelltrack. "Any at all."

"Oh, you've got rights. So does the little girl. If she's your daughter, she has the right to membership in your tribe."

"Her adopted father is Wyatt Archer," Teri said, her tone flat. "He's Sioux."

"Your mother was Sioux, too, wasn't she, John?" the judge asked. John nodded, aware that Shelltrack already knew the answer.

"The Sioux have an old saying. 'We're all related.' And it's true." The old man steadied himself on the table as he stood up. He turned to Teri. "So now we know you are the child's mother and John is her father, and we have John's request for the tribal court to intervene in his behalf."

"You can really do that?"

"I can really do that. And I think Mr. Archer will bring the child to my chambers because he is a Sioux. And he knows I can really do that."

She planted her hands on her hips and whirled to challenge John. "How can *you* do this? If they have to bring Rachael to court, they'll have to tell her why." She shook her head, and her hair shimmied like tall grass. "John, she's too young."

Shelltrack sighed. "There are many things to be considered in a case like this, including her age. And the fact that the natural mother willingly gave up her rights, while the natural father..."

"Went off to be a soldier," Teri finished dismally.

Shelltrack signaled Chuck that it was time to leave. "I hope we can settle this quietly, without making a spectacle," he told John. "You can do that over land, my boy. Make a loud fuss over the land. But in the matter of the child, I want no police and no newspapers." He turned to Teri. "I hope we can all agree to that."

Her face was red, and her eyes glistened with unshed tears. Chuck muttered his goodbyes, offering John a sympathetic glance as he followed the old man out the door.

Their proximity had turned from ecstasy to ordeal. She avoided his eyes, and he avoided hers. The kitchen walls closed in. Outside, a car engine turned over. Inside, John's stomach did the same.

"I have caused all this. It was a mistake to tell you," Teri said finally, her voice thick with tears. "I will never, never trust you again."

He didn't know what to say. Her anger scared him. Her pain tore at his very soul. He could only stand there, staring at her like some dim-witted fool, and let her cuss him out.

"Call it off, John. Call Judge Shelltrack back and tell him you've changed your mind."

He glanced out the window and caught a glimpse of the car's billowing dust wake. He hadn't changed his mind. He'd done some stupid things in his life, and he'd paid. Time after time, he'd paid. But he hadn't changed his mind. The more he thought about it, the more determined he was to meet his daughter.

"You sound like Wickery," he said absently. "Call it off. Crawl into a hole. Who do you think you are, John Tiger? You think you've got a right to speak up?"

She groaned. "What is it? You've come this far, and you can't back down?"

"For the love of God, I'm her father!" He turned to her and extended both empty hands. "How could you give my baby away, Teri? You got my letter. You could have written to me and told me you were pregnant. You could have told me you were going to give her away."

"Why? I wanted my child to have the kind of family children are supposed to have. With a mother and a father." She backed away. "You left me. I didn't take that as a good sign that you were anxious to be a family man. Not with me, anyway."

"If I had known you were going to have a baby—"

"It would have made a difference?" Controlling the crack in her voice had become a lost cause. Her tears spilled over and coasted down her cheeks as she shook her head. "I don't think so. It made no difference to *my* father."

"It makes a difference to me."

"You're just trying to prove another point, John. At Rachael's expense." She took a swipe at her tears, using both palms. "Please fix my car so I can leave."

"You can leave now." He turned to the window. "I put it back together after you'd gone to sleep the first night."

"You could have told me," she grumbled on her way to claim her purse.

"Right," he tossed back. "That's what *I* just said."

Chapter 9

Wyatt Archer was a Lakota Sioux who had left his own reservation for boarding schools and "mainstream society" long ago. Only recently had he pursued his growing interest in his own culture, but he had taken several college courses before he'd felt qualified to teach in a field that should have been his birthright. He knew little more than what he'd studied in books about the Arikara, Mandan and Hidatsa people. Other than John Tiger, he had few acquaintances on the central North Dakota reservation that was shared by the "three affiliated tribes." And Wyatt certainly wasn't anxious to get to know these people in court, especially not with Rachael's future hanging in the balance.

He thought over the alternatives as he parked his car in front of the tribal office building. The one that tempted him most would have been a flat refusal to comply with the judge's order to bring Rachael in for "an informal meeting." But then he would soon be sitting behind a barricade the way John Tiger was. He could probably still take his wife and daughter and find a place to hide, dye their hair, change their name. He'd changed it once already—back in the days when he'd been embarrassed by his Indian-sounding name—but he could easily do it again. This time he might have real cause.

He didn't know Judge Shelltrack from Adam, but on the phone he'd seemed like a reasonable man. Since Wyatt Archer was also a reasonable man, he'd opted for cooperation.

If that didn't work, he had a drawer full of maps.

"Ready to pay a visit to a real courtroom?" he asked his three girls. He glanced at his wife first, then Teri and Rachael in the back seat. Rachael was the only one who nodded cheerfully.

Wyatt and Lavender had tried to prepare the child without scaring her. The time had come, as they had always known it would, to explain to her that she was adopted. The adults, fretting over their carefully chosen words, had breathed a sigh of relief when Rachael took the initial news in stride. Now it was time for part two. The plan was to make a good impression on the judge and deal with John as best they could. They couldn't imagine anyone missing the obvious fact that Rachael was well adjusted, well provided for and well loved.

Wyatt had consulted an attorney, who thought the request for an informal meeting was a good sign. But Wyatt understood the Indian Child Protection Act. He had taught classes on the subject. As a member of the Sioux nation, he understood that too many Indian children had been taken away over the years, and he had defended the very law the judge could now use to take his own daughter away.

Rachael wasn't scared. She had no need to be. She was with her parents. It was a sunshiny summer morning, and she was anxious and eager to explore. She skipped along the sidewalk, staying ahead of her family as she took particular care to avoid all cracks in the cement. This was like a field trip. The tour of the educational places would come first, then the fun.

"You ladies go on inside, and I'll catch up."

Rachael stopped midskip and turned to watch her dad cut across the grass and offer his hand to an Indian man who had very big shoulders and long hair. Her dad was probably telling the man he shouldn't be smoking. "Healthy young man like you," Daddy always said. "You oughta come out for the wrestling team."

Rachael knew for sure that *she* would never smoke. The man with the long hair didn't seem to be paying as much attention to whatever Daddy was saying as he ought to be, though. He was looking at her instead, and a funny expression came into his eyes, as though maybe she reminded him of some special person. Then he sort of smiled. Rachael didn't usually smile at strangers, but her dad was there, and the man seemed to need a friend. She smiled back.

"Let's go inside, sweetie," her mother said as she took hold of Rachael's hand. "Daddy'll be along in a minute."

Teri also noticed the expression in John's eyes. She wanted to stay angry with him. She needed her anger to carry her through the coming ordeal. But it was hard to feel any anger as she watched John's eyes meet Rachael's for the first time. Her heart swelled tight against her ribs as his gaze drifted from Rachael to her. She saw the glimmer of pride, the claim, the connection, and she wanted to respond with just a tiny nod, a quiet *yes*. She dug her nails into her palms, hoping a good puncture would let the air out of all her self-indulgent fantasies. Determined, she tore herself away and followed Lavender and Rachael through the double doors.

The judge was expecting them. He shook hands with each one in turn, and when Wyatt brought up the rear, he greeted him, too. Teri wondered whether John would come to the meeting right away, wait to be called, or would be called in at all? Good Lord, was he simply waiting to take Rachael home with him?

"This is the little girl I wanted to meet." Judge Shelltrack bent stiffly to shake Rachael's hand. Briefly the little girl attended to protocol. Then she peeked around the old man's legs to get a look at a toddler who'd just pulled away from his mother and was headed for the pop machine. She glanced at two photographs of stern-looking men hanging on the wall, and she surveyed the chairs in the waiting area before she finally confided in Judge Shelltrack. "I've never met a judge before, but I've seen a lot of them on TV. I might want to be a judge."

"It's a hard job," he told her.

"I could do it, though. I'd put all the murderers away for life." She glanced over her shoulder to make sure Lavender and Wyatt were still close by. "We can't stay too long because we're going to have a picnic at the lake today. Daddy took the day off."

"It's a good day to go to the lake, but don't you want to see a judge's chambers first, so you'll know a little more about being a judge?"

"Well, I've seen *People's Court*," she said, obviously unimpressed with what she was seeing here so far.

Shelltrack signaled the group to follow, but he held the door to his office open for Rachael first. Clearly, she was his main focus.

"This is a little bit different. This is where I keep my desk and my books. You have to read a lot of books if you want to be a judge."

"Oh, I like to read books. I got forty-four stars on the 'Books and Beyond' chart last year."

"She also likes to talk," Lavender warned as she filed past their host. "So I think you're going to get an earful."

"Good. That's what I want." With a gesture he directed Rachael to a chair at the end of his big gray desk. He took the desk chair, and everyone else found seating against the back wall.

"Why did you come to visit me today, Rachael? Did your parents tell you what we need to talk about?"

"Well, they said you invited us. Daddy said you wanted to know how I'm doing. He said part of your job is to see how kids are doing." She clapped her hands together and jammed them between her knees as she leaned forward in the big chair. "So, I'm doing fine."

"I can see that."

"And you want to know how I'm doing because I'm adopted, right?" She didn't notice the hush that fell over the room. "That's what Daddy said."

"Do you understand what 'adopted' means?"

Rachael nodded and sighed, as though she was reluctant to take the time to enlighten the old man, since the whole thing was self-explanatory. "It means that my mom and dad didn't have me in the regular way because my mom had something wrong—" She peered around the back of the chair, one braid nearly reaching the floor as she checked with Lavender. "Is it okay if I tell him?"

Her mother's nod gave her permission to turn to the judge and tell the rest. "See, my mom had something wrong inside her womb, where babies grow, and she had to have an operation, and then she couldn't have any babies, because she didn't have a place inside her for them to grow anymore. But my mom and dad really, really wanted a baby, so they looked and looked, and they asked God to help them and all that stuff.''

"And they found you."

Rachael giggled, shaking her head vigorously. "You know what Becky Snustad said? She said storks bring babies. Isn't that the dumbest thing you ever heard? I told her God brings babies, but not always the regular way because some people, like my mom..." She leaned forward and lowered her voice. "Like I told you, but I'm not supposed to tell everybody because it's personal, but my mom didn't have a place where God could put the seed inside her. So He put it inside another woman's womb." She paused. "And you know who that was?"

"Who?"

"Teri!" She peeked around the chair again, grinning at Teri this time.

Rachael's smile was so perfectly guileless, so thoroughly cheerful, that Teri wondered how she herself could ever have regarded their relationship as such a deep, dark secret. Her throat tingled as she rewarded the little girl with a confederate's wink.

Rachael whipped around excitedly in her chair and continued to regale Judge Shelltrack. "I didn't know that, but my mom just told me it. So, I was this little seed." She demonstrated with her forefinger almost touching her thumb. "And I grew and grew, and then I was born, and Teri gave me to my mom and dad to be their baby. But, of course, I'm not a baby anymore."

"Of course not," the judge agreed.

"I'm going to be in second grade already."

"You must be making good grades. You're a very smart girl."

"All S and S-pluses." Distracted by the discomfort of bare thighs sticking to vinyl, she rocked back and forth in her chair, peeling first one thigh, then the other, off the seat. Primly, she adjusted her khaki shorts. "My dad's a teacher, you know. And a wrestling coach."

"I've always wanted to meet your dad. I've heard a lot about him."

"My dad's an Indian, and so am I."

"So am I," the judge told her. "You live in Bismarck, where there aren't too many Indians. We've got a lot more Indians around here."

Rachael bobbed her head.

"There are a lot of different tribes of Indians."

"I know that. My dad teaches Indian studies, you know. He says the real name for his people is Lakota. But I'm only part Lakota. Let's see . . ." She enlisted the help of her fingers to make her calculations. "I'm about one-fourth Lakota, one-fourth Arikara . . ." She did a little rubbernecking her father's way. "Arikara?" Wyatt nodded, beaming proudly as his precocious daughter turned once again to the judge. "And one-half Scandinavian."

"You have a lot of good parts," Shelltrack said.

"I'll say," Rachael agreed happily. "What kind of Indian are you?"

"I'm Arikara, like you. And Mandan," he added. "Here on this reservation we have the three affiliated tribes." He slid a sly glance at Wyatt. "Some of us even have a little ornery Sioux mixed in."

"My dad's not ornery," Rachael retorted. "Not unless he catches Jasper getting into the cereal, like he did this morning."

"You have some Arikara cousins. Did you know that?"

She thought about that for a moment. "Are they my age?"

"Some of them might be. Do you already have a lot of cousins?"

"I have nine cousins on my Archer side, but most of them are named Uses Arrow, because, see, my dad changed his name to Archer, because..." She peeped around the chair again, eyes wide, braid dangling. "Why did you change your name again, Daddy?"

"Because I was young and..." Wyatt searched for the word. Chagrined, he glanced at the judge and tried, "Struggling."

"Oh." The explanation was good enough for Rachael. "Anyway, I have three cousins on my Holland side, but they mostly live pretty far away."

"Well, with your cousins you have here, you might just have a bigger family than anybody in your school."

"I bet I do. Wait 'til I tell Becky Snustad. She gets to go to her grandma's whenever she wants to."

"Mrs. Archer, there's a pop machine at the end of the hall." Shelltrack took some change from his pocket and handed it to Rachael. "After all this talking, Rachael probably wants to wet her whistle."

Wyatt whispered reassurances to Lavender, who took Rachael by the hand and led her from the room. Once the door was closed, the judge tapped his finger on a file folder close at hand on his desk.

"I am considering John Tiger's petition, and I want to give him the chance to meet her. Here, today, in my presence."

"What does John want?" Wyatt asked tightly.

"His daughter." Shelltrack waved a gnarled hand to cut off any protest as he recounted, "She is entitled to be enrolled here. Her natural father is enrolled here. The tribal court can take custody of her. You know that."

Wyatt folded his arms over his neatly pressed sport shirt. "Not without a fight."

"Well, we can have that." Judge Shelltrack bobbed his head reflectively. "We can surely have a fight if you want one." He stared at Wyatt for a moment. Teri, as far as the two men were concerned, was not even in the room.

Shelltrack pointed to the door. "I like that little girl. She's got spunk. She has Arikara blood, too. Not many of us left, you know. Put the three tribes together, we still don't have too many left. First the Sioux, then the small-pox, then the Corps of Engineers and their dam, eatin' up all the land...." The old man sighed deeply. He eyed the folder as though he could see through it. "John Tiger is a good boy. He's a fighter, too."

"I know he's a fighter. I taught him to—" Wyatt caught himself glimpsing the issue from the wrong side. He shook his head. "He's not going to take my daughter."

"The judge is right, Wyatt," Teri offered quietly. "John is a good man. Did you explain to him that we are going to tell her who he is, but that—"

"I told him she doesn't know yet." He spoke to the man behind the desk, taking pains to be more patient. "We're taking this one step at a time, Judge."

"The next step is for her to meet him."

"If I could—" Teri sensed Wyatt's readiness to object, and she laid a hand on his arm. "It's my job, Wyatt. She's your child, but she was our... John and I were the ones who..."

A good man, too, Wyatt took a moment to accept what had become inevitable. "You sure you're okay with it?"

"I'll be fine." There might have been a touch of false brightness in her smile. "We've come this far, and Rachael's still Rachael, isn't she?"

"You're damn right. She's something else."

"John *is* a good man, Wyatt. I know he is."

Lavender brought Rachael back to the judge's chambers while Shelltrack fetched John. When they were all assembled, Teri sat down next to John, then turned to reach for Rachael's hand.

Sporting a fresh orange-pop mustache, Rachael edged closer to Teri's knees.

"We want you to meet someone from your Arikara side, Rachael," Teri began. "You've got your Archers and your Uses Arrows, your Hollands and your Scandinavians." Fearful of spoiling the moment with tears, she had carefully avoided John's eyes until now. Cautiously she met them, found a smile in them and returned it. She was quaking inside, but she would not cry. Not now. She shared her smile with Rachael. "And now you've got your Tigers. This is John Tiger."

Rachael looked at him curiously.

"Hello, Rachael."

The gravel in his voice knocked Teri's heart for a loop.

"Hello," Rachael said, putting her small hand in his. "I saw you smoking outside. You shouldn't smoke, you know. It's bad for you."

"I know." John cleared his throat as Rachael's hand slid away. "I'd like to quit."

"I think there's a kind of gum or something you can chew." She shoved her hand in the pocket of her shorts. "I have some gum. You want some?"

"Sure." He held out his hand, and she pressed a stick of gum into his palm as though she were dealing cards. "Thanks."

"How come your hair's so long?"

John crumpled the gum wrapper in his palm as he flashed a smile, regaining his easy charm. A child's frankness worked wonders. "Guys can wear their hair long, can't they?"

"I guess so." Rachael looked over at Wyatt's scrupulous hairstyle, then considered John's again. She tipped her head to one side, reached over and touched the end of a lock that was almost the same color as her own. "I guess it looks good on you. My mom braids mine. Do you braid yours?"

"Sometimes I wear a headband to keep it out of my face." He popped the gum into his mouth and watched her watch him chew. It was a gift put to use—acceptance all around. "Did you know that—" he glanced at Wyatt, seeking more of the same "—your dad used to be my wrestling coach?"

Rachael's eyes widened. "He used to be Teri's teacher. Didn't he, Teri?"

"Mine, too." For a moment the feeling was there, the way it used to be. Wyatt Archer was the greatest man alive, Lavender the most understanding of women, and Teri was... "Teri and I went to school together. A long time ago." *...still so beautiful.* "She was my girlfriend back then."

"She's a model now." Rachael flipped a braid behind her shoulder and asked the obvious. "Are you my cousin or my uncle?"

"We're pretty closely related," John said, his burgeoning joy quickly subdued.

"The Indian way, everybody's related," Shelltrack put in. "We have big families, and you're a special part of the Tiger family." He seated himself at his desk again, muttering, "Lots of cousins. Lots of aunties and uncles."

Rachael drew away from Teri and stepped closer to John. "Do we have any cousins who are my same age? Any girls?"

"Yes." A flash of belly warmth made John smile. Bound up in the word *we* was a sense of shared blood. He glanced at Wyatt, whose face was unreadable. "There's Missy. She's about six, I think."

"I'm seven. I bet you don't know when my birthday is."

Needing a hint, he glanced at Teri, who pressed her lips together and looked away. John's glimmer of warmth paled like winter sun.

"It's May first, and my daddy always goes around saying, 'Mayday! Mayday!'" Rachael supplied happily. "You missed it already."

"I know," John said, and for Teri's sake, "I'm sorry."

"That's okay. I'll invite you next year. And Missy and... Who else?" Rachael rested her hand on John's knee and allowed him half a second to offer more suggestions. "I'll bet Missy can't ride a two-wheeler yet if she's only six. My daddy's teaching me to ride a two-wheeler, but it's hard because I fell off already and got two skinned knees. See?"

John checked the nearly healed wounds she presented for his inspection. He smiled sadly, remembering the incident at the bridge, remembering his coach finding him, getting him to the hospital, then keeping the vigil at his bedside. "What did your dad do when you fell off?"

"He took me inside and washed my knees and put on some medicine, and I stopped crying, and we had but-

terscotch ice cream *before* supper." She took a breath.
"Do you think Missy could come to my house? I live in
Bismarck."

"I don't know. We'd have to ask her mom." He
stopped himself from looking to Teri for permission,
turning to Lavender instead. "And yours."

"Where do you live?"

"I live here, by the lake. I have a little ranch."

"We're going to have a picnic by the lake. Maybe we
can go to your house. Oh . . ." Rachael clapped her hand
over her mouth and shrugged her shoulders as high as her
ears as she stole a sheepish glance at Lavender. "I wasn't
inviting myself. That's rude."

"I want you to come to my house." Tentatively he
touched the back of her hand, which was no longer than
his middle finger. "I want you to come anytime you feel
like it. Bring your . . . bring Teri, too."

"Teri lives in Minneapolis, but I can bring my mom
and dad. Do you have horses?"

John nodded.

"I told my dad I wanted a horse, but he got me a two-
wheeler instead." Spinning on her heel, she suddenly
skipped out of his reach.

"Mommy, we could go to John's house after we have
our picnic, and I could see his horses." She crawled into
Lavender's lap, threw her arms around her neck and
whimpered petulantly, "I'm getting hungry."

"We all need a break," Judge Shelltrack announced as
he carefully unfolded the bows of his reading glasses. He
opened the folder, peered down his nose and examined
the top document as if it were something he had not yet
read. "This was just an informal meeting, but the next
step—"

"There's no next step, Judge," John said quietly. "Let's just drop the whole thing."

Shelltrack looked up from the paper. "You want to withdraw your petition?"

"Yeah." John's face burned. He stared steadfastly at the paper in question. He felt the heated attention of all eyes, the pressure of breathing suddenly suspended, the quickening of everyone's hopes but his. The room suddenly felt crowded, and the words came hard. "This isn't the way."

"It's the only way you have any leverage," Shelltrack reminded him. "You know that."

"Yeah, well . . ." John raised his chin and injected his voice with new starch. "Me and Coach Archer, we know all about leverage. You've gotta make your move," he recited with a snap of his fingers, "*that* quick, and don't look back. If you make a mistake, you have to let it go. Do it right the next time." He looked straight at Wyatt. "Isn't that right, Coach?"

Wyatt nodded, his eyes shining with a teacher's unqualified pride.

John grinned. "That's a switch. He doesn't have his speech ready."

"Neither do I," the judge said. "You just took me off the hook, Johnny boy." He slapped the folder shut. "I want you to see that all the papers are completed to get Rachael enrolled."

The old man tipped his chin up at Rachael. "You'll come back and see me, won't you, granddaughter? In the Indian way, you are my granddaughter, so I will want to see how you are doing again."

After everyone thanked the judge, the leave-taking became awkward. In the hallway, Wyatt hung back a little, while Lavender took the cue to shepherd Rachael along, out of earshot. Teri traded needy glances with John, but the exchange escaped Wyatt's notice as he laid his hand on John's shoulder and took prior claim.

"I don't know what to say, John. She's my little girl. But, damn, she looks more like you all the time. There isn't a day goes by that I don't think about you and wonder what I would do in your place."

"I want to fight for her." John stole one last glimpse as Lavender ushered Rachael out the door. "But I can't win. Not with her in the middle." He looked at Wyatt again. "I want her to know her family. She doesn't have to know all the details. Just that we're..." He smiled as he repeated the common Indian expression. "...closely related."

"We'll work it out, John. I promise. Today it was your turn to teach me some moves." John accepted Wyatt's handshake. "It doesn't have to be a fight."

John nodded distractedly. He wasn't letting Teri go without a private word. He just wasn't sure what it would be.

"How long do you expect this standoff to last?"

"Standoff?" Oh, yeah, he thought. *Wait a minute, Teri!* "I don't know. Some lawyer's working on it. Meantime, we stand our ground."

"I respect you for that. I would have backed down by now, even if I had a handful of aces." The statement took John by surprise. Wyatt Archer's respect was like the Holy Grail. Wyatt gave a quick nod as he backed away. "You've got guts."

More guts than brains, John thought, along with a childless house and a cold bed. But, hell, he was doing the right thing, wasn't he?

With Wyatt heading for his car, John knew he had only a minute to say goodbye to the only woman he'd ever loved. One short minute in a public hallway. He was having one hell of a character-building day.

"Teri?"

He spoke as though he was afraid to startle her.

She turned, her blue eyes brightening for him.

He moved close to her and said, for her ears only, "She's a great kid."

Teri nodded quickly. She took a stab at smiling, but her lips quivered. For all the good things Rachael was, she belonged to another mother. And now she was the daughter they might have raised during a life they might have shared.

He wanted to fight for his child, he had said. John had guts, Wyatt had said. But in the presence of Teri's quiet strength, he felt like a wretched lightweight.

He tucked her under his arm and whisked her across the hall, where the door to a vacant, windowless room stood open. In the dark he heard the catch in her breath. She tried desperately to stifle a small whimper, tried to drive it back with a vigorous shake of her head. It was no use. The cry of a woman in pain literally tore from her throat as John's own tears filled the deep well in his heart.

"I know," he whispered. He took her in his arms and hugged her tightly. Her face felt warm and damp against his neck. "I know."

John leaned heavily on his mother's walking stick as he climbed the last few steps to the top of the hill. It was almost sundown, and he was bone weary. After he'd left the courthouse, he'd spent the rest of the day stacking the square bales one of his neighbors had cut for him and brought in off the right-of-way. He'd worked past fatigue, past hunger, past thinking about much of anything. But he owed somebody a visit before he turned in for the day. He owed somebody an apology or a confession or some damn thing. He'd done what seemed right today, but he wasn't feeling real great about it.

He hadn't had a chance to replace the older crosses the way he'd planned, but he had cut the grass with a scythe, and as soon as he could go to a store that carried more than the basics, he would buy some wildflower seeds. His mother's freshly turned plot looked pretty barren.

Sun-faded ribbons rustled amid withered carnations as an evening breeze stirred among the graves. Spirits in the grass, John thought. He dropped one knee in the soft earth and righted one of the paper pots that had tipped over.

"I saw my daughter today, Mom," he said quietly. "I never thought I'd have any kids, but I've got a daughter. A sweet little kitten with long braids and big brown eyes. Her name is Rachael. Coach says she looks like me, but she really looks like you. Remember that old picture we used to tease you about? You and Auntie Edna sitting on that swaybacked plow horse. Rachael looks like you in that picture."

He speared the willow cane into the ground and pushed himself to his feet. God, he felt like an old, old man. Sighing, he shook his head. "I don't have any excuses, Mom. 'Bout as bad as Buckshot. Somebody else is raising my kid.

"You think you're going to do things differently," he mused, echoing Teri's regrets. Probably wasn't a good idea to mix regrets and spirits on one hill, but then, nobody was accusing him of having too many good ideas lately.

"I don't know about the right or wrong of it, but I know I couldn't go through with it today. I couldn't take her away from her—her parents. They're gonna tell her about me when the time is right. And I'll tell her about—'' he directed the end of the stick toward the collection of markers silhouetted against the red evening sky ''—the ones who came before.''

Chapter 10

John slept in the back of his pickup under the stars that night, parked by the barricade. The standoff, as Wyatt had called it, had been pretty low-key since the funeral, but John had made his bed with an uneasy, eye-of-the-storm kind of feeling. The sun beating on his face woke him the next morning, along with the sound of early-morning traffic. He sat up and opened one eye. What he thought he saw was a camouflage vehicle. He squeezed his lying eye shut and gave it a moment to get real.

He gave it another try, but the damn thing was still there. A truckload of troops from the North Dakota National Guard! There was a jeep in tow, making it a convoy of two, followed by Woody Whitestaff's ragged red pickup pulling an old hay mower. It would be him and Woody against a whole damn platoon packing army-issue M-16s. The troops' boots were already hitting the pavement. Their captain, alighting from the jeep, puffed

his chest up with fresh morning air and adjusted his aviator glasses.

John's black pup scooted out from under the pickup
and yapped gallantly. John calculated his odds as he
vaulted over the wall of the pickup bed and dropped to
the ground. A couple of squads of part-time soldiers
against two full-time Indians. He decided they were just
about even, so he reached back into the pickup box for
his hunting rifle. Since he generally hit what he aimed at,
he figured he now had the advantage, as long as he stayed
on his side of the fence.

He ambled over to one of the building blocks of his
barricade, a dead-engine pickup, and leaned his backside against the open tailgate, waiting for the captain to
come to him. The pup took up his post next to John's
boots. Woody had the good sense to hang back and
watch from his pickup. John wanted him to be able to
take off if things turned sour.

"You guys out on maneuvers?"

"In a manner of speaking." The pudgy man seemed to
think he needed no introduction. According to the GI
name tag on his crisply pressed fatigues, he was Captain
Kohler. "I have orders to hold this position and wait for
instructions."

"Strange way to spend the taxpayers' money." John
knew damn well the captain had no interest in his political opinions. They were sizing each other up, and the
pretext was unimportant. John's rifle was pointed at the
ground. The Captain's sidearm was holstered. John gave
a quick chin-jerk. "That highway belongs to the state, so
I guess you can go ahead and hold it, just in case."

"Just in case what, Mr. Tiger?"

"Just in case somebody decides to come looking for
trouble." And just to irritate the captain, John smiled.

Woody slammed his pickup door shut, turning John's smile into a scowl.

"Our job is to be ready for trouble."

"It pays to be ready. This road might just turn out to be a real vital artery." *And this toy soldier might turn out to be a real jerk.* Off to his left, a shrill whistle sounded amid the ground nesters, and John grinned. "See? The prairie dogs know something's up."

"Something's been up ever since you cut off access to the lake," Kohler clipped. "Now, we don't like this any more than you do, but you people started it."

"Come on now, Captain, you like it plenty. Gives you something to do with all your hardware." He was glad to see that Woody wasn't packing any. "And we like it fine, too, don't we, Woody?"

"What's up?"

John shook his head in mock reproach. "You forgot your caution sign on the back of the mower, Woody. Big mistake. They sent the Guard out."

"If you guys would just dismantle that barricade, we could all go home," the captain suggested. "I have a feeling it'll come down today, one way or another."

John glanced at the troops, some stretching after the long ride, some hitching up their pants. "You think you'll have to shoot anybody first?" he asked Kohler casually.

"I sure hope not, Tiger."

"I sure hope not, too. We kinda let our guard down here. Yesterday I actually got some work done, and this morning..." He pushed himself away from the pickup and sauntered closer to the fence, the butt of his rifle resting easy in the hollow of his cutoff denim sleeve. "Well, you can see, it's just me and my dog against all you guys. The dog's still got his milk teeth. I'm on my own land. My neighbor here's a witness. It's not gonna look good if you shoot me."

"It doesn't have to come to that."

"It does if you try to open up that little road there." John smiled. "And I'll shoot back, Captain."

"It won't come to that if we keep our heads." Kohler stepped back slowly, as though he wasn't quite sure it was safe to turn his back. "We'll all just sit tight and wait for our orders."

"*Your* orders. I know what I'm doing here." He turned to Woody, then shot a puzzled glance at the mower.

"I, uh…" Woody looked back at the mower, too, then shrugged. "Ted told me to bring that to you. He's sending his boy over with that little Ford tractor of his. Thought we'd get after that alfalfa patch and knock it down in a little while, since things have been pretty…"

John shook his head. "You go tell Ted to keep his boy home today. Quiet time's over, looks like. Right, Captain?"

Kohler stood on the shoulder of the road, hesitating, adjusting his glasses again. "Why don't you just take your damn wall down and let people drive through?"

"People can drive around." And Captain Kohler could drop what was left of his soldier act, since John wasn't buying it. "Maybe the governor could put you guys to work cutting a road. Wouldn't that make more sense?"

"I don't believe Lake Sakakawea is included in your treaty rights, Mr. Tiger. The Corps of Engineers—"

"Just so you know, Captain." John pointed out all the perimeters as he spoke. "This is a state highway. The right-of-way belongs to the state. My land starts right here. So you stay over there, put up your pup tents, have your little bivouac. Tell the guys to police the area, okay? Keep North Dakota's highways nice and clean."

"I don't like smartasses, Tiger."

"I never met a captain who did." John gestured toward Woody's pickup. "Get going, Woody. Find out if Chuck's still around, and tell Ted not to—"

"Now listen here, Woody. We don't need a lot of people getting hurt here, so why don't you just stick around?"

"You can't keep him here, Kohler. He's just a neighbor delivering a piece of machinery. I'm the one you guys wanna keep a close watch on." A breeze swept his hair back from his face, and he smiled. "The Cat is armed and dangerous."

Within the hour, John's stand gained more teeth. Woody returned with a dozen men on horseback. When they appeared one by one on the crest of the hill, John raised his rifle in the air and cut loose with a whoop of welcome. His buddies' answering cries made his blood run hot. He counted at least three rifles.

Chuck led the string of horsemen full tilt down the hill. Well versed in the fine points of protesting, Chuck would have told them to keep the number of weapons to a minimum—enough to keep the Guard from walking over them, but not so many that they posed a threat to the tourists. The key to all this was to get the right kind of media attention. Tactics had changed over the years, but Indians had always found ways to make the best use of whatever was available to them.

Into the heat of the afternoon the troops kept watch. The highway had been blocked off, and the confrontation amounted to a lot of posturing, a lot of eyeballing, but not much noise. John would have traded his only pair of boots for one cold beer, but beer would have made for negative press. And the press, Chuck had assured him, was on its way. He was glad Woody had brought fresh water.

Chuck handed out "Crimson Eagle burgers," while the troops sent out for lunch. The aroma of pizza wafted across the road as John bit into his bologna sandwich. The pup whined pitifully. Pizza and beer would have tasted great, John thought wistfully as he gave half the dry sandwich to his dog.

The noise started when the press arrived from Minot. Captain Kohler didn't have the authority to make any comments, but John had plenty of authority. He explained his problem once again and expressed his surprise that the Guard had been called in, considering that *his* property and *his* livelihood were being threatened. He chuckled when the TV cameraman wanted a shot of the dead cow, but Woody volunteered to show the way.

The Bismarck reporters arrived later. Captain Kohler made some rumblings about "securing the area," but he was already too late. He had no control over Indian land, and the press had sashayed right through the roadblock on state land. He grumbled to one of the corporals that if this kept up, he was going to have a crowd here when the order came to move in. A crowd of civilians would not be good.

John was repeating his statement for another reporter when he saw Wyatt and Teri getting out of one of the cars. She was wearing her own jeans and T-shirt this time. Her long, sunny hair fluttered in the breeze like a bright yellow banner as she marched toward the fence with Wyatt at her side.

Kohler was on their heels as soon as he realized they were headed for John's side of the fence. "Hold up there! Unless you're members of the press...."

Wyatt made a space for Teri to crawl through the fence while he glared at Kohler, who turned on his heel and shouted to his men to form a line across the road. "Check with me before you let anyone else through!"

John reached them in time to stretch the wire for Wyatt. "What are you two doing here?"

"We heard about this on the news." Wyatt straightened as he turned to watch Kohler make a belated production of deploying his men. "What do they think they're doing?"

"They think they're gonna open up this road. And they might just try it, so would you take her—"

"I already missed my flight, John." Teri's eyes glistened with excitement. "I might as well stay and make coffee, load guns, whatever you need."

"This is no joke." She had no more sense than the pup yapping at his heels, and the man he'd once counted on to know everything had even less. "Have you lost your mind, Coach? This is no little sheriff's posse. These guys have much bigger guns."

"Bigger than yours?" Teri asked with a coy moue.

He was stunned. Actually shocked. Coach turned a smirk into a cough as John sidled up close to her. His heart raced, and he was holding back a smile for all he was worth. "I'm going to kiss that sassy smirk off your face, and then you're gonna turn around and go back where you came from."

She touched his arm. "I'm on your side, John. Wyatt said he was coming up here, and I wouldn't let him come without me."

"She's tough," Wyatt assured him.

John slid Teri's hair back, tucked it behind her ear and touched one small, heart-shaped earring. "Are these the same ones I gave you for your sixteenth birthday?"

"The same ones." She searched his eyes, and he knew what she was looking for. She knew damn well that smile was always there for her. Somewhere. "I wear them a lot."

"You shouldn't be here. You should be running as far away from me as you can get."

"Maybe tomorrow," she said softly. Her hair smelled like strawberries, and he forgot all about pizza and beer. "Today they've got guns pointed at you. Very bad time for me to leave."

He glanced across the highway. The guns had suddenly taken on new meaning. "I don't know what's gonna happen here."

"We're not going to let them move that stuff, right?" Teri jerked her thumb over her shoulder.

"That's the idea." But John was also looking at the barricade in a new light. That pile of junk wasn't going to stop sixteen armed men.

"Then I'd say you either need more guns or more bodies to stand in the way." She smiled sweetly. "Since I didn't bring a gun, you can have my body."

John passed a hand over his face and groaned. "Now she tells me."

"For the cause," she added. "Wyatt says I have to be careful not to get too wild, because they can arrest me on Indian land, even though they can't touch you."

"If they arrested you, they'd get me, too, 'cause I'd be flyin' after them so fast—"

"Shh." She touched two fingers to her pretty pink lips and made him ache when she took them away, smiling. "Don't give them any ideas."

It was hard to wait when no one seemed to know exactly what they were waiting for. Kohler had moved his vehicles to block the road, and he had a couple of men manning checkpoints, but the rest were finding places to sit and ways to pass the time. A couple of the guardsmen had broken out a deck of cards. Another one had brought along his Walkman, and there were two who'd had the foresight to bring paperback books along.

On John's side of the fence, the guys liked to joke around, no matter what was at stake. Most of his friends had done a hitch or two in the army, so they knew what it meant to hurry up and wait. They'd also seen the same Westerns the guardsmen had seen, and, lo and behold, here they were again, brown eyeball to blue eyeball, just like Crazy Horse and Custer. John knew these guys. They didn't need cards for entertainment.

"What do you think, Tex?" Chuck asked one of the guardsmen. "You ready to lose your scalp over this here wagon trail?"

The soldier lit a cigarette and stared humorlessly across the fence.

"He's not gonna fraternize with the enemy," Woody observed. "Hey, Tex, you think we'll hit in broad daylight or wait—" he paused for effect, then added ominously "—'til *nightfall?*"

"You'll know for sure when you hears the drums," Chuck said.

"You guys don't like to fight at night," a second guardsman supplied. "Everybody knows that."

Woody punched Chuck's arm. "Hey, they brought along ol' John Wayne. Best damn Indian fighter ever was."

"Nah, Jimmy Stewart's got John Wayne's body count beat all to hell."

"No lie?"

"I'm talkin' 'skin count, now." Chuck offered Woody a cigarette. "Am I right, Tex? Who's your favorite Indian fighter?"

"Captain Kohler" was the stiff reply.

"Captain Kohler," Woody echoed, then glanced at Chuck, eyes smiling.

"Hey, we've got Wyatt Archer now," Ted LeBeau announced from his perch on top of the hay wagon. "Plus the Cat."

Wyatt had found a comfortable seat in the shade. "Why don't we put the guns away and go at it barehanded, huh? No holds barred."

John had little heart for bantering now. He wanted this thing settled, and before Teri had shown up, he would have welcomed a fight just to move the whole mess off dead center.

He decided to put Teri in his pickup. "You've gotta stay behind the front line," he explained as he handed her his keys. "Otherwise I'll be a nervous wreck."

"Do you have to be in the front line?" He nodded. "So if they decide to shoot somebody..."

"They don't want to shoot anybody." With one arm on the open door, the other on the roof of the cab, he ducked his head inside and offered a reassuring smile. He liked seeing her behind his steering wheel. He could imagine her driving his pickup out to the hay field to pick him up and take him home for supper. "I just don't want you out there stealing all the press."

"Should I talk to the press? Tell them how unfair all this is?"

"That's up to you."

She rested her hands lightly on either side of his waist, tipped her chin up and looked into his eyes. "I want to tell them I'm on your side. Do you think they'll care?"

"I think I care." He touched her cheek. "I *know* I care." He studied her for a moment. Then he bent down and plucked the pesky black pup off the toe of his boot. He handed him to Teri. "This guy's more trouble than a woman."

"Really." She scratched his ears and got her face licked for her efforts. "He ought to have a name."

"Think of a good one while you're waiting." He closed the door. "You'll stay put?"

Teri nodded.

John needed a cigarette, but he couldn't bring himself to have one in front of the coach. He felt like a kid sneaking a smoke behind the barn when he copped a quick drag from Ted LeBeau. But before he'd gotten rid of the smoke, he realized that Wyatt was watching. And laughing at him.

John held up his hand. "I'm gonna quit, Coach. I swear."

"Not before this is over." Wyatt jerked his chin toward the fence. "Woody should maybe tone it down a little. Some of these guys put on a uniform and lose their sense of humor."

"If they had any to begin with," John grumbled. He turned and called out, "Hey, Woody, you might have more luck with the reporters." Then, to Wyatt, he added, "Reporters don't understand Indian humor, either, but if you laugh, they kinda laugh, too, like they know it's supposed to be a joke."

He glanced back at his pickup and at Teri, who was trying to keep the pup from jumping out the window. "Did she really miss her flight?" he asked Wyatt.

"Yeah, she did." They were headed for the fence together, walking slowly. "It didn't take much. Just the news that you were looking down the barrel of an M-16."

"Does she visit you guys very often?" Wyatt glanced at him sideways, and John felt like an intruder. "I mean, do you think she'll be back for...?"

"Thanksgiving, probably. Where will you be?"

"Either here or in jail."

"We can always bring the turkey to you," Wyatt suggested. It was John's turn to send a sharp glance, which Wyatt met head-on. "The night you took a nosedive off that bridge, you said you didn't want Teri to see you like that. And then later, when you were bandaged up like a mummy, you said the same thing again. There was no stopping her then, any more than there was today. She's determined to be there for you."

John flinched. "There's never been much in it for her, has there?"

"When did you stop loving her?"

"Stop loving her?" John gave a dry chuckle. "It could happen when I stop breathing." Poor choice of words, he thought. "But probably not."

"Then you oughta stop running, John."

"I have. This is where it ends, Coach. Right here, on my grandfather's land." He stopped, as if to prove his point, and gazed wistfully back at the pickup again. "Trouble is, she's got places to go and things to do."

"Did she say that?"

John's answer was lost in the rising heat of voices. One coarse taunt flared like a match headed for an oil drum. John muttered his own string of expletives as he started for the hot spot along the fence.

A sharp *whack!* split the dry heat like thunder. Before the echo faded, a second shot was fired. A moment's wide-eyed paralysis gave way to a flurry of bodies hitting the dirt, fingers fumbling for weapons.

"Get down!" John shouted.

Chuck lunged for the hay wagon. Woody was on his back. At the sound of another crack John sprinted as though he'd just hit a pop fly. He slid into base—Woody—at the same instant something wicked whizzed overhead.

"Woody! You all right?"

"I don't know." He sounded mostly surprised. "I'm bleeding."

John examined the bloody hand Woody extended, then the soggy sleeve, then the blanching face. "Is it bad?"

"Burns like a bitch, man."

"Hold your fire!" Kohler was shouting, but some fool on the other side of the highway didn't get the message.

John looked back and satisfied himself that Wyatt was covering some ground on his belly, then turned again to his wounded friend. "You're gonna be okay, Woody," John muttered. Coach would take care of him. He signaled for help even as he focused several yards behind Wyatt's position. He couldn't see much of his pickup, couldn't see anybody in the cab.

His legs got moving under him. "Teri!"

Another shot rang out, and John dropped into a crouch. Chaos swirled around him.

"Hold your fire!"

"Keep that camera rolling!"

"Teri!" Still crouching, he tore open the door. His mouth was dry, and he was choking on mind-numbing terror. The cab was empty. The far door stood open. He heard a puppy whine.

"Get down, John! For Pete's sake, they're *shooting* at you!"

Following the blessed sound of her voice he dropped to the ground and connected with her huge blue eyes peering around the pickup tire. The black pup's floppy ear was pressed to her cheek. John crawled under the truck and caught her in his arms, warm relief flooding his icy veins.

A police siren came like the voice of God, quelling the storm. Kohler managed to reel his men back under control, while Wickery crossed the fence, blatantly ignoring everything it stood for.

"Anybody hurt?"

"Just one o' them flesh wounds, Sheriff." Woody sat up, checking himself over to be sure. "'Preciate your concern, though."

John and Teri emerged from their cover, the puppy at their heels. John's scattered supporters peeled themselves off the ground, rubbing bruised elbows and looking at one another in utter amazement.

"Your lawyer got you your injunction, Tiger," Wickery said. "I've still got orders to arrest you if you step into my jurisdiction, but I got no authority to open this road. So I guess you made your point."

"Captain, I got the Colonel on the two-way," a corporal called out from the jeep.

Sheet white and speechless, Kohler headed for his call.

Like flies on honey, the reporters flew out of hiding and buzzed around John. He wasn't sure when Teri had managed to back away, but she was the only person he needed to talk to now, the only voice he wanted to hear. He introduced his brother to the reporter from the Minot newspaper.

Then he took Teri aside. "When's the next flight to Minneapolis?"

She looked at him for a moment before she glanced away, as if his eyes had somehow burned hers. In the small bit of voice her better judgment hadn't squelched, she said, "I don't think I can make the last one out to-day."

He took her chin in his hand and turned her face toward him. The asking was hard, because he knew she wouldn't refuse. Her eyes betrayed a kind of regretful willingness, as though she had resigned herself to loving him. It wasn't the way he wanted her to come to him.

But he would take what he could get.

"Give me tonight. I'll get you back down to Bismarck tomorrow."

Chapter 11

"I named him Wimpy."

John laughed, and the black pup, apparently just as delighted, romped around John and Teri, barely keeping ahead of their toes as they strolled across the yard.

"We made a fine pair when the bullets started flying. I went from Teri to *Teary*, and he was Wimpy." The dog's oversize paws thudded against her thigh as she bent to tousle his flapping ears and greet him nose to nose. "Weren't you, my little Wimpy-wimp?"

John groaned. As a liberating gesture he had taken off the dog's stiff collar and his own sleeveless denim jacket and tossed them both in the back of the pickup. Barechested, hands on his hips, posturing as though he had the world by the tail, he stood for a moment taking stock of a dog who had proved unworthy. John's Sioux ancestors might have tossed the miserable whelp in the stew pot.

"Poor mutt." John chuckled. Now that his place was his own again, he was feeling generous with his sympathy. "It's gonna take some real heroics to live that name down. You've got your work cut out for you, boy."

"I'm sure you do, too. Running a ranch by yourself." Teri stood and surveyed John's holdings, which were now officially no longer under siege. "Big job." But she had no doubt that John was up to it.

"It's not a big ranch, but it is a big job." They came to the rail fence he'd started putting up along the driveway last summer. In April he'd put up two more sections, and he had enough materials for one more. The posts cast long shadows into the stubbly yard. Once the project was complete, maybe in a year or so, he was thinking about trying to grow a real lawn.

"It feels right for me to be here. It feels good, watching the calves grow, piling up the winter feed, riding across a stretch of grass and thinking, 'On this little piece of ground, what I say goes.'"

"Really?" She plunked her elbow on the rail and turned with a flirty smile. "Make it rain."

"Now that comes from up there. All I can do is ask." He tipped his head back and considered the purpling sky. "I don't want to be Wyatt Archer anymore. Today I stood my ground, and he showed up to back me." The thought of it made him feel just fine, but looking at Teri, still there, still with him, made him feel even better. "So did you."

"Does that surprise you?"

"Yes." He had to be honest with her, even though he could see a trace of hurt in her eyes. "It still does."

"You're a slow learner, John Tiger." Her voice was as hushed as the slow settling of light on the horizon. "I'm glad you've found yourself here."

"I was here all along," he said. She didn't understand that it hurt him, too, to doubt the way he sometimes did. He slid his hand over hers. "Except the part of me that was part of you."

"Where is that part now?"

"Still part of you. You'll take it with you when you go back to the city. Every time I see your picture, I'll feel like I'm right there in that picture, too." He was doing his damnedest to make up for his shortsightedness. She pressed her lips together and gave a tight little nod.

"Hey, not like this." With his thumb he smoothed her fine hair back from her temple. "Not with a sad look in your eyes. I'll be in your smile."

"I don't have to leave tomorrow. I could stay another day or two." Her eyes drifted closed for a moment as she pressed her cheek into his palm.

"That's some job you've got, where you can come and go as you please."

Her eyes opened, smiling. "I can't come and go quite as I please, but I can afford to cancel out once in a while. I've worked very hard. I've—"

"Made a bundle?"

"I've reached a certain level of . . ." She waved all that away. "Anyway, if you asked me to, I might consider staying another day."

"Things have changed." He turned and leaned back against the fence, catching himself on his elbows. "You're flyin' the coop, and I'm staying right here, *if*—" his mocking grin was, just between them, for all his critics "—I know what's good for me."

"At least I'll know where to find you."

"One night," he said firmly. "That's all I'm asking you for, and even that might be pushing my limit. Because when you go, I'm gonna be left with all kinds of crazy ideas running around in my head." He bumped his hip against hers, teasing, making sure he had her full attention. "Like going after you."

"You can't," she reminded with a saucy smile. "You have to let me come to you."

"You can't live like that, Teri. Neither can I."

Her smile slid away, and they shared a long look, full of anticipated loneliness. "Then how will we live?"

"We'll live." Starting tomorrow it wouldn't be easy, but he wasn't about to waste tonight. He slapped his hand on the fence rail and forced a note of cheer. "Come on, hop up here and sit for a little while. We'll watch the sun set on our night together."

Teri cast him a doubtful glance as she scrambled up to the perch he'd indicated. "That's a rather ominous way of putting it."

"Not if you think of the sunset as the beginning." The burnished colors promised a fevered summer night. He stood behind her, put his arms around her and tipped her shoulders back against his. "You get sunsets like this in the city?"

"No, not like this." And she had missed them, among other native Dakota things. She relaxed her shoulders and let her backbone slip against his bare chest.

He moved her hair out of the way and nuzzled the side of her neck. He captured her earlobe with his teeth as he slipped his hands under her T-shirt. Quickly dispatching the clasp between her breasts, he brushed the cups of her bra aside, drawing his hands slowly across her breasts.

"Oh, John, that's...distracting."

"Doesn't have to be. Just don't close your eyes." He caressed her breasts in circles, closing in.

"Mmm, I think I'm...slipping down."

"Hang on," he whispered. "Watch the sky."

He touched her teasingly until she drew a deep breath, lifting her chest. Her nipples ached. He molded her breasts delicately, nearly pinching. Nearly touching the tips. Nearly, but not quite. His tongue flicked over her neck and just behind her ear. She moaned, and he used his thumbs, deftly flicking while he murmured, "Look at that rosy sky. That's the color of your nipples. I know, because I've seen them. I've loved them with my mouth."

He slid one hand over her belly, unbuttoned her jeans and ran the zipper down. Her thighs came together, trapping his hand as she groaned his name. He caressed her breast and whispered, "This is my gift," and then, closer to her ear, "Don't fight me."

Her body had become boneless. She gripped the rail. "I might fall."

"Not a chance. I've got you." He slid his hand into her jeans, pushed satin and lace aside and cupped her protectively. "I've got you, baby. Open your eyes. The sun's sinking."

But she was rising, and he was sliding deep. She rested her head on his shoulder and whispered, "You're sinking, too. Into me."

"Like this?" He stroked carefully, touching what needed touching, melting her down, melting her deep until she gasped.

"That's right. The sun's comin' down, baby."

Down to raw nerves and real need.

"So am I."

Down from the fence and into his arms. She kicked her shoes off and pushed herself away from the rail. He caught her under her knees and lifted her, then lowered her, letting her slide belly to belly, catching her mouth with his as soon as the two came within reach of each other.

It was a desperate kiss on the fly. She shucked her jeans, tossed them on the fence and stood before him in her scanty T-shirt. She was a Greek goddess triumphant. She was the sexiest woman on earth. She raised her arms and slid her hands into her hair, lifting it in two silken sheaves and releasing it in two feathery cascades.

John swore a lustful oath and reached for her. She stepped back, charged to the hilt with her own erotic energy. "That should be my line after what *you* did."

He grinned. She smiled back, and before he saw it coming, she'd snared his belt buckle, flipped it open and unsnapped his jeans. "And now *you*—"

Without interfering with her hands he grabbed her hips and pulled her closer. "Let's go inside."

"You started this." She pushed his pants down over his hips and took him in her hand, touching him as intimately as he had touched her. His grip on her hips tightened as she pressed her lips against his chest, then harassed his nipple with the tip of her tongue. Pitched a foot above ground level, he groaned.

"You started this, John."

"I'll finish it, too," he promised.

But it was she who tumbled him to the ground and straddled him. "You think so?"

"Have it your way." He laughed and made a stab at struggling, wrestling with a frisky woman and the requisite condom both at once.

Rising above him, she paused. She wasn't sure what her way was. Then laughter faded, his eyes met hers, and he sat up slowly, meeting her with a kiss. They guided each other. *This way. Our way.*

"Take as much as you can," he whispered, easing his way.

"I can take a lot," she answered, boldly guiding him her way.

He closed his eyes and savored warm, sensual sanctuary. He looked up and saw heaven. Rising above him against the pink-and-gold backdrop of the evening sky, Teri was the embodiment of all that he wanted to give her.

"Everything."

It was nightfall when they came to their senses and realized that there were more comfortable places to recline than this prickly front yard. They shared a shower, a towel and a bed, and they loved long and slow, taking the time to cherish each other with lips and hands and hearts. There was no time for sleep. Too soon it would be morning.

They refused to speak of the future. The past rested more easily with them now, and there was no objection when, lying abed beneath the moonlit window and stirring her hand soothingly over John's chest, Teri decided to bring it up.

"You have the makings of a good father," she said.

He lifted his head and looked down at her, puzzling. "How do you figure?"

"Wyatt said that if you hadn't withdrawn your petition, the judge could have decided to take custody of Rachael on the spot."

He let his head fall back into its pillow nest. "He wouldn't have done it that way. Shelltrack has more finesse than that."

"Did you go in there intending to take her?"

"Yes." Head up again, he sought her eyes. "I did. Does that surprise you?" She looked at him, saying nothing, but he knew it did. "I wanted to make it right,

Teri. Erase the mistakes. Put things back the way they belong.''

"We can't go back and do it over."

"Would you want to?"

"It would happen the same way every time. You would leave me. You were restless. You were unsure of me, unsure of—" she drew a deep breath and sighed "—of what you wanted."

"I was unsure of myself." He lay back again, studying the texturized pattern in the ceiling. "I was so damn young and stupid, I wasn't worth—"

"We were both young."

"And now we're old?" She laughed, and he shook his head, laughing, too. "Well, I think I'm gettin' there. My body feels like it's lived twice as long as my mind. But yours..." He touched her smaller breast, lying sweetly against his side. "Yours just gets younger."

"You mean flatter?"

"No, I don't mean flatter, I just mean..." He groaned and did the only thing a man could do when he was messing up his words. He wrapped her close in his arms. "I love every inch of it, okay? So take better care of it. Stop starving it to death."

Instantly she went as stiff as sun-dried rawhide.

He leaned back, looking for cause before asking, "What's the matter?"

"Nothing."

"I was just kidding. I didn't mean...that you look like you're..." She pulled away, taking to her own side of the bed. He followed, like a bloom yearning for sun, bracing himself on his elbow. "I don't know what to say, Teri. I think you're beautiful. I always have."

"But?"

He shook his head. "Too beautiful sometimes. Fragile. Breakable." With a tentative finger he stroked her eyebrow. She closed her eyes. "I want to take care of you. I feel like a fool saying that, because what have I got that you can't buy ten times over, but…" Her eyes flew open again. "But when you're with me, I want to take care of you. Protect you, keep you warm and safe." He smiled wistfully and spoke gently. "Make you eat."

"You can't." She turned her face away. Her voice turned thready. "Nobody can make me eat. I have to make myself eat."

"*Make* yourself eat?"

"I thought I had to be thin to get accepted, to be really successful. And I do. I *am*. Thin and successful."

The two words rang hollow. On that unconvincing note she cleared her throat and collected herself, launching a recitation. "Actually, I thought I had to be thin for modeling, for my mother and for—" she offered a tight smile "—the man that got away. I learned all that in counseling."

She remembered the therapy sessions during which she'd been invited to vent her anger on empty chairs. Anger came hard for her. She'd felt as though it was wasted on her mother's chair, and she'd been afraid to hurt the chair that was supposed to be John.

"Counseling?" he asked softly.

"I used to be thinner than this. I dieted every way there is to diet until I finally ended up in the hospital." Her hand went to her concave stomach, protecting it even as she said lightly, "I'm much better now."

Caressing her arm, shoulder to elbow and back again, he sought to put a cap on his alarm. He wasn't sure he understood how a person would have to make herself eat. He'd known some hungry times, and he didn't even like to think about them, so he suspected there was more to this than just getting her to eat, and it scared him.

"Have you...does Lavender know?"

Teri shrugged. "I've never told her, but she's probably guessed. She's noticed that I'm not a big eater, and that I've lost..."

There was a time when she would have told Lavender if she told anyone. It seemed strange to her now, after all that had happened, that she should choose to confide in John first. Maybe even laughable, but somehow happily so.

"I said I was never going to trust you again, and here I am, trusting you again." She touched his cheek, as though to comfort him. "This is a very fragile part of me, John. Please..." She drew an unsteady breath and looked him in the eye. "Please be careful with it."

He would, but he was so damn clumsy. He hated the thought that he might make a mistake and hurt her again. Sweeping his big thumb across her fine-boned face was like using a squeegee on the good dishes. He pulled her into his arms and whispered, "Just tell me how."

"I'm not sure. I guess...don't be disgusted with me because I'm not always beautiful."

"You get disgusted with yourself. That's when it hurts the worst." It hurt him more knowing she had suffered, too, the way he had over all the things he'd thought he had to be. "That's when you try to run and hide."

"Or disappear altogether." And she tried now, pushing herself deeper into the envelope he made for her with his body. "John, I couldn't tell Lavender about my eating problems because it would make her feel bad because..." Her confession came quickly and quietly, whispered in broken syllables against his chest. "Because it hurt so much to give our baby away."

All he could do was hold her. She wasn't crying, at least not visibly, but she shared the hurt readily now that he had stopped blaming her. None of the circumstances mattered. None of the reasons made a damn bit of difference when it came down to bare bones. And he imagined Teri had been just that when she hit bottom. Bare bones without her baby. Bare bones without her confidence.

Bare bones without the man who on more than one grand occasion had vowed his willingness to die for her. But stay by her side for life? Hell, no, he hadn't been up to a challenge like that.

"Tell me about when she was born."

"Are you sure?"

He looked down. She waited. He nodded once.

She turned, pillowed her head on his shoulder and drew his arms close around her. "I went into labor early in the morning. I wasn't sure at first. I didn't know what to expect, but there were fingers of pain sort of poking around here." She put his palms to her sides, then stroked the backs of his hands. His fingers overlapped at her navel. "Of course, I had this huge belly, if you can imagine."

"I'm imagining." He pressed his lips against the top of her head and closed his eyes for a moment, bracing himself for a bumpy ride. "I'm imagining myself in bed with you, and it's getting light outside. Was it—" he steadied himself on a deep breath "—getting light?"

"Yes. It was the first day in May. It was still cool, but I had the window open, and it was raining."

"I imagine you'd say, 'John, it hurts right here,'" he said, moving his hands lovingly over her. "And I'd say, 'Maybe we're going to have a baby, Teri, what do you think?'"

"I think..." She swallowed hard, and he was glad they weren't looking at one another. Only touching. Only, at long last, listening. "I woke Lavender up. I was staying with them. We had taken the Lamaze classes together. Wyatt drove the car right up to the step because he didn't want me to slip or get wet or..."

"I imagine I would have carried you. I would have wrapped you in a big star quilt. Pink and blue."

"I was in labor for twelve hours. It felt like twelve days. I did the breathing right up until the end." She sighed. "Then, I have to admit, I did a little screaming. I called your—"

She went very still. Beyond the window screen the crickets' song became deafening, warring with the sound of her breathing and his thudding heartbeat.

"Did you call for me?"

She took two quick breaths. "I screamed, 'John, I need you! John, where are you? John...'"

"I'm right here. I'm with you." His throat burned horribly. He heard no tears in her voice, and he felt ashamed.

"It hurt more than any pain you can imagine." She moved her hands over his, massaging his knuckles, his wrists, his forearms. "But you know what pain is like."

"Not that kind of pain. But I imagine I would hear it in your voice and see the way it gripped you." Feeling helpless, he held her fiercely. "And I would want to die for you."

"But only for a short time, because when the baby is born—" she pushed his hands hard against her belly, then released them "—the pain subsides. It's like a miracle. She squalls like a little lamb, and she's all red and wrinkled."

"Did you hold her right away?"

"They put her on my stomach. After they cut the umbilical cord, I held her. I was crying, and so was she. She was mine then, and I wasn't going to let her go. I was the first to hold her. I held her close to my..."

She moved his hands to her breasts. His tears broke free.

"Now I can imagine...handing her to you." She turned in his arms and lifted both hands to touch his damp face. She knew how dearly his tears cost him, and she pressed her lips to his cheek to taste them. "Seeing her helps, John. I'm never sad when I see her, because she's doing well."

"I'm not sad." Amazingly, it was true. "I just had a baby."

He dreamed without sleeping. He contented himself with holding her until just before first light, and then he had to move, to stretch and have a smoke. He didn't want to disturb her, so he put his jeans on in the living room and opened the front door to the cool, dew-laden air. He lit a cigarette.

Wimpy came bounding around the corner of the house with a mouth full of old shoe. Good ears, John thought. The dog opened his mouth and let the shoe drop in the yard, ready to play if he had any takers.

John leaned against the doorframe and sucked a deep drag. He figured Wimpy should have been *his* name, the way he'd acted. Not that he wasn't glad about the way she'd let him in on the experience—he was. But cowboys never cried. Any four-year-old Indian boy could tell you that.

In the face of her courage, he had always been a coward. No longer. He knew what he had to do.

"John?" *Speak of the angel.* "What are you doing?"

"Singin' the blues." Past the screen and into the dark he smiled at the pup. "Me an' ol' Wimp, we've got the moon on the run."

"I didn't hear any singing."

"We're wimps, see. We're howlin' so high-pitched, we're way above your frequency."

He could hear her bare feet treading lightly.

"Are you okay?" she asked.

"I'm terrific." He turned and stretched his arm out for her, inviting her to take the last few steps and come to him. "How about you?"

"I missed you. Couldn't you sleep?" He shook his head as she claimed her niche under his arm. He liked the way she looked in his T-shirts. "I couldn't, either," she said with a sigh.

He chuckled. "Coulda fooled me. Who was doing all that snoring, then?"

"I don't snore," she said with absolute certainty.

He smiled.

"Do I?" She tried to read the truth in his eyes, but he wasn't giving any more than that smile. She shook her head. "No, I never snore."

"Tell you what." He took a last puff and stubbed the rest of his cigarette out in an ashtray he'd left on the windowsill. He sent the smoke off into the night and turned to her. "You never snore if I never cry. That's our story. Got it?"

"It's a lot to trust each other with, isn't it?" They were standing almost face-to-face. She braced her back against the opposite side of the doorframe, reached out and brushed his hair back, grazing the top of his ear with her little finger. "It's nothing to be ashamed of," she said.

"What?"

"Crying. I do it myself on occasion."

"I wasn't crying. Cowboys get the blues, honey. They don't cry."

"Okay." She pushed herself away from her support and leaned into his arms. "Ladies don't snore."

"Okay." He brushed his nose back and forth over her hair. "What time is your flight?"

"Around noon," she said quietly. "Will Woody be taking me back?"

"No. I will."

"It's too risky, John."

"It's no risk at all. I'm not running anymore. I'm going to put you on your plane, and then I'm going to turn myself in."

"But you're safe here." She tipped her head back to look up at him.

"I'm a prisoner, Teri. I can't leave the reservation, so I'm not free."

Out in the front yard Wimpy had started his own game of toss the shoe. John turned to watch. He remembered the old expression about a dog's life, and he figured having only one shoe was part of the beauty of it. The second one would never drop.

"It used to be that way, you know," he mused absently. "Years ago, when they started the reservation system, Indians couldn't leave without special permission."

"But it isn't years ago anymore. It's now. And you haven't done anything wrong." She shrugged winsomely. "I mean, really, what's one little pickup? Besides, it was Woody who—"

"Nooo, no. Woody didn't do anything he didn't think would please me."

"They'll call him as a witness. He'll have to explain his part in it."

"And I'll explain why I was responsible and hope they don't ask for more than I can pay in damages."

"Oh, John, I could help—"

"No."

"Loan—"

"No. I'll handle it." He spoke with more conviction than he felt. He would have to arrange for someone to watch his place for a while, maybe even move in for a while, in case "handling it" wasn't possible. "And as for the shooting incident, I guess it's my word against theirs."

"They were warning shots," she insisted.

"They *were* warning shots." He smiled. She had made the claim as though she'd seen it firsthand.

I will never, ever trust you again.

He hugged her fiercely, praying that if he ever had to be judged in this life, let it be by this jury of one.

"I hate airport scenes," she said, trying for glib smoothness. "Especially with people who like to cry at the drop of a hat."

"You are one coldhearted woman."

"And you are one bighearted cowboy." Her arms went around him, her hug as fierce as his. "Which is why you can't turn yourself in. Tomorrow's too soon."

"It's today." Rubbing her back, he repeated sadly, "It's already today."

"Today's not a good day. For one thing, you need a lawyer."

"I'll get one." He sighed. "It's not gonna get any easier. I want to get it over with." He straightened away from the doorframe, taking her with him, her slight shoulders in his hands. "And I don't want to waste any more time talking about it."

"I could stay one more—"

He devoured the bittersweet suggestion with a kiss, breaking it off only when he was sure she was breathless. Eyes still closed, she flicked her tongue over her lower lip and whispered, "One more."

"How about one more something else?"

"Yes." Smiling, she whispered, "One more something else."

Chapter 12

Woody didn't mind taking care of John's place. In fact, he liked being the one to get asked. But he didn't like the way the Cat was sticking his neck out, and he told him so. "Get a lawyer to cut a deal with the court," Woody said. "Like you read about. And don't do nothin' crazy 'til it's all in writing, signed and sealed."

John wondered aloud how many years that might take. He wasn't having an easy time of it, dealing with Woody's mountain of advice and trying to usher Teri out the door. She was still giving him static, too. So was the dog. John carried his mother's walking stick, partly because he didn't want to leave it behind, and partly because he thought it gave him an air of authority. He brandished it at Wimpy and made an attempt to hiss the dog out of the way as he got into the pickup. A quarter mile down the gravel road he had to turn around and head back to the house. He didn't want Wimpy to run himself ragged trying to follow.

"Hang on to him until we're way the hell down the road," John barked as he plopped the squirming pup into Woody's arms. "Don't tie him up. He'd probably choke himself. And don't—"

The big black eyes got to him. He couldn't resist giving a quick scratch, then patting the flat spot between those floppy ears. "Don't forget to feed him twice a day." Backing away, John added with a shrug, "His name's Wimpy. You know, he's just a pup yet."

The soulful last look between man and dog tugged at Teri's heartstrings. John had tried to assure her that everything would work out, but she knew he didn't believe his own line. They drove in silence. He'd elected to use the main highway, brazen as you please, and he smiled at her every time she slid a test glance his way. Her smiles, she knew, were somewhat tighter, causing his to fade. He would set his jaw as he set his sights on the road ahead. Each time one of those looks was exchanged he would take a firmer grip on the steering wheel with both hands, steadfastly maintaining his hold.

Out of the corner of his eye John could see Teri's hair fluttering in the open window. God, it was a pretty sight, especially with the tall roadside grass waving back. Off to his left there were cloud shadows sliding across a field of tan stubble. A scattering of pale green square bales waited to be collected, probably today, he thought. They looked dry enough, and a guy wouldn't want to see them get caught in a rainstorm and have to go through all the trouble of turning them over to dry out again.

In the last few hours he'd been thinking a lot about rain, among other things. It had been raining when Rachael was born on May first. All these years he hadn't realized that day was anything special. Now he knew better. It didn't matter whether she knew he was her father; he could still give her some kind of a gift next time around. She knew he was *somebody*.

She knew he was family.

Another hay field slid by. The owner was out early this morning, mowing the grass down. Bluestem with a little sweet clover mixed in. The yellow blooms were just beginning to open. It bothered John that he hadn't finished bringing his hay in. He wondered whether he would still have the chance to get it done.

He was glad he'd made his decision. There was a sense of relief in knowing that it would all be settled soon, one way or another, and he could get on with his life. The summer work would get done somehow. He would see to it. He was glad the choice he'd made had nothing to do with running this time.

Another cloud shadow passed across the hood of the pickup. Teri shivered, but she wasn't chilled. She was scared. In the distance she could see the radio tower. They were almost there.

The siren speared the silence like an icicle.

Teri whirled toward the back window. She saw the flashing light, and she allowed herself the feeble hope that it was meant for someone else.

John cursed roundly under his breath, easing down on the brake. He turned the front wheels toward the shoulder of the road.

"Were you speeding?" Teri asked softly, as though someone might overhear. "Maybe it's just—"

"Do you have some ID with you?"

"My license."

"Good." He shifted into neutral and jammed on the parking brake. "I'm just giving you a ride to Bismarck, okay? Don't try to..." He glanced over his shoulder. The lights were flashing right behind them, and he figured the lawman was already running a check on his plates. "They've got nothing on you, so be a good girl and just be along for the ride, okay?"

"I'm going to do what I can to help you."

A second patrol car pulled a U-turn in the middle of the highway. John's stomach felt queasy. This wasn't the way he'd planned it, but he'd known all along this was the risk he was taking.

"You can help me by playing it real cool," he said. "No dramatic stuff, okay? No brave lady throwing her body over the condemned man."

She was only half listening as she watched in the side-view mirror. "Oh, John, they're getting out of the car."

He touched her shoulder. "I want you to call Coach and tell him to come and get you right away, because I don't want you hangin' around the police station. You've got a plane to catch."

"I'm not going—"

An amplified voice cut her off. "Get out of the car. Keep your hands up where we can see them."

John cursed again and sighed. He could have done without the guns. He slid his fingertips the length of Teri's arm, touched her hand and whispered, "Do what they say, honey. Take that cane with you." She glanced at the willow stick, propped against the seat between them, then looked up at him, skeptical. "Keep my mother's walking stick for me," he said.

Their gazes caught and held. He hooked his elbow behind her neck and pulled her to him for a quick, hard kiss. "I love you," he told her, more gruffly than he'd intended.

With guns drawn the two patrolmen approached each side of the pickup, while a third stayed back near the car. John and Teri emerged slowly, exactly as they'd been instructed. They complied with the order to put their hands on the side of the pickup box. It was the command to spread their legs that broke John's control.

"We're not armed. The woman's got nothing to do with this. She's just—"

"Nothing to do with what? Are you the owner of this vehicle?"

"I'm John Tiger. My license is in my back pocket." He lifted his chin and risked a glance across the open pickup box. Teri's eyes, full of fear and confusion, met his.

She was looking at him. John Tiger. The man who'd fed her all kinds of pretty words about wanting to protect her. Surely those words were echoing pathetically in her head now, the way they were in his, and turning her stomach.

One hulking cop laid hands on John at the same moment that his partner reached for Teri.

"I'm not going to hurt you, ma'am, but I have to—"

All John had to see was that hand, and he was halfway into the pickup box. "Don't touch her!"

The towheaded young officer standing near Teri looked a little startled.

But the bigger one had John by the shoulders, and a third man managed to twist his right arm behind his back. The big man finished pat-searching John as he spoke to him calmly. "You're not giving the orders here, son. Just keep your shirt on."

"She hasn't done anything," John said. "It's me you want. You don't have to..." He twisted around to catch a glimpse of the blond guy running his hands over Teri's back pockets. "You don't have to do that!"

"Well, you're right, Mr. Tiger. You're the one we want. There's a warrant out for your arrest. Did you know that, Miss...?"

"Teri Nordstrom." She didn't miss the warning blazing at her in John's eyes. *You don't know anything.* "I know John, Officer. He's not a criminal."

"Well, he's under arrest."

"The lady's clean," the young cop reported.

"Come on over here, then, and help us with the cuffs. Mr. Tiger, let me tell you about your rights...."

The manacles tethered John's wrists to a chain around his waist. The sight of them made Teri's stomach churn. Once he was locked into them, he refused to look at her, and her heart went out to him. He was a proud and beautiful man, bound in chains. She knew he wouldn't want her to cry, but the prickly pressure rose quickly in her throat, along with breath-stealing panic.

Don't tie him up, he might...

"We're not arresting you, Miss Nordstrom, but we're impounding the pickup. When we get to the station, you'll be free to go."

When they got to the station, Teri called Wyatt, who called Paul White, the attorney who had established the legitimacy of John's claim to the access road. John would appear in court the following day, where he would be charged. The judge would determine his bond. Until that time, only his attorney could see him. After meeting with John, the lawyer paid a visit to the Archer home and delivered John's request that Teri stay away from the courtroom altogether.

"Is it a public courtroom?" Teri asked.

"Of course it is, but John doesn't want you to—"

"See him there, I suppose." She'd been down this road before, and she knew all the signs. She sat across from the two men, balancing the diamond-willow stick across her knees, caressing the worn wood. It was all she had—all he'd left her to hold on to. "What kind of bond do you think it will take to get him out?"

"I'd be surprised if you could get him out with a king's ransom," Paul said. "I can't exactly claim he has a history of cooperating with the law."

"He's not a criminal."

"I know that." The helpless look the lawyer gave Wyatt didn't win him any points with Teri.

Nor did his legal assessment. "This is a political thing, pure and simple." Nor his strategy. "We'll just have to wait and see which way the wind is blowing in Indian Affairs this week."

Early the next morning Teri dressed for court. She put on the same navy-and-white coatdress she'd worn for John's mother's funeral, but she added a string of pearls and a lacy pocket scarf. Lavender stayed home with Rachael, and Wyatt drove Teri to the courthouse. He made no attempt to dissuade her. He knew better.

They arrived before Paul White did, and they waited for him on the bench in the lobby. When he finally showed up, he offered polite greetings, followed by an exasperated expression of disapproval.

He set his briefcase beside the bench, adjusted his glasses and perched tentatively next to Teri on the bench.

"Let me tell you what happens," Paul began. "They bring him into the courtroom wearing those damned orange coveralls. You know how he'd feel if you saw him in those?"

"I've seen him in bandages, head to foot." The man didn't seem to understand. She was on John's side. What difference did orange coveralls make? "If he's held without bond, will I be able to see him at all?"

"Let me talk to him." The attorney patted her hand as he stood. "I'll tell him I couldn't keep you away."

"He knows that's par for the course," Wyatt said.

"Let's see what he says."

Paul returned within fifteen minutes with word that they were waiting to meet with the federal prosecutor and the judge in his chambers. The move had clearly taken him by surprise. "I don't know what it means," he told them as he started back down the hall. "But keep your fingers crossed."

They waited, the hands on the big wall clock seeming almost arthritic. They paced. They drank coffee. They paced faster.

Paul White appeared suddenly, his brown eyes brimming brightly. "I've got a surprise for you folks." He gestured with a flourish. Wyatt and Teri waited, both of them afraid to move. Finally bootheels sounded on the linoleum.

He was dressed in the same white shirt and jeans he'd been wearing the day before. No prisoner's orange coveralls. He was walking tall, and he had eyes only for Teri. Wyatt was standing closer, so he jumped in for a handshake, then stepped back as though he'd forgotten himself. John was already halfway across the room, catching Teri in his arms as she came up off the bench. They buried their faces against each other's necks and whispered one another's names. After a long, blissful moment, they leaned back, made sure, then turned to the two men who stood grinning from ear to ear. Finally John turned back to Teri.

"Every time I get myself in a tight spot, I turn around and there you are." Buoyed by the marvel of it, John tucked her under his arm. "I tell them, 'Don't bring her *here,* for God's sake.' These big guys, you know what they tell me?"

"They can't keep me away," Teri recited.

"I must be some prize, huh?"

"You must be." And she hugged his waist, just to prove that it was true. Then she tipped her head back. "Are you all right?"

"I'm free." He looked at Wyatt. "Can you believe it? The charges were dropped. Paul figures the government is fighting too many Indian claims—water rights, access, easement, all that. They lost this one when they couldn't come up with an easement, and they want it to die quietly. They don't want any publicity over a trial this time around."

"They figure they're better off stopping up the hole in the dike by building another road," Paul explained.

Teri was amazed. After all that worry. "So they let you go, just like that?"

John did a double take for her benefit. "Too easy?"

"I was already planning what I was going to wear for Sunday visits to 'the big house.'" She squeezed his slim middle once again. "And what kind of cake I should bake a file in."

"I can tell you're disappointed."

She squeezed harder, this time catching him off guard with an exuberant kiss that missed its mark and landed on his chin.

He laughed, pulled her close to the wall and kissed her back the same way. And then he kissed her his way. The long way.

Wyatt busied himself with congratulating Paul as the two courteously edged away.

"Did you miss your plane again?" John asked. Teri nodded happily. "Can I buy you lunch?"

"If you pick up the tab, I suppose I'll have to clean my plate."

"Damn right." He leaned down and spoke close to her ear. "But I'll feed you a little at a time. I was thinkin' along the lines of room service."

Before the day's last flight, they stopped at the Archers' so Teri could pick up her luggage and say goodbye. Then John took her to the airport, where they stood together by the big plate-glass window and watched her plane taxi toward the gate. People started gathering up their belongings and getting in line. There wasn't much time left.

Teri took a few steps backward toward the other gate. The empty one. John followed reluctantly. He wanted to kiss her again. He'd kissed her lips into soft putty by now, but he would never be able to say he'd kissed them enough. He just didn't want to kiss her goodbye.

She wasn't looking for another kiss. She had things to say. "Remember when you told me you loved me, just before you got arrested?"

Fine time to spill his guts, he told himself, especially after he'd been the one to warn her against getting dramatic. But now he could chuckle about it. "Just like in the movies."

"I didn't get a chance to say that I loved you, too." She slipped her arms around his waist, ignoring her flight's first call. "I do, John. I love you. It's a fine time to tell you, I know, but—" her voice dropped to bedroom soft "—I love you so much."

"It *is* a fine time to tell me." He took her face in his hands. "Anytime is a fine time. Take care of yourself for me. Remember how beautiful I think you are."

"Is this another brush-off?" she asked. "Another dramatic parting?"

"You're the one who's doin' the parting this time. You've got places to go and things to do. Whenever you come back to see Rachael, you just remember I'm..." He kissed her lingeringly, then whispered, "...real close by."

"Why haven't you asked me to stay?" He closed his eyes, and she knew that wasn't fair. "Okay, then why don't you ask me to come back to you?" She placed her forefinger in the center of his chest. "To *you.*"

"Because you'd have to make a choice, and what I've got to offer you isn't a whole lot by comparison."

"I guess 'I love you' must have seemed like the right thing to say at the time, hmm? The right line?"

"It wasn't a line." Her flight was called a second time. His hands trembled as he slid them into her hair. "I've always loved you. I never wanted to leave you, but I wasn't worth a damn back then." He nodded once. "I am now."

She wanted to be as sure of herself as he was, but it was a conviction she was still working on. She could not allow anyone to work against her. Softly she asked, "Am *I?*"

His eyes glittered. "You mean everything to me, Teri. You're worth my life."

But that was not enough. "How about your trust?"

"That, too." He smiled sheepishly as he cupped his hands around the back of her neck. "If I knew how. You were teaching me, weren't you? I was doing pretty good, wasn't I? I was listening better."

Then maybe he would listen to a new plan, one that would allow her to accept herself and come to believe that there was more to Teri Nordstrom in the flesh than in photographs. Therapy was a start. John's love surely helped. And a good talk with Lavender had spawned some wonderful ideas. At first this was all "food for thought," but when "prospects for change" had gone down better with food-shy Teri, she and Lavender had fallen into each other's arms in a fit of laughter. Such good medicine.

But when it came to sharing the idea with John, she was hesitant. She avoided his eyes and spoke softly. "Lavender says I can come to work with her. She says she wants a partner, and it would be just exactly the kind of work I'd love to—"

He spoke softly, too, as though he was afraid too much excitement might scare her away. "If you lived in Bismarck, I could see you...."

Neither of them heard the final call. There was too much to say, too much that had been saved for far too long.

"I have places to come back to and things to try again," she said hopefully.

"I've been thinking of adding on to the house. I mean, I haven't really been thinking about it, but I could. If I ever needed more room."

He could make room for her. And she could risk offering him the space in her life that only he could fill. They could surely try, Teri told herself. "I have some commitments in the city. Professional commitments. But if you were to invite me to come back..."

"I don't want you to go back at all." He dropped his arms around her back and pulled her close. "And I'll die a lonely, blues-singin' cowboy if you don't come back to me."

"We wouldn't want that," she whispered into his shirtfront. She didn't want to cry, but her throat was doing it to her again.

"I wasn't gonna ask you for another chance. I didn't think it would be fair after the way I let you down, you and Rachael." He pressed a kiss into her hair. "But if you're not afraid to take another chance..." He pulled back, sought her eyes and promised, "You'll be able to count on me this time."

"I want to have more children, John. Lavender and Wyatt are Rachael's parents, and they always will be. But I think we can love her, too. And if we *did* have more children..." She scanned his face as she made the suggestion. He was afraid to hope, as she was. But the hope was there. "There would be room for brothers and sisters in Rachael's life, and for her in theirs. I believe it could work that way."

He smiled. "See, I'm learning, and you're learning. Both of us. I think Judge Shelltrack would wanna give us a damn medal."

She smiled, too. His fingers were locked together at the base of her spine. Hers were laced together at the back of his neck. They smiled with lips and eyes and hearts, and their time stood still.

"Wait!" a woman dashing through security called. "That's my flight."

"Better hurry," said the gate attendant.

"Oh, gosh, my plane." Teri came to her senses, feeling a little foolish as she turned and adjusted her purse strap on her shoulder. Her other arm slid along John's as she started away. "Oh, John, I'm going to miss my plane."

"Will you stay another day..." He caught her hand, and she turned expectantly. He offered a gentle smile. "...if I ask you to?"

"My luggage is already on board."

"I've got an extra T-shirt." He tugged. She watched the gate attendant stamp the latecomer's ticket. John's voice came low and soft and insistent. "Will you stay another day?"

She turned to him. The chain rattled as the gate attendant roped off the jetway. Teri stepped back into John's arms, tipped her chin back and gave a self-satisfied smile. "Just one more?"

"For now," he said, smiling as he watched her plane back away from the gate without her.

"It sure wasn't easy getting you to ask."

"I keep telling myself that I'm not asking for much," he said. "Just get me past the roadblock. Just get me through the night. Just give me one more day. Love me one more day."

"And after that?" He looked down at her, waiting for her to answer her own question. Smiling, she shook her head. "You know I can't stop loving you after one more day, any more than I could drop you off on some long, lonesome highway."

"That's what I'm countin' on, honey," he confided, and he tucked her under his arm and gave her a quick squeeze as they started toward the escalator. "I'm countin' on making this pretty woman my wife."

* * * * *

For all those readers who've been looking for something a little bit different, a little bit spooky, let Silhouette Books take you on a journey to the dark side of love with

If you like your romance mixed with a hint of danger, a taste of something eerie and wild, you'll love Shadows. This new line will send a shiver down your spine and make your heart beat faster. It's full of romance and more—and some of your favorite authors will be featured right from the start. Look for our four launch titles wherever books are sold, because you won't want to miss a single one.

THE LAST CAVALIER—Heather Graham Pozzessere
WHO IS DEBORAH?—Elise Title
STRANGER IN THE MIST—Lee Karr
SWAMP SECRETS—Carla Cassidy

After that, look for two books every month, and prepare to tremble with fear—and passion.

SILHOUETTE SHADOWS, coming your way in March.

Silhouette®

SHAD1

INTIMATE MOMENTS®
Silhouette®

CONARD COUNTY

CONTINUES...

Come back to Conard County, Wyoming, where you'll
meet men and women whose lives are as dramatic as
the landscape around them. Join author Rachel Lee for
the third book in her fabulous series, MISS EMMALINE
AND THE ARCHANGEL (IM #482). Meet Emmaline Conard,
"Miss Emma," a woman who was cruelly tormented
years ago and now is being victimized again. But this
time sheriff's investigator Gage Dalton—the man they
call hell's own archangel—is there to protect her. But
who will protect Gage from his feelings for Emma? Look
for their story in March, only from Silhouette Intimate
Moments.

To order your copy of MISS EMMALINE AND THE ARCHANGEL, or the first two Conard County
titles, EXILE'S END (IM #449) and CHEROKEE THUNDER (IM #463), please send your name,
address, zip or postal code, along with a check or money order (do not send cash) for $3.39
for each book ordered, plus 75¢ postage and handling ($1.00 in Canada), payable to Silhouette
Books, to:

In the U.S.

Silhouette Books
3010 Walden Avenue
P.O. Box 1396
Buffalo, NY 14269-1396

In Canada

Silhouette Books
P.O. Box 609
Fort Erie, Ontario
L2A 5X3

Please specify book title(s) with your order.
Canadian residents add applicable federal and provincial taxes.

CON3

AMERICAN HERO

It seems readers can't get enough of these men—and we don't blame them! When Silhouette Intimate Moments' best authors go all-out to create irresistible men, it's no wonder women everywhere are falling in love. And look what—and who!—we have in store for you early in 1993.

January brings NO RETREAT (IM #469), by Marilyn Pappano. Here's a military man who brings a whole new meaning to macho!

In February, look for IN A STRANGER'S EYES (IM #475), by Doreen Roberts. Who is he—and why does she feel she knows him?

In March, it's FIREBRAND (IM #481), by Paula Detmer Riggs. The flames of passion have never burned this hot before!

And in April, look for COLD, COLD HEART (IM #487), by Ann Williams. It takes a mother in distress and a missing child to thaw this guy, but once he melts...!

AMERICAN HEROES. YOU WON'T WANT TO MISS A SINGLE ONE—ONLY FROM

IMHER03R

Take 4 bestselling love stories FREE

Plus get a FREE surprise gift!

FC